DISCLAIMER

This is a work of fiction. Names, characters, organizations, places, events, and incidents are either the product of the author's imagination or are used fictitiously. Any resemblance to actual persons, living or dead, or actual events is purely coincidental.

This book contains satirical content intended for mature audiences. It includes depictions of exaggerated or absurd behavior for the purpose of commentary and dark humor. The views and actions of characters in this book do not reflect the views of the author or publisher.

EPIGRAPH

Columbine High School, 1999

Red Lake Senior High School, 2005

Virginia Tech, 2007

Sandy Hook Elementary School, 2012

Marjory Stoneman Douglas High School, 2018

Robb Elementary School, 2022

Michigan State University, 2023

The Covenant School, 2023

Perry High School, 2024

"America, I implore you: end this."

—Theo W. Pitchstead

CONTENTS

PRELUDE

Outside the windows, the brightness of the day cast a comforting warmth over the deep hues of green on the playground, stubbornly resisting the typical loss of color that accompanied autumn. The sun hung low in the sky, making little effort to climb any higher. The coolness and comfort of the seasons had settled—if only for a moment—between the change into the pending winter.

In Classroom 1B at Hope Valley Elementary, the morning routine had progressed smoothly. Attendance and the Pledge of Allegiance were completed without issue, followed by an enthusiastic acknowledgment of Max's seventh birthday—the room erupting in a chorus of *Happy Birthday!*
The teacher, young and not yet disillusioned or wearied by the bureaucracy of education, smiled warmly with genuine happiness, enjoying the moment and the lively banter about the very best part of a birthday.

With the class settled, it was time to begin the literacy component of the morning. Today's text was *The Lost Puppy*, and she used some of the words within to support the class's phonetic understanding, sounding out *puppy*, *found*, and *home*.

It was somewhere toward the end of the picture book that a distant sound reached her ears. A sharp, staccato *pop*—short, unnatural. She paused the story, the class of small children instantly engaged by the sudden break in the lesson.

POP. POP. POP. POP.

It was closer now. Much louder.

And then came a rapid, relentless barrage of sound—louder than anything should be. The teacher froze in place, the students murmuring excitedly, shifting in their seats.

She knew now. Oh God, she knew what it was.

Twenty-eight young faces in front of her, all glued to their desks. It was so close—maybe the next classroom down the hall. She tried to scream at the children to hide, but nothing came out. Her stomach plummeted, fear locking every muscle in her body. Her heart pounded so hard, so fast, it incapacitated her ability to function.

"Everybody hide!" she screamed, her voice finally breaking free.

POP. POP. POP. POP.

The classroom erupted into chaos, her own terror spreading to them like wildfire. They scrambled, knocking over chairs, tripping over each other. Even at their young age, there was a terrible understanding: there was nowhere to go, no way out.

The door to the classroom flew open.

He was just a kid.

Vacant. Expressionless. Angry and confused.

A rifle gripped in his hands like it belonged there.

For a moment, time slowed. The world shrank to the space between her and him. A sick, twisted inevitability hung in the air. She was looking at death itself—not some abstract idea, not something far away, but real, standing in the doorway. Breathing. Moving. Watching.

She stepped in front of the children huddled behind her desk, her arms spreading wide—an instinct older than thought itself.

A useless gesture. A meaningless sacrifice.

The gun rose, and she turned away from the shooter.

The first shot hit her—a force like a sledgehammer to the chest. It slumped her over, knocking the air from her lungs. Another. And another. She collapsed to her knees, her vision tunneling, pain flooding through her.

The screams of the children rang in her ears.

More gunfire. Fewer screams.

Her desk now a brace against the inevitable fall into death.

Her fingers twitched, reaching for something—there was nobody to help. They were all alone.

There was nothing.

Only darkness.

And silence.

CHAPTER 1: MR. PRESIDENT?

November 24, 2025.

Lauren smoothed the front of her blazer and tugged at her cuffs, ensuring everything was perfectly in place. Acutely aware of the small number of friendly news reporters and cameras lingering at the back of the room, she crouched down, careful to maintain composure, as he intently watched a group of children in some small-town backwater school perform a play they had written especially for him.

"Mr. President... Excuse me, Mr. President?"

Despite the childlike entrancement of the president, her own mind raced. She had lost her place in the performance, but she knew from the briefing prior to arrival that the young students had put their all into a brief musical titled *The History of America – Speed Edition.* It was somewhere around the part about the Founding Fathers—delivered in a suspiciously American accent rather than the historically accurate British enunciation—brushing over any mention of slavery.

Moments earlier, she had received an urgent security alert from the Big House, the contents of which visibly impacted her. Lauren's normally stoic face flashed with fear and worry; her eyes darted toward the president as she quietly attempted again to deliver the message into his left ear. The official White House photographer raised his camera, sensing something was off. Lauren glared at him directly, shaking her head just slightly—almost imperceptibly.

"Mr. President, there's been another school shooting. Intel reports at least 35 currently unaccounted for... it's an active shooter situation."

The president didn't react—at least not in any physical way. Lauren couldn't tell if he had mentally registered the message. She remained crouched next to him for another moment before pressing again.

"Mr. President, shall we conclude this visit?"

His head turned ever so slightly. Irritated, he raised his hand, signaling her to stop speaking. Then, realizing that onlookers were recording his actions, he finally responded.

"Let's watch this play out. Great American theater—really terrific."

Lauren stood, her face tightening as she wondered how her life had come to this. It hadn't been by accident. No one rises in the halls of power by accident. This chapter of her life began as an ambitious teenager, carefully curating her education, extracurriculars, and volunteer work. Sometimes all your dreams come true—and you live unhappily ever after.

Outside the classroom windows, she spotted a large black helicopter waiting to transport the president and his team back to the airport. Marine One—his preferred mode of travel: bold, obnoxious, and overbearing. The perfect companion piece for his visit to an elementary school. The children's play dragged on, far beyond the strict limits they were given. For them, it was history. For Lauren, just another Tuesday.

After some time, the children concluded their performance, and the president clapped with enthusiastic obliviousness to the tension around him. The aides in attendance all looked to Lauren. After a series of photo ops, she gently placed a hand on the president's back and guided him toward the exit. She approached the situation again.

"Sir, I need to brief you on the shooting... We've got... well, we don't know how many dead, but it's going to be bad. Sir, it's an elementary school. The police are in a standoff with the shooter—he's barricaded in. The media is all over it."

The president stopped in his tracks. After a moment of consideration, he spoke.

"Children. Alright. Tell me about the victims—who are they?"

"Sir? They're elementary school students."

Lauren was briefly taken aback. His brow furrowed as it often did when he didn't like what he was hearing. Lips pursed, he considered the information.

"Terrible news. Terrible. What a disaster," he muttered.

"Okay, but are these, like, real Americans? Hardworking, tax-paying? Or are we talking, you know... something else?"

"Sir, no—Hope Valley's just a typical suburban town outside Philly. Pretty affluent, I believe?"
The president was more attentive now, his beady eyes locking onto Lauren like lasers, as if trying to will her into saying what he wanted to hear.

"Wow. Thirty-five dead white kids? Unbelievable. The suburbs, you say? You know, they don't always love me out in suburbia, but I think they could learn to. We're gonna get involved here. We're gonna sort this out. What do we know about the shooter? I need details—and let's make this quick. What I want you to do is call whoever is in charge on the ground and tell them how we're going to solve this problem."

They reached the helicopter—its rotors already spinning. Two security agents motioned for the president and his entourage to board. With her headset on, Lauren responded.

"One moment, sir. I'll try to get a line to local police on-site."

A few moments later, after a secure call back to the White House, Lauren had a direct line with Police Captain Evans, who was on the ground at the school.

"Captain, Lauren Chalmers—Chief of Staff to the president. Can you give me an update? What do we know?"

His voice was shaking, nearly shouting down the line—lacking the control the situation demanded.
"Ma'am, it's bad. It's really bad. We've got at least four classrooms worth of kids unaccounted for, and about a dozen teachers and staff. It's an active shooter."

The crushing weight of the news left Lauren momentarily flustered. Her shoulders sagged as she sank deeper into the seat of the chopper. Across the cabin, the president opened his arms dramatically—palms up. He wanted details. Now.

She nodded to him without emotion.

"Captain, what do we know about the shooter?"

"Hold on, ma'am." Evans' voice became muffled as he spoke to someone nearby. After a pause, he returned.

"Ma'am, it's chaotic. We think we have a possible ID—witnesses inside say it's a fourteen-year-old male, Lamar Williams. Former student, expelled a few months back. His father has registered firearms at home. But ma'am, don't quote me—I don't want the media on me if this ID is wrong…"

"Captain Evans, I'm not the media, and I don't care about their involvement right now. Hold for a moment."

Lauren switched her headset channel.

"Mr. President, numerous classrooms unaccounted for, along with teachers. Possible shooter ID is a former student, fourteen years old." The president sat silently, glaring at her before speaking very calmly.

"Lauren, patch me through directly to the person in charge over there." She nodded, slightly relieved. She patched him through to Captain Evans.

"Captain Evans, President Reign. Okay, real quick—what are we dealing with here? Is this a good kid who's a bit misguided, or is this, you know... one of the bad ones?"

Evans hesitated, clearly thrown by the escalation. "Sir, the suspect is a fourteen-year-old male, we're still confirming—" Reign cut him off.

"No, no, no. Don't give me the politically correct nonsense, Captain. What's his deal? Is this a gang thing? A cartel beef? Maybe a little... Middle Eastern situation? I mean, we have to ask. We have to know."

"Sir...we don't have any information on that at the moment."

"Come on, Evans. You're on the ground. You must've seen a picture. Does he have one of those names—you know, the ones that make you go, 'oh boy, here we go'?"

"Sir, that's not relevant—"

"Of course it's relevant! Everything's relevant! Look—if it's some white kid, maybe it's mental health, maybe a bad home. Very sad. But if it's, uh, let's just say *not* a white kid—this could be a whole different situation. A terrorism situation. A gang situation."

"Mr. President, our priority is locating and removing civilians and apprehending the shooter."
Reign sighed loudly. "Unbelievable. This is the problem. Nobody wants to ask the real questions. I have to do it myself. So frustrating."

He turned to Lauren and switched back to the internal

intercom. "Find out if this kid has priors. Or if his parents snuck in under the last administration. I want all the info." And then Reign focused his frustration back to Evans:

"Now Captain, what resources do you have? What do you need to end this situation before more kids die? You got any problems with DEI in your department, or do you have the right people for the job?"

"Mr. President, we've got about two hundred officers here, but we need SWAT and heavier equipment. The shooter's barricaded inside. We had to pull back—officers were under fire."

"You pulled back because a kid shot at you? You can't get in because he locked the door? And the big police force is scared of the little kid? Terrible leadership. Absolutely the worst."

Evans snapped. "Sir, this 'kid' has two AR-15s and enough ammo to hold us off for hours. No clear shot from outside. No easy way in. You want me sending my officers in blind?"

For a moment, Reign was stunned. He didn't appreciate the tone. But he recovered quickly, rage filling his voice.

"What the hell are you talking about, Evans? Two hundred officers?! And you had to pull back from a fourteen-year-old? Are you kidding me? This is a disgrace. An absolute disgrace. You've got kids in there, teachers in there—and you're standing around waiting? What do you need, a damn tank?!"
He didn't let Evans respond.

"I don't want excuses. I want action. You've got a door? Breach it. You've got weapons? Use them. I don't care if he's barricaded —get in there and end this. Every second you wait, more kids could be dead. And if this goes south, I won't be the one taking the blame—you will. Do your damn job, Captain. Go in. Right now."

The channel went silent for a moment. Only the white static of the radio crackled softly before Captain Evans finally retorted:

""With all due respect, sir... I don't know or care how you think this works, but I don't take orders from you during an active shooter situation. Now I'm going to go do my job—without your suggestions."

Evans terminated the communication. He was right, of course. The president didn't have any actual authority to direct a law enforcement operation. And although Reign might occasionally lose a battle, he had an uncanny ability to win the war. Hanging up on President Reign was a miscalculation on Evans's part—he'd be lucky to avoid prison by the time Reign was through with him. At best, he might end up working as a traffic cop in a town without any traffic.

In any case, Lauren already knew how this was going to play out. Evans was about to become public enemy number one —more so than the shooter—because he dared to argue with Reign and had the audacity to end the call.

The thing with Reign was, he enjoyed conflict more than anything. Sometimes, Lauren wondered if he was truly a psychopath. He sat very still in his seat, anger burning on his face, held tight beneath a tense veneer.

"Lauren, get on the line with some of our preferred news channels. Let's make sure America knows what's happening here," he said, leaning in as if revealing a grand strategy.

Lauren, well-versed in his meaning, nodded. "You want me to reach out to Liberty Channel?"

"Yes—and PatriotVision. Freedom News. The real ones. The ones that know what's at stake."

He straightened his tie and continued, "We're going to get ahead of this. I gave the order, Lauren. I told them to end it. The police? Weak. Pathetic. They refused to go in. You make sure the American people know that. Evans hesitated, and because of that, people died—and more will die before this is over."

Lauren scribbled notes as Reign raged. "Understood, sir. You want to push the narrative that you took command but Evans defied you. That you tried to save lives, but they ignored your leadership."

Reign smiled, pleased—that goofy, boyish, closed-lip smile. "Exactly. I want words like *betrayal* and *failure*. Evans didn't just hesitate—he abandoned those children. He personally stood between me and saving their lives. You understand?"

Lauren nodded, although she didn't truly understand what was happening at that moment.
"Lauren, one more thing," Reign said, leaning forward with a look of absolute certainty. "We're ending school shootings. Effective immediately." He pointed the index finger of his right hand at Lauren, dropping it like a loaded gun. "Find out what it takes. Budget, logistics, legal—it doesn't matter. We're doing it."

He checked his watch. "I want options on my desk by the end of the day."

He nodded slightly to himself, chin tilted, lips pressed together in satisfaction.

"Yes, sir. I understand." She felt like vomiting, but held it down.

She placed a call through to the White House to connect with their friendlies in the media.

CHAPTER 2: HOPE VALLEY

In Hope Valley, Pennsylvania, crouched behind a police SUV, Sergeant Jordan Peck grew increasingly agitated. His partner of three years, Officer Victor Rodriguez, bore the brunt of his escalating abruptness and anger. Jordan checked his phone repeatedly, hands shaking with adrenaline, searching for something he couldn't find.

Two hours earlier, they had been called to a domestic dispute. The woman was so badly assaulted they couldn't leave her—she'd likely die if they did. Jordan had paced the living room, waiting anxiously for the paramedics. Vic was downstairs, the boyfriend cuffed in the back of the car. The call came in over the radio less than ten minutes after they arrived.

They couldn't leave. It took another half hour for the EMS team to arrive. Jordan knew every available badge had answered the call; the rest of the district was manned by a skeleton crew. The moment the paramedics arrived, Jordan bolted from the apartment like a baton had been passed in a relay race. His heart pounded, his breath came in short gasps—but his focus was razor-sharp. Then it was back to the station to drop the punk off at the holding cells. Another twenty minutes lost. Jordan fumed with rage, barely restraining himself from pulling over to strangle the guy before dumping him on the sidewalk to save the trip.

After handing the punk off to the booking officer, Jordan barreled through the station and back into the patrol car. He tore through city streets on the far side of town, opening it up on the outskirts to reach the outer suburbs.

In the few short moments since Jordan and Vic arrived at Hope Springs Elementary, it had become obvious: there was no clear plan of attack, and no leadership on the ground. Sporadic bursts of automatic gunfire pierced through the cacophony of police radios and shouted orders, grim reminders amid the sea of flashing lights muted by the clear, bright sky. Countless law enforcement vehicles were scattered around the entrance, but confusion reigned. Command was paralyzed. Every passing second could mean more death. Evans—brought in from another precinct—was nominally in charge.

"Jordy, all the screaming..."

Jordan turned toward the restless crowd of civilians behind the barricades. Parents. Grandparents. Brothers. Sisters—wailing like tormented souls in the depths of hell. The two men locked eyes, faces drawn tight with tension and fury.

"Vic... someone's gotta..." Jordan struggled to say it, stumbling over the words before firming his resolve. "Vic, we have to go in. We have to end this."

Still crouched behind the SUV, Jordan nodded to himself. His right hand gripped the watch on his left wrist. At first, his movements were small and restrained, but they quickly grew more pronounced—his whole torso swaying in silent agreement.

Captain Evans interrupted again, shouting across the assembled officers. "Does any law enforcement have family or kids in there?"

Jordan looked back at the crowd—at the parents, the siblings, the faces lined with horror. Rage surged in his veins. Adrenaline flooded his system, electrifying every nerve. He suddenly stood up, sucking in several deep breaths. His abrupt motion drew immediate attention.

Across the small parking lot, Captain Evans yanked his megaphone to his mouth. In a howl that cracked across the chaos, he screamed: "Officer! Get down, now!"

But Jordan didn't respond.

Evans turned to the officers near him, furious. "Goddammit, what the hell is that asshole doing?"
Sergeant Jordan Peck clenched his fists, arms heavy with fury, muscles tight, veins bulging. His chest heaved visibly from a distance. Evans toggled his mic again—but as his eyes met Jordan's, he froze. The megaphone let out a weak squeal of feedback. He didn't say a word

.

Sensing the weakness, Jordan surged forward. He sprinted around the SUV, pushing through the barrier of cops crouched behind bulletproof shields. He was a big man, and none of them tried to stop him—least of all Evans. He broke across the open ground in front of the school, fully expecting to catch a bullet. But nothing happened.

He hit the stairs at full speed. At the top, he slammed his right foot into the doors—once, twice—and the lock gave way with barely a protest.

Vic was right behind him.

Captain Evans slumped behind a patrol car, sighing heavily as the two officers disappeared through the doors.

"Those two fucking assholes are going to get killed," Jordan heard him mutter as he passed.

At the front of the hallway stands a reception counter, and leaning back in an office chair is a middle-aged woman, her eyes frozen wide in a look of absolute terror. Multiple bullet holes have torn through her blouse, now grotesquely marked with bloodstains and fragments of body tissue. Vic glances at the name badge pinned to the left side of her chest. It reads: "Carol Robinson." She's somebody's mother, a wife to someone. Now she's dead.

Already intoxicated by the flood of adrenaline and fury coursing through his body, every nuance of Jordan's senses sharpens to a heightened state. He releases his Glock from its holster, raising the weapon, his index finger pressed against the frame outside the trigger guard, his left hand steadying the grip. He moves past the reception counter and into the hallway, noting the classroom doors on both sides.

Scurrying along one side of the corridor, the two officers approach the first classroom door. Pressing their backs against the wall—Jordan in front—he inhales deeply, steeling himself for whatever lies beyond. With a burst of adrenaline, he pivots into the doorway, weapon drawn and ready.

The scene inside hits him with the force of a physical blow. His mind fragments like pieces of a jigsaw puzzle. The room tilts. His vision narrows. His perception ricochets against some invisible threshold—his brain disconnects, unable to reconcile the image before him with any conceivable version of reality. The death inside this room, the horror that has unfolded, is so utterly inhumane that, for a moment, his brain refuses to process it.

A wave of disorientation crashes over him, and for a time, he is dumbstruck. His right arm—still holding the handgun—drops limply to his side.

Slowly, as if waking from a deep sleep, Jordan begins to process the scene before him. Bodies. Tiny bodies. Blood. A pile behind the desk. The teacher in front. His mind stalls, refusing to comprehend. *This isn't real. It can't be real.*

They're all huddled behind their teacher—a small blonde woman, her blue eyes frozen in shock, mouth slightly agape.

She tried to save them by standing in front, a futile attempt to protect them. The bullets tore through her body.

As the ghastly reality begins to pierce his shock, a visceral response overtakes him. His stomach lurches, and he vomits violently into a trash bin just inside the door. Gasping for air, the dryness in his mouth burns. Pain rips through his body—the overwhelming agony of such senseless violence.
Jordan doesn't know how long he stands there in the doorway, torn between the deepest sadness—tears streaming down his face—and a rage he can barely contain. Confusion and shock consume him.

Vic, standing a few feet away, watches as his partner frantically checks his phone over and over, returning it to his pocket, only to pull it out again. Jordan fidgets with the watch on his wrist, mouth agape, head gently shaking from side to side, until all emotion and movement leave his body.

Vic pulls him from his trance—as gently as a partner can in that moment.
"Come on, man, we have to keep moving."

The dread twisting in Jordan's stomach is debilitating. He's in a daze now. Vic studies him closely, his eyes flicking back and forth, reading his partner's face.

They continue down the school hallway, Jordan moving senselessly, his pistol hanging limply at his side. He stumbles, unfocused, aimless—until Vic notices.

"Man, come on. I need you to pull it together. We've got to watch our six."

Jordan nods, slowly heeding the point. The instinct to survive begins to rise. He falls back on his training—this isn't his first war zone—and reverting to field tactics gives him something to hold on to. He knows what happens if you freeze in a skirmish. There will be time to deal with his broken mind later.

For now, he is numb—but nothing lasts forever. Eventually, you pay the bill for the sins you witness... if you make it out alive.

He shakes his head hard, sucks in a breath through his nose, and raises his Glock, tightening his stance. The two cops repeat their routine from the previous classroom and arrive at the next door. Empty. No one is inside. Open books lay sprawled across the small desks, but there are no signs of violence.

"They would've heard the gunfire up the hall and run," Vic speculates.

Jordan mutters through gritted teeth. "Run, hide, fight." That's what they train these kids to do.
He shakes his head, exasperated. The thought of children and teachers defending themselves against some asshole with an assault rifle—using only the contents of a classroom—would be laughable if not for the consequences.

Exiting the classroom, Vic suggests it might be a good time to sign up with God. He begins to mumble, "Dear God... please," but trails off.

"There's no point starting now, Vic." It's obvious he doesn't know how to pray anyway—and if he's about to die, Jesus isn't going to be fooled by a last-minute repentance.

The weight of his weapon grows tedious as he continues holding his aim high. The third classroom is just ahead.

"Slow is smooth, smooth is fast," he mutters quietly, a display of compensatory bravado.
With Jordan still dazed, Vic enters the room, sweeping the area —then freezes at the sight inside.
"It's clear, Jordy. Don't come in."

His breath hitches. His stomach twists. Tears fall. He pulls the door shut and turns away.

"It's clear, Jordy. Don't come in."

Vic's stomach clenches. Tears spill. He shuts the door and swallows hard. Closing his eyes, he breathes deeply before pulling himself out of the room. Two tough guys—ex-military, Philly beat cops—both reduced to tears within minutes of entering the school. Nothing they've seen before compares to this.

Time is suddenly of the utmost importance. They begin moving down the hallway again with escalating efficiency. More classrooms checked—most empty, some grotesque theaters of death.

Eventually, they reach the school bathrooms.

Moving swiftly to maintain an element of surprise, Vic sweeps across the tiled walls from a wide angle. Four stalls in front of him are locked.

"If anyone is in there, my name is Vic, and I'm a police officer with Hope Valley PD."
His voice is far more tremulous than he'd like. The silence—and lack of movement from within the stalls—confirms his fears.

"I know you're scared—and I am too. But I'm going to get everyone out. I understand nobody wants to come out, but can anyone tell me about the shooter? Where they are now? Anything at all?"

Silence lingers—until sobbing can be heard from the far stall. The voice that eventually answers is not that of a child, but a much older man.

"It's a kid... we heard him in the classroom up the hall."

Near the bathroom exit, the half mirror above the sinks catches the involuntary raise of Vic's brow.

With urgency tightening his voice, Vic presses the speaker. "I need a description of the shooter—weapon, location, anything you can tell me."
Again, silence.

Jordan's patience wears thin. He struggles to maintain coherent thought, his mind fractured by the flashing images of death and destruction.

He snaps. "Goddammit, tell me where this fuckin' kid is! NOW!"

Immediately, he hears sobbing from one of the stalls. A child—half-screaming while trying to whisper—hisses back at him.

"Please. Just shut up. He's going to hear you."

Then the adult voice returns. "The last I saw, he went into the library. I don't know guns—it was a big rifle. Please. Just get out there and kill him before he kills us."

His voice breaks as he finishes. He begins sobbing again, a low, guttural groan escaping between breaths. Jordan pauses for a moment, then addresses the concealed group.
"Wait here. We'll be back when it's over."

He storms out of the bathroom, rage surging through his veins. He needs to find the shooter—but there are still classrooms to clear. They're alone. No backup. No one else has entered the school.
The library lies ahead, its signage visible well before they reach the doors. A row of tall windows in the hallway reveals shelves and desk space inside. The windows are a massive risk. Jordan knows the shooter could be anywhere—concealed behind the books, rifle aimed through a gap, waiting to pick off officers as they enter.

They need to draw his attention.

Jordan darts into a nearby classroom and grabs two metal

chairs from behind a couple of desks. Holding them tightly, he uses the wall nearest to the library as cover.

"I'm going to smash the windows and see if we get any movement in there. Spot me, Vic."
Vic nods, moving farther down the hallway to cover the angle. Jordan, his nerves fraying, creeps closer to the glass. His grip tightens around one of the chairs—the weight of his rage pushing him forward.

With a maddened roar, he hurls the chair through the window. The deafening crack of shattering glass echoes through the hallway, followed by the violent splintering crash of shards scattering across the floor. The noise seems to freeze the air— and for a moment, everything is still.
Except for the pounding in his chest.

"I'm going to break another one, Vic."

He hurls the second chair at a farther window. It hits but doesn't break—too far, too angled. There's no clean way to do this.

Bracing himself, Jordan sets his left foot slightly behind his right. He pushes off hard, pounding down the hallway, launching himself through the broken frame, crashing into the small library—ready to throw the full weight of his body at anyone in the tight aisles.

Nothing.

The room is empty.

Vic holds position in the hallway, gun raised, eyes scanning the interior for any movement.
There is none.

Jordan's heart pounds so hard he feels it in his throat. Gradually, the rhythm slows.
He suddenly becomes aware of how quiet the hallway and

rooms around him have become. He can't bear to look inside any more of them. He begins to run—past another series of classrooms, rows and rows of nondescript metal lockers. He knows where to find this kid.

At the end of the hallway stand two large swinging doors with small vision panels. A sign above them reads: "Herbert R. Cunningham Gymnasium." Jordan doesn't know who that is, but Herb is going to hate the infamy about to be associated with his name.

He stops short of the doors, his mind racing. *Is this the only way in?*

For fuck's sake, he doesn't even know the layout of the school. Why is there an army of cops outside while he's alone— standing between a wooden door and some psychopath with an assault rifle?

This is a goddamn ambush.

Once he pushes those doors open, he's dead. Fear overtakes any remaining courage that carried him this far. He's scared—more scared than any other time in his life.

Vic appears beside him, puffing from the run.

"Jordy, you've gotta get under control, man. Shit...I know, but come on. You're my partner. We both need to get out of this."

"Yeah. Okay, Vic. I got you. It's gonna be alright."

It's not going to be alright.

Jordan runs the numbers in his head. The classrooms behind them are either empty, or everyone in them is dead. The captain, running the shit-show operation outside, has no idea how many are missing. If there are more victims—or hostages —they're in the gym.

The school is old, maybe built in the fifties. *Is this really the only entry and exit point?* Maybe additional exits were mandated later. Maybe they exist—and they're barricaded from the inside.

He reaches into his left front pocket for his phone—no signal. Probably a network overload. He has no way to call for help. He considers retreating back to the front of the school. He's taken so many risks already, and there's very little gained that might change the outcome. He wants to run—to leave the next step to someone more capable.

But despite every part of him screaming against it, he creeps toward the gym doors.

He presses himself into one corner and, as slowly as his fraying nerves allow, peeks through one of the small vision panes.

Nothing. It looks empty. He pulls back into the corner again.

Relief washes over him. His anger subsides into heartache. He's tired. His body is rigid from adrenaline. Without the power of rage, he just feels scared.

The shooter isn't in there. Jordan is certain he's searched the rest of the school. The kid probably escaped during the panic —blended in with the survivors. Stashed the guns somewhere. Probably in the gym.

Jordan doesn't know if he's lying to himself or thinking rationally.

He slowly brings his eyes back up to the vision pane.

He jerks back violently, chest heaving. Raising his left arm, he looks at his watch—180 beats per minute. He's pushing it. Staring straight ahead, he works to control his breathing. He presses his index and middle fingers against his neck, feeling the rapid pulse while watching the numbers on the screen.

Slouched in the corner of the hallway, just outside the gym doors, he whispers to himself, "Get your shit under control."

It's obvious what needs to be done. He inspects his weapon, releasing and reinserting the magazine before pulling back the slide slightly to check for a round in the chamber. He speaks quietly under his breath.

"Drop the weapon."

"Drop the weapon."

"Hands in the air. Hands in the air."

He slowly rises to his feet, checking the straps of his bulletproof vest.

"Center mass," he whispers.

Then he rushes the gym doors, gun aimed at the shooter's back —center mass. The kid stands midway across the gymnasium. A row of children huddles against the wall closest to him.

"DROP THE WEAPON! DROP THE WEAPON!"

The sheer force of the command startles Vic.

The shooter stands. Motionless. Emotionless.

"DROP THE WEAPON AND GET YOUR HANDS IN THE AIR!

Vic, get those kids out of here!"

Vic, keeping his weapon trained on the shooter, uses his free hand to guide the students toward the main doors. Within seconds, they're gone. Jordan and Vic are alone with the shooter.

"DROP THE WEAPON! LAST TIME I'M GONNA ASK!" Jordan screams.

Slowly, the teen turns. His rifle dangles loosely from one hand, barrel pointed toward the floor. In the other, he holds up his phone, its screen glowing. His movements are sluggish— almost dreamlike, like he's underwater.

The officers advance, closing the gap. The kid drops to one knee, placing the rifle down with exaggerated care—but keeps the phone raised.

"PUT YOUR FUCKIN' HANDS IN THE AIR, NOW!"

He just stands there. Staring. Past them. Through them.

A slow, eerie smile creeps onto his face.

"I'm... I'm gonna surrender now," he murmurs, voice flat, like he's reading from a script. "You're gonna take me... I want you to take me in."

Vic's breath catches. Something's off. The kid's pupils are blown wide, his skin damp with sweat—but there's no fear in his voice. No desperation. Just... detachment.

"Do you understand me, cops?" His speech slurs, as if forcing his tongue to move. "Arrest me..."
He lifts his wrists, pushing them forward in a mechanical motion, palms up. His fingers twitch. His head cocks slightly, as if listening to something only he can hear.

Jordan tenses, watching the shooter's eyes flick toward the rifle at his feet.

Beside him, Vic inhales sharply, his knuckles white around his gun. The rifle is several feet away.

The kid has no chance. He's done.

Jordan stares at him. The kid's eyes close.

A bolt of rage shoots through Jordan, burning in his veins. His jaw clenches. His brow furrows.
Hatred.

Jordan's Glock fires. Once. A pause. Then again.

The shooter staggers. His eyes snap open—wide with surprise

and confusion. His legs buckle. He crumples to the ground. The phone slips from his hand, the screen cracking against the floor.

The officers rush forward, Jordan's gun hovering inches from the teen's forehead. Blood pools beneath him, his chest rising in shallow, uneven breaths.

"What the fuck, Jordan?!" Vic's voice cracks. His body shakes as he paces.

Jordan doesn't answer.

The kid is dying. Fast. His lips part, mouthing something incoherent. His eyes flicker—not with pain, but with... nothing. Empty. Detached. Like he's already gone.

Jordan raises his boot over the kid's skull. He hesitates. Then lowers it.

No need. There's nothing left.

He stands over the shooter, waiting. Watching. Until the kid stops breathing.

He knows he's dead.

Jordan kicks the rifle closer to the body. He looks over at Vic but doesn't speak. He just stares at the shooter, blood pooling underneath him.

Vic snaps to attention. "Jordan. His phone—was he livestreaming?"

Jordan bends down and picks up the kid's phone, staring at the screen for what feels like an eternity before speaking.

"No. He was just recording it. It's not live."

He slips the phone into his pocket without saying anything more.

The two men stand in silence.

There's nothing more to be said.

CHAPTER 3: NO GOOD DEED GOES UNPUNISHED

Night of 24th November 2025

It was how they tried to get him. He should've seen it coming —recognized the tricks he'd used on suspects countless times before. His own captain had walked him in, arm around his shoulders, leading him into the interrogation room. Jordan knew the drill—casually dismissing the need for a lawyer or union rep. He'd only done it with guilty parties, not wanting to waste his time with lawyers and their games. Just get the confession, laid out in a well-worded spiel, with the assurance that the police were here to help.

He could've focused more if he'd been able to reach her. No response to his texts. Her phone was switched off. He needed her right now more than ever. First responder to a massacre —one thing. But what really had his mind racing was that he couldn't contact her. He had to focus on the issue at hand, put her out of his thoughts. There would be a perfectly reasonable explanation.

They had led him to believe it was just a routine interview— standard procedure after an officer-involved shooting. Captain Evans had even mentioned Garrity rights, assuring him that nothing he said could be used against him criminally in an interview like this.

But Jordan was too tired. Too exhausted to think straight. His mind was drained, overwhelmed by the horrors of the school. The images from today had burned themselves into his brain and would haunt him in his sleep. Like a horror film on a loop, the nightmares would lie in wait, striking at his most vulnerable moments.

But this... this was a different kind of nightmare.

After the introductions and the usual casual dismissal of the process—"just a routine procedure to protect you"—he knew what this was really about. The questions came fast, relentless, trying to crack his resolve.

"So, tell me again, Jordan. The shooter, Lamar—turned around 180 degrees. What happened next?"

Jordan slouched in his chair, opposite the two Internal Affairs detectives. He had been in this room countless times before, but never like this. Never under the cold gaze of the one-way mirror, and never with these two. The sterile room, devoid of personality, felt suffocating—mismatched chairs, a dented metal table, a welded metal rail on his side of the table. But no cuffs. Not yet.

His mind was a battlefield, the weight of the day crashing down. He wanted to sleep, but there was no escape from reality. The questions came again and again, pushing, prodding for a crack.

He didn't understand why he was here. Maybe Captain Evans had a bruised ego, or maybe it was because of rumors that President Reign had personally intervened. The operation had been a disaster—law enforcement was everywhere, and the kid had free rein to run around the school with a rifle because no one had a plan.

Why was he here? Why now? He didn't know. But one thing was clear: he had to stay focused. There was something these two didn't know, and it would stay that way. His life, his business. No one else had the full story. Vic didn't even know all the details.

As the silence dragged on, Jordan's thoughts strayed. He began ridiculing the detectives in his mind. Bitch Barrett and Pussy Pierce. Barrett could've been attractive, if not for her rigid personality and uptight demeanor. Her hair was pulled back too tight, makeup too minimal, and she wore one of those cheap women's suits that every detective seemed to love. Her yellow fingernails hinted at an addiction to cigarette breaks.

Pierce, on the other hand, was the epitome of a guy nobody liked. A pudgy, washed-up failure who had joined Internal Affairs to cement his place at the bottom of the barrel. His gut hung over his belt like dough overflowing from a pan. His flushed red complexion suggested he was fueled by something stronger than coffee, and his wife... well, she probably wondered how she ended up with someone like him.

Barrett cleared her throat, pulling him back to the present. "Ahem." Jordan sighed and answered.
"The same thing I told you. The gun was at a 45-degree angle to the floor. I shouted, 'POLICE, DROP YOUR WEAPON!' He raised the rifle, and I fired—two shots to the upper chest. He went down. I kicked the rifle away." His voice was hoarse, fatigue creeping into his words.
Pierce scribbled something on his notepad, tapping his pen twice. Was that a signal? Maybe, maybe not. The dread was building inside him.

"I see. And your partner, Vic—where was he?" Barrett asked, clearly enjoying the repetition of her questions.

"My left. Six feet away," Jordan answered, his voice rising involuntarily.

"What exactly made you feel threatened? Walk us through your mindset." Barrett's voice was smooth, but there was an edge to it.

Jordan leaned back, suddenly aware of the trap closing in. "This is sounding more like a criminal investigation."

"No one's saying that," Barrett said, feigning calm. "We're just trying to understand your decision-making."

Jordan felt the pressure mounting, like a noose tightening with every word. They were digging, searching for a hole in his story, but he wouldn't give them one.

"So, you discharged your weapon," Barrett noted, scribbling in her notepad. "You were certain lethal force was necessary?"

Jordan slammed his palms down on the table, the metal chair scraping violently against the floor as he leaned forward. His eyes locked on hers. "Listen, detective. I've been in this damn room for two hours, answering the same questions over and over. Yeah, lethal force was necessary."

Barrett didn't respond. Pierce didn't flinch. They were waiting, both of them, like predators circling. Jordan felt the rage building.

"You two idiots have spent two hours going around in circles!" he snapped. Barrett cut him off, her voice icy.

"Officer, today you broke rank, ignored direct orders from your captain. You and your partner took it upon yourselves to enter a school with an active shooter, not knowing the situation or the shooter's location. And then you engaged with a black teenage suspect, killing him. What do you think the problem is?"

Jordan shot back, his voice shaking with fury. "The problem is you're more worried about covering up the shit show that was this operation than the fact that little kids died today!" His blood boiled. He was done being calm.

"Maybe I'll just do an interview with the media outside," he muttered, glaring at them.

Barrett's expression hardened. "Officer Peck, if you walk out and talk to the media, you're done. You'll never work as a cop in this state again. That's a direct order."

Jordan shoved his chair back with force, the metal screeching against the floor as he stood. He pulled his police shield from his wallet, slamming it onto the table with a loud crash. He stormed out of the room, slamming the door behind him.

Barrett glanced at Pierce, who was still staring at his notepad, no longer pretending to take notes.
"Interesting," Pierce muttered. "I bet his friend next door heard him leave. Let's let him cool off for a bit."

Barrett nodded thoughtfully, then broke the silence. "You still think there's something off about the events?"

"Yeah. I do," Pierce replied, opening his phone to check the news. Outside, the media was swarming Jordan, interviewing him like he was a hero.

"That asshole is acting like he just won the Super Bowl," Pierce muttered, shaking his head.
A small smirk tugged at Barrett's lips before she wiped it away, her face growing stern again. "Goddamn it, this is gonna turn into a circus."

Twenty minutes later, the detectives entered the adjacent interview room. Vic Rodriguez sat hunched over, his forearms propped on the table, his face buried in his hands. He looked exhausted—defeated.

Barrett spoke first, her sarcasm sharp. "Good news! Your partner's resigned, leaving you to clean up this mess."

Vic barely looked up. "What mess, ma'am? We risked our lives when nobody else wanted to go in, and we stopped the shooter before he could kill more kids."

Barrett didn't flinch. "I disagree, Victor. The shooter's dead, and you and your partner are lucky not to be in the morgue too."

Vic's gaze shifted to the camera in the corner, then back to Barrett, his voice low and defeated. "The morgue? Most of those kids are probably piled up in refrigerated trucks. Thirty, forty dead? Do you even know? Christ, the evil shit I saw in that school today…"

Barrett nodded solemnly. "Look, Vic, I get it. Nobody's calling what happened here anything but pure evil. But we can't let the focus shift from the shooter to you and your partner for disobeying orders. The shooter's dead, and we don't want a wrongful death lawsuit on our hands."

Vic snorted. "Apprehend him? The kid had an automatic rifle pointed at us!"

Barrett leaned forward, eyes narrowing. "Tell me what happened inside that gym."

Vic slammed his forehead into his hands. "Fine. We went in, didn't know where the shooter was. We found him in the center of the gym, facing away. We yelled, 'Police, drop the weapon.' He turned, rifle at a 45-degree angle, started raising it, and Jordan shot him. He went down, we kicked the rifle away, and we tried to give first aid."

Barrett leaned back, studying Vic. "And why didn't you take the shot?"

"It happened too fast. Jordan shot him, and I knew he was neutralized. He went straight down."

Barrett turned to Pierce, who shrugged slightly.

"Officer Rodriguez… don't leave town," she snapped as she stood up and stormed out of the room.

CHAPTER 4: MORE GUNS, MORE GOD.

Richard Garrison pushed open the heavy oak door and stepped into the war room of the United Firearm Advocates Association. The leather seats creaked as board members shifted, their eyes locking onto him. He took his place at the head of the stately wooden table. Behind him, the American flag draped across the back wall, its bold colors glaring against the dark mahogany decor. To his right, a plaque bore the Second Amendment in raised brass letters; to his left, a reproduction of the Declaration of Independence hung beside portraits of Jefferson, Madison, Henry, Franklin, and Teddy Roosevelt.

Garrison settled into his chair, his bulky frame filling the last vacant seat at the table. He cleared his throat—a deep, resonant sound that demanded attention. The thirty or forty members in attendance sat forward, silence falling like a guillotine.

"Ladies and gentlemen, thank you for attending this extraordinary meeting," he said, his baritone voice cutting through the air. "For the record, present today are Vice President Lucas Kim, Treasurer Dr. Jason Caldwell, Chief Lobbyist Alicia Turner, Legal Affairs Chair Nathan Booker, Public Relations Manager Wyatt Dalton, and Secretary Elaine Vasquez."

A cell phone in the audience rang, its owner scrambling to silence it. Garrison shot them a cold glance. This was no time for distractions.

"Last week, we watched a tragedy unfold," he began, his voice steady but thick with underlying fury. "Forty-five lives lost to the criminal actions of a man with a gun. Who knows how much worse it could have been without the actions of two good men, armed with the strength of God and the finest American nine-millimeter bullets?"

Applause broke out, the room nodding in agreement, their faces lit with grim satisfaction. Elaine silently prayed, mouthing, "Thank you," her eyes cast upward as if Jesus personally intervened at some point to end the massacre.

Garrison let the silence stretch. "We know the media, the left, the politicians—they'll point fingers at us, at our rights, trying to blame the tools, not the criminals. They'll demand our surrender. But we won't bend. We won't give in." His voice hardened, each word deliberate. "We'll offer thoughts and prayers to the victims, but we'll also remind America that it's not the guns that kill—it's the criminals."

A pause. The murmurs in the room quieted, nods of approval mixing with sharp glances. A few cleared their throats, sensing the weight in Garrison's words.

"And let's be clear," he continued, his voice rising, "the fight for the Second Amendment is no longer about hunting, it's about survival. Our forefathers didn't give us the right to bear arms so we could protect ourselves from deer. They gave us that right to protect ourselves from tyranny—men like Lamar Williams who want to strip us of our freedom." He shot a glance at the portrait of Jefferson on the wall.

A few members stood and clapped, but the applause felt stiff, mechanical.

"All right, let's go around the table," Garrison said, the edge of his tone still sharp. "Alicia, what's the play?"

Alicia turned, her eyes bright with anger. "Thank you, Richard. Well, we know what's coming. The media's already spinning this into another anti-gun circus. The freedom-hating commies will come out in full force, blaming you, me, guns—everything but the criminals who commit these atrocities."

The room murmured in assent. The air buzzed with unity and simmering contempt.

Alicia's words cut through the chatter. "Mass shootings are good for us, statistically speaking. Donations surge. New memberships flood in. But we need to play this right. The public needs to see that we stand for the victims, not the violence. But we also need to stand firm. We can't let them take our rights because of one deranged bastard."

She paused, taking a sip from her water glass, struggling to balance it in her hand. Garrison's eyes briefly flicked to the microphone she gripped with two hands, nestled against her chest. His gaze lingered just a moment too long, a small smirk tugging at his lips, as though savoring a private joke.

"Let's be clear," she continued. "Schools need armed guards. Every damn school, all the time. We need to push the narrative that the only way to stop bad guys with guns is good guys with guns. And let's not forget—teachers should be armed, too. It's time to make that happen."

The Vice President raised his hand, leaning in with interest. "What do you think, Lucas?"

The Vice President spoke slowly, his voice dry. "How many lives could have been saved if, when Lamar Williams entered that school, a receptionist had said, 'Not today, buddy. You're not getting through here.' And then pulled out her S and W." He mimicked the motion, holding his hand up in a mock gun stance, then blew imaginary smoke from his fingers.

Garrison laughed, the sound deep and approving. "Good ol' Smith & Wesson—always protecting the good guys from the bad." He turned to Wyatt. "Wyatt, you've been quiet. Thoughts?"

Wyatt nodded, keeping his voice even. "This is tragic, no doubt. But we can't let it undermine everything we stand for. We need to control the PR, make sure the media knows where we stand. We can show compassion for the victims, but we can't let these events weaken our position on gun rights. That's the real fight."

Nathan Booker, the Legal Affairs Chair, had been sitting silently for most of the meeting, his arms crossed and his face set in a serious expression. But now, he leaned forward, clearing his throat to make his voice heard.

"You know, we haven't really hit the video game and movie angle lately," he said, his tone slow but deliberate. "Every time one of these tragedies happens, the media goes straight for the guns. But we haven't made enough noise about the real poison —the culture of violence we're feeding our kids. These damn video games and movies glorify violence and desensitize young minds. It's a damn shame."

He paused, shaking his head as if reflecting on a lost time. "And it's not like the old days, when we had good, wholesome American movies that showed right from wrong. Now all we get is trash that teaches our kids to glorify the bad guys. We've got to start calling out this toxic culture. It's time we push that narrative—guns aren't the problem, it's what people are watching and playing."

Garrison raised an eyebrow, intrigued by the suggestion. He nodded, his eyes glinting with a calculating look. "Not a bad angle, Nathan. It's been a while since we've hit that one. Let's make sure we highlight the importance of protecting our kids from this garbage. Wyatt, what do you think?"

Elaine, sitting quietly at the table, spoke up. "What about a donation to the victims' families? A scholarship fund, maybe? Help promote educational opportunities in their names?"

Garrison sat back in his chair, arms crossed, his eyes narrowing. His demeanor shifted from thoughtful to icy resolve.

"Elaine, no. We're not funding school shootings. It's not our fault that criminals are turning schools into shooting galleries. We won't sponsor that kind of nonsense. We stand firm on our core message. This is about preserving the Second Amendment, not playing into their hands."

Garrison, his head still shaking in frustration; "does anyone have anything intelligent to ask? Dr. Jason?"

Dr. Jason Caldwell, the Treasurer, sat back in his chair, his gaze steady but with a hint of frustration. Finally, he spoke, his voice low but deliberate.

"You know, we've been dancing around the real issue here. It's not just the guns—it's the culture. And what's feeding that culture? These goddamn rappers and their glorification of thuggery. The music today is full of filth—promoting violence, disrespect, and this whole 'gangsta' mentality. Look at what these kids are listening to. Look at what they're idolizing. They're being taught that violence is power, that swagger is more important than integrity. It's poisoning their minds."

He paused, allowing the words to sink in, then leaned forward, his hands gripping the arms of his chair. "You think this kid, Lamar Williams, was some outlier? Hell no. He's the product of a culture that worships criminals, we need to get these kids back to listening to real music, you know, some Glen Campbell, Merle Haggard- you think anyone ever listened to Rhinestone Cowboy and went out committing massacres?"

Caldwell shook his head, disgust evident in his voice as he looked around the room of attendees—all of whom were white. "I remember when music used to mean something— something decent. Something that taught respect, patriotism. Now it's all about disrespecting authority. You know, all this 'F the po-lice' talk, acting like prison is glory. It's no wonder these kids are out of control. I mean, did you see the halftime show at the Super Bowl this year? That rapper, Kendrick Lamar, mumbling nonsense, lewd dancing in front of our children. Now that's the real national tragedy."

He looked around the room, his eyes lingering on Garrison. "If we're really going to fix this, we need to start calling out that trash. You can't just blame the guns. We've got to address the poison they're listening to, the poison that's turning them into this."

Garrison's eyes narrowed slightly, a dark smile playing at the edge of his lips. "I like where you're going, Jason. Let's put that in the mix. It's time people start seeing the full picture. Wyatt, thoughts?"

He looked around the table, making eye contact with each member. "Alright, I think we've got enough to move forward. Let's take a short break. Afterward, we'll come up with a clear plan to rally the troops, lobby the politicians, and draft our responses for the media. We have work to do."

CHAPTER 5: THOUGHTS AND PRAYERS

The President skimmed over the speech again, printed on crisp white sheets, double-spaced, with massive font. The teleprompter was ready, displaying the carefully crafted words meant to guide him. The work was probably redundant; he liked speaking off the cuff anyway.

Behind the camera, Lauren took a deep breath. "Are you ready, sir?"

Reign straightened his tie, puffed out his chest, and fixed his gaze on the lens.

"Lauren, I'm always ready." His face hardened into what could only be described as his version of presidential seriousness.

The camera operator began the countdown. "And recording in five, four..."

Reign inhaled deeply and launched into the speech.

"My fellow Americans... Today, I stand before you not just as your President, but as a father, as a leader, and as a man who loves this country. And today, something truly disgusting happened. Something horrible. An atrocity. A total disgrace. Innocent children... little kids, were gunned down at Hope Valley Elementary in Pennsylvania. You know, they're telling me 45 dead? Some teachers and mostly students? Terrible. Absolutely terrible."

He shook his head, lips pressed tight as if personally offended.

"We have had ENOUGH of this. Enough! Every time, they say, 'thoughts and prayers.' Every time, they say, 'we have to come together.' Well, I say NO MORE! We are not coming together. We are going to take ACTION. And folks, let me tell you, it is NOT going to be pretty."

Lauren shifted in her seat. This wasn't the script. He'd deviated after just two sentences and was now careening toward an unpredictable route.

"Now let's talk about how this happened, because we all know some of the media won't tell you the truth. Who's to blame? WHO is responsible? Because let me tell you, this is not just some random act. This is systemic. This is a FAILURE at every level."

He jabbed a finger toward the desk, as if it too required discipline.

"We have soft-on-crime, weak police leadership—like Police Captain Evans, who, I gotta say, folks, is just... a complete disaster. A total embarrassment. Should've NEVER been in charge. NEVER. And now, look at what happened. The blood of these kids? It's on his hands. It's on the hands of the people who let this happen."

Lauren sucked in a breath. Oh, Jesus. Blaming a police captain for the massacre.

"You know who else is responsible? The radicals. The lunatics. The criminals flooding into our country. The woke mob, the activists—they don't want law and order. They don't want strong schools, safe schools. And we see the results, don't we? We see it every single day." He held up a hand, shaking his head.

"And let me tell you something else: this shooter? This shooter didn't act alone."

Lauren sucked in a breath so forcefully, she felt as if her lungs would explode. Unable to exhale.
"Oh no. No, no, no. He was assisted by the failures of the past administration and their failures towards mental health and education."

Lauren let go of her held breath. She never knew if he was going to sprout some iniquitous conspiracy or just wax lyrical, musing about things he didn't fully understand. She turned to the staffers, who looked just as shell-shocked. The camera operator hesitated but didn't stop the feed. No one dared interfere. At least he wasn't naming any individual on national TV, but the broader political attack was undeniable.

"Now, before I continue, I have to say something about the heroes of today. Because let's be honest, without them, this would have been even worse—if you can believe it. Officer Victor Rodriguez. Officer Jordan Peck. Two BRAVE men. VERY brave men. They ran in, no hesitation, no fear—just pure, raw American COURAGE. And they took this shooter down like the rabid animal he was." Reign spread his arms wide.

"You know, folks, some people might say, 'Oh, maybe they shouldn't have used deadly force.' And to those people, I say: SHUT UP. Shut your mouths! If it were up to me, we'd be giving these guys medals. Medals! Because in MY America, we don't mourn for monsters. We celebrate the heroes who put them down."

He paused, letting his admonishment sink in.

"You know this was some kind of record? I think a record for the most children killed in a school shooting? Who would have thought?"

There it was, the musings of the president, on live television.

Then, abruptly, he froze. The energy shifted, and the room

went silent. Tension stretched like a rubber band ready to snap. Lauren tilted her head, trying to discreetly signal him. Just stick to the script, that's all you need to do. Reign blinked, and just like that, any pretension toward following the script evaporated.

"You know what? No. No more speeches, no more fake sympathy. I'm sick of it. I'VE HAD ENOUGH."

Lauren's stomach dropped. Oh no. No, no, no.

"Tomorrow morning—first thing, I am summoning my people. Homeland Security, the Defense Secretary, the NYPD, every damn person who can actually get things done. We are ending this. And if we need to bring in the military, we bring in the military. If we need to change the laws, we change the laws. And let me tell you, if people don't like it? TOO BAD."

His fist slammed against the desk.

"No more dead kids. No more excuses. No more WEAKNESS."

He let the words hang for a moment, then leaned forward slightly.

"Thank you. God bless you. And God bless the United States of America."

The camera kept rolling for a few lingering seconds before the operator called it. "And… we're clear."

Lauren shot up from her seat.

"Sir… I don't know what just happened, but I don't think that was…"

Reign cut her off with a wave of his hand. "Lauren. Listen. I don't care. I don't care! This is happening. First thing tomorrow, I want a round table, in person. Get me DHS, get me the Defense Secretary, get me anyone you have to—I don't care. We are getting this done." Lauren opened her mouth, then shut it. She had nothing.

Reign smirked. "And get me those two cops. The ones who took down that son of a bitch. I want to talk to them personally. Maybe I give them an award, maybe I give them a promotion. Who knows? We'll figure it out. But get someone to set up a meeting with them, I love meetings."

Lauren sighed, rubbing her temples. "Yes, sir. I'll set it up now."

"Good." He straightened his cuffs. "And Lauren?"

Her head tilted slightly forward. "...Yes?"

Reign grinned. "Tell the press it was the best speech I've ever given. You know, I didn't use the script? I just made it all up on the spot. I wouldn't be surprised if that goes down in history as one of the greatest presidential addresses ever."

CHAPTER 6: A BAD MAN WITH A GUN.

16th May 2024

It was a scheduled callout in the inner city, part of a police outreach education program. Still, Sergeant Jordan Peck felt uneasy as the crowd in front of him glared back with trepidation. He was confident he could incapacitate the entire room single-handedly if tensions rose too much, but that would be a gross excess of force. Around the room, oversized furniture with soft edges and bright colors contrasted against the scaled-down desks and tiny chairs.

"Okay, everybody, Officer Peck is here today to talk to us about a very important subject: what to do if something scary happens at school."

The teacher smiled at Jordan, and he suddenly realized he found her quite attractive. His train of thought briefly derailed.

"Officer Peck, are you ready?" she asked in a perky tone. Her voice was small and sweet, almost childlike.

"Yes, thank you, ma'am," he replied, moving to the center at the front of the room. Twenty-eight young students sat peering at him.

"I'm here to talk to you today about staying safe when bad or scary things happen at school. This could also apply when you're not at school. We're going to discuss what you should do. Have you ever participated in a fire drill before?"

A chorus of young voices droned in response, "Yeeessss."

"Okay, so just like when we practice a fire drill, we're going to practice what to do if we ever have a situation where there's a bad person at the school."

A student in the second row gingerly raised their hand. "What if it's a bad lady?"

Jordan was bemused. The question, in its innocence, was almost facetious. Actually, kid, he thought to himself, considering that most mass shootings in this country have been perpetrated by men, the chances of you, as an eight-year-old, being slaughtered in your classroom by a woman are next to none.

"Yes, it could be a bad lady too," he answered.

A little girl raised her hand and, before Jordan could prompt her, called out, "Could it be a teacher being bad?"

"Uh, well, no. Statistically, perpetrators are usually not current faculty members..." Jordan started to explain.

The teacher cut him off. "Boys and girls, perhaps we can wait until the end to ask Officer Peck questions, okay?"

He appreciated the backup on this one. He was a large, physically intimidating man, but he had no idea why he was always assigned to these kinds of education programs. Then he shuddered at the thought of a teacher going postal and the catastrophic effect that would have on these kids. Lambs to the slaughter. He refocused.

"Right, so back to what we do if a bad person, even if they are a member of the faculty—is present. We're going to learn about something called 'run, hide, fight.' Now, it's very rare that we would ever have to use it, but it is important to learn, okay?"

The students murmured in agreement.

"If you see or hear something that doesn't feel right—like loud noises, bangs, something unusual—the first thing we should think about is 'run.' This means moving away from the noise as fast as you can in the safest way possible. It might mean not taking the usual route but finding the safest one.

You always head toward a safe place. Does anyone know what a safe place might be?"

"Your house?"
"The police station?"
"The library?"

"Good answers, but sometimes it depends on what's happening. A safe place is anywhere you feel out of danger and where there are adults who can help you."

Jordan glanced at the teacher. He was in the zone now, commanding the presentation, holding the room.

"What if we can't run to safety? That's when we 'hide.' Have you ever played hide and seek? That's what we want to do here, find somewhere to hide where no one will be able to find you. It could be a closet, behind something, or even just under your desk. The key is to be as quiet as possible until someone you trust, like a police officer or a teacher, tells you it's safe to come out."

He scanned the room. The mood had darkened. He saw it in the children's eyes, in the way they shifted in their seats. Then he caught the teacher's expression—the lightness in her demeanor replaced with solemnity.

This was the part he hated. He hadn't become a cop to teach elementary school kids how to fight back against a perp with an assault weapon. He took a deep breath.

"The last option, and this is something we only do if we absolutely must, is 'fight.' Now, this doesn't mean trying to punch or hurt the bad person. It means doing anything you can to stay safe. It could be yelling or screaming to get someone's attention. But if you really have to, you can find something to scare them away."

The absurdity of this lesson weighed on him. His eyes darted around the classroom for objects that could be used as weapons. His hand instinctively brushed his own gun holster, reassuring himself while knowing they would be helpless if there was an active shooter. He clenched his jaw.

"Okay, remember, the most important thing, more important than running or hiding—is that if you see or hear anything out of the ordinary, you must tell an adult immediately. You won't be in trouble for speaking up, even if it turns out to be nothing. Whether it's someone behaving oddly near the school or overhearing something that just doesn't sound right, you need to let us know. Does everyone understand?"

The children voiced their agreement in a chorus of "Yes!"

"Thank you, everyone. You listened so carefully today and did a great job. I'm so proud of you.

Remember, the police and your school staff are here to help you and keep you safe. Come to any of us anytime you're worried about something."

Jordan looked at the teacher, his gaze meeting hers. They held eye contact for a few seconds before she broke into a smile and looked down.

If he could just get rid of these kids for a minute, he had a few questions he wanted to ask her after this presentation. Maybe he'd stop by after school.

Where the hell was the bell when you needed it?

CHAPTER 7: AMERICA DEMANDS ACTION

28th November 2025

Lauren was seated within the West Wing of the White House, inside the Situation Room. Looking around, she marveled at the technology that enveloped the space; large digital screens were mounted on the walls, accompanied by the audible hum of electrical equipment. She recalled the press release detailing the complex's upgrade, highlighting how construction extended five feet downward to accommodate the enhanced power and technological requirements. Constructed in 1962, following President Kennedy's directive for a streamlined intelligence feed into the White House after the Bay of Pigs Invasion, the Situation Room had since been the epicenter of critical decision-making. It was here that Kennedy navigated the Cuban Missile Crisis, Bush coordinated the response to September 11, and Obama watched the operation to capture Bin Laden live.

God only knows what Reign will do. The prospect of solving the epidemic of school shootings by holding a crisis meeting with a collection of equally clueless, hamstrung, and constrained middle-aged men, each battling both literal and figurative impotence, was a joke she found almost amusing. The faintest hint of a smile curled at her lips, but the realization of what was coming crushed it. As the thought sank in, she couldn't ignore the sinking feeling in her stomach. It wasn't just the meeting itself that disturbed her, it was the impending stupidity that she knew would come with the

President speaking without a script.

Suddenly, a phalanx of powerful-looking men entered the room, a moment later followed by their respective advisors and staff. The men all moved forcefully to take a seat at the table, some exchanging curt greetings with Lauren. After a few minutes, the President entered the room.

Lauren took a measured breath, ensuring her posture was upright and her expression neutral. She had done this before, but this was different. The weight of the school shooting loomed over the room like a specter, and every person present knew why they were here.

"Gentlemen," she began, her tone measured and professional. "Thank you for assembling on such short notice. I will proceed with introductions." She glanced at her notes, though she had memorized every name long before entering the room.

"Vice President Bruce Sinclair," she said, nodding to the man seated to Reign's right. "National Security Advisor General Nathan Pierce. Secretary of Defense Admiral Carter Hammond. Secretary of Education Dr. Hector Alvarez. Attorney General Douglas Newman. Director of National Intelligence David Bishop. Director of Homeland Security Julian Crest. NYPD Commissioner John Martinez. LAPD Chief of Police Angela Richardson. Ethical Affairs Policy Advisor Dr. Anika Patel. And finally, United Firearm Advocates Association President Richard Garrison."

She took a calculated pause before continuing. "We are gathered today to discuss an appropriate course of action following the tragic events at Hope Valley Elementary."

Garrison leaned back in his chair, the leather creaking under his weight. With a dismissive wave, he interrupted her.

"Doug, what the hell is this meeting for? We're wasting time, believe me. This is just nonsense. Everyone knows what we need. You know it. I know it," Garrison said, slapping his hand against the armrest with emphasis.

"Richard, two days ago, we saw the worst school massacre ever. It was a disaster, folks. And I mean, just—nothing like it, alright? But we're going to fix it. We're going to use the best, most incredible law enforcement, the military. The best technology. We're talking about scientists, engineers, folks, the smartest people, and we're gonna fix this problem. It's gonna be huge. We're going to end this problem for good."

Lauren bit her lip, stifling an eye roll. The screens around the room flashed with live feeds from news channels, but she couldn't focus. She had always assumed that this president's legacy would be his endless, mind-numbing gaffes and embarrassing faux pas. Yet now, he was determined to leave his mark as the one who failed at solving gun violence in schools, all while rubbing the UFAA's back. Her gaze shifted across the table to Garrison, who was staring directly at the President, his face contorted with impatience.

"Doug, listen. These shootings? They're rare. They're extremely rare, okay? What do you think is more likely? More people get hit by cars on the way to school than by shooters. It's just a fact, people. It's a fact," Garrison said with a gesture, like he was sharing a top-secret truth. "What we need is more armed guards in schools. More teachers armed. You're gonna see it. Trust me, it's gonna work, it's the only solution that works."

LAPD Chief Richardson slammed her hand onto the wooden table with a force that made everyone in the room jump.

"For Christ's sake, Garrison! Are you out of your mind?" She leaned forward, her voice raising in incredulity. "You want teachers to walk into classrooms with guns, and then, if an intruder shows up, you want them to shoot that person in front of kids?"

Garrison stared at her, unfazed. "Let's not get emotional here. I know over in California, you're all peace and love, but in the real world, we aren't all out here driving electric cars, smoking pot and hugging one another, okay? We can fix this, just train the teachers, simple. It's really simple. We've got to educate them. Have you ever seen a gun shoot somebody by itself? Listen to yourself, y'all blaming an inanimate object when it's the criminals we need to worry about. It's just about education, my friends. Educating teachers, faculty staff, whoever really—educating them to shoot sure and straight."

Dr. Alvarez, unable to let that slide, quickly cut in. "Mister Garrison, with all due respect, you're talking about arming teachers like they're police officers. This idea is ridiculous. You might as well hand out matches and tell them to prevent fires. Guns have no place in a classroom."

Garrison waved him off like he was dismissing a trivial concern. "Exactly! That's what I'm saying! You can't stop a fire unless you know how to use matches, right? Guns are no different. We train people, we make them safe, and we'll solve this problem. Trust me, it'll work."

Lauren, with her patience wearing thin, stepped in before Garrison could derail everything further.
"Mister President?"

The President looked at her, momentarily stunned by her interruption. Then he straightened in his chair, ready to put his mark on the discussion.

"Richard, listen. I love guns. America loves guns. Everybody loves guns. We're not here to reduce gun rights, no. It's not happening while I'm president. More guns is the answer, folks. The more guns, the better. We all know it. Guns equal safety. More safety."

"Exactly! That's right," Garrison chimed in, his face lighting up with pride. "More guns! More safety! You know it, I know it, everyone knows it. And let's not forget, the Second Amendment is sacred. It's the most important right we have! You take that away, we're not America anymore. What are we? Some trash country that doesn't have any freedom? You want to be like Canada? What about Australia? They don't even have guns—a whole continent living in fear. The founders knew what they were doing. They wanted us to have the firepower to stand up to tyranny."

Lauren exhaled sharply. Tyranny? Was he seriously suggesting that the ability to buy an AR-15 at their local gun shop was going to keep the government in check?

At this point, a soft voice interrupted, the first attempt at a more measured approach. It was Dr. Anika Patel, Ethical Affairs Policy Advisor, who had remained silent up until now.

"Gentlemen, with all due respect, I think we need to pause and ask ourselves: will giving more guns to teachers really stop violence, or could it escalate the situation? We know that many school shootings have been carried out by people with access to legally purchased firearms—more guns doesn't always equal more safety, and sometimes it could just—"

"Antifa, listen," Garrison snapped, cutting her off. "You can't be serious. More guns, better trained people—it's not rocket science. Don't overthink this. The answer is simple. We make sure everyone's armed, and we won't have any problems. You can talk all day about what-ifs, but the bottom line is that guns protect people. Period. How are you going to shoot me if I shoot you first? We don't need defense, we need offense. We don't need to be crybabies about it—we're not gonna score a touchdown sitting on the bench, are we?"

Reign, nodding vigorously, chimed in, his tone committed and firm.

"Richard's right. Folks, I'm telling you. More guns. We're gonna be the safest country in the world. Just imagine it. Nobody's gonna mess with us. More guns equal more safety. No one's gonna dare try anything. Believe me."

Lauren felt her stomach twist as she watched the room devolve into chaos. The President's simplistic "more guns" mantra was being met with a cacophony of voices, some in vehement agreement, others in horrified opposition. She wondered how the nation could come together if the best people the country could assemble couldn't have a civilized conversation in a hallowed room. She needed to do something, something crazy to counter these arguments and focus attention. Something so stupid, it would derail the meeting.

"Mr. President," she interjected, her voice cutting through the noise. "Perhaps we should consider your idea about using robots?"

The room fell silent, all eyes turning to Lauren. She could feel Garrison's glare burning into her, but she pressed on.

"President Reign, you and I had an interesting discussion about robots protecting our schools. Do you think this is something we should explore further?"

President Reign sat silent for a moment, the room following suit, waiting for the president to speak.
"That's true, folks. Listen, guns are great, nobody can deny that, I have a great idea for ending gun violence in American schools..."

CHAPTER 8: WE DON'T TALK ABOUT HOPE VALLEY

November 30, 2025

"Jordy, you nervous, man?" Vic broke the silence between them. They sat at a small table in the Liberty Grand Hotel bar, away from the other patrons. Through the large windows next to their table, the White House loomed a short distance up the road. Jordan swirled his glass of scotch and Coke, watching the last remnants melt into the ice. He shot the drink back and set the empty glass aside before signaling to a waitress to bring another round.

"No, it'll be okay..." His voice was stoic, but a sense of dread gnawed at him. He hated feeling this way, the unease creeping up on him until the weight felt immovable, crushing down on him.
Vic nodded. "I can't believe that bitch took your badge... After everything you've done..."

This wasn't entirely accurate, but in the past few weeks, Jordan had unwittingly become a national hero. The story had been shaped by misleading facts, hidden behind internal affairs' privacy rules.
Suddenly, a man approached their table.

"Excuse me, sir? Are you Jordan Peck?"

Jordan looked up, quickly scanning the man's waist. No signs of a gun or holster. He relaxed, then nodded.

"I just wanted to thank you for everything you've done, sir.

You're an American hero."

Jordan stood, shaking the man's hand. "Oh, hey, thanks, buddy. This is my partner, Vic Rodriguez. He went in with me that day."

The man smiled. "Right. Nice to meet you. Hey, would you mind taking a picture of me with Officer Peck?" His tone was eager, like a child meeting a celebrity.

Jordan hesitated. "Actually, why don't we ask someone to take a photo of all three of us?"
He raised his hand, signaling a nearby waiter, who approached to take their picture. Afterward, the man shook their hands and left.

"This shit has been happening non-stop, Vic. Is it happening to you?" Jordan asked.

"A couple of times, man. The news really blew up about you, but, huh, when we meet the prez, you might want to let him know you're gonna take his job."

Jordan laughed. "No way. Too many problems for me. I'll stick with being a cop."

He quickly caught the slip, and his smile faded.

"What are you going to do now, Jordy? Think you'll get your pension?"

"No. No pension. Money won't be an issue for a while, though. That donation site they set up raised a couple hundred grand."

"Holy shit, Jordy, that's a few years of paychecks right there."

"Yeah, but I don't want charity. I just wanted to go to work, do my thing, you know? After we discharged, there weren't many options. Now, I'll never work in this state again in law enforcement—unless it's as a mall cop or something."

"What about other states, man? Maybe somewhere warmer?"

"I heard chatter about other departments offering me a job, but they're all backwater hellholes with half the salary... I don't know. Maybe I'll hit up the president and see if I can be Secret Service." Jordan smiled at the thought.

"Jordy, you gonna take a bullet for the prez?" Vic asked, sincerely.

"Nah, man. But it won't come to that. I'm proactive, not reactive! Shoot first, ask questions later."
Vic stared at him, and the mood shifted. The conversation died. Jordan felt a surge of anger. He didn't appreciate the lack of support.

"Look, Jordy. I'm not here to judge what happened that day. Shit went down, and it's done."
Jordan's anger flared, dread twisting in his gut. It hit him without warning, engulfing him. A pulse of rage surged within his chest. The words boiled up inside him until they shot off his tongue without restraint. "Don't ever fucking bring it up again. Not now, not ever. Don't think about it, don't question it, and don't fucking talk about it. Got it?"

"Jordy... I..." Vic froze, taken aback by the sudden rage. He struggled for words as Jordan pressed on.

"You saw what that piece of shit did. If you didn't like it, you could've sold me out to IA. But you didn't. Now, unless you want to call 'em up and tell them you lied during the IA investigation... Maybe incriminate your partner? Is that what you want?"

Vic stared, mouth slightly open, struggling to find words. Finally, he said, "Jordy, I got your back. Ain't nobody gonna tell those assholes anything about that day. The truth is, that kid raised his weapon, and you took him out. You're a hero, Jordy.

Plain and simple."

"Yeah. That's fucking right, Vic. Don't ever bring it up again, alright?"

"Yeah, alright, Jordy. It's cool. We don't ever need to talk about it again."

The two men sat in silence, sipping their drinks until only the ice remained. Finally, Jordan broke the quiet.

"Vic, look, it's just... It's hard, man. I don't want to talk about it or think about that shit. But you know..."

"It's all good, Jordy. We're good. You're my partner, with or without your shield."

Jordan nodded. The mood lightened, and Vic attempted to change the subject.

"So, you still seeing that girl, Jordy? The one you never introduced to me?"

Jordan didn't answer. He sat, twisting his watch around absentmindedly, his gaze distant. After a moment, he blinked, like waking from a dream.

"I could go for another drink. You want a round, Vic? Let me grab it."

As arranged, at eleven a.m., the vehicle organized by White House aides arrived precisely at the designated time at the drop-off area outside the hotel. The late-model black sedan was immaculately presented, as was the staff member who exited the front passenger seat and briskly walked around the rear of the car to open the back door for the two men, acknowledging that they were indeed Mister Peck and Mister Rodriguez. The dark, tinted windows hid the interior of the vehicle. Upon opening the door, the detailed stitching and soft leather struck Jordan with the level of opulence it presented.

The minibar was stocked with decanted spirits and appointed with crystal glasses. The staffer turned in his seat to face the two colleagues.

"Gentlemen, we will now proceed to the Northwest Gate of the White House. Travel time will be approximately fifteen minutes. At the gate, you will be subject to identification screening and a metal detector. If you have any weapons on your person, they will be held at the checkpoint and returned at the completion of your visit."

The staff member returned to his forward-facing position and nodded to the driver. As promised, the vehicle pulled up promptly to the gate of the White House at approximately quarter past eleven. Upon exiting the vehicle, the men were thoroughly screened by security officers at the gate. They were quickly escorted to a secondary security station, where they were subjected to a metal detector scan, pat downs, and residue tests. At precisely eleven forty a.m., the men were escorted down a hallway towards the doorway of the Oval Office. At the end of the hall, a tall, slim woman, perhaps in her thirties, stood, her sharply presented suit providing a pop of red color against the decor. As the two police officers approached, the woman extended her hand to greet them, her familiarity with the two men evidenced by greeting each with their correct names.

"Mister Peck, welcome. Officer Rodriguez, my name is Lauren Chalmers, I'm the chief of staff for the president. Thank you for this meeting; it's an honor to have you here."

"Thank you, ma'am."
"We're honored to be here, ma'am."

"Right, so now I'll take you in to meet with the president... Mr. Reign. Please, don't be nervous; we'll make sure everything goes smoothly here. Now, there will be a number of members of the White House media team present as well. They'll take photos and video recordings of the meeting that may be released to the general media—obviously, outlets that are friendly to our side of things. I understand you've been briefed on how to conduct yourselves during the meeting: keep it simple, no politics, don't be controversial... anything goes off track, the meeting will be terminated immediately. Everyone understand the rules here?"

"Yes, ma'am," Vic answered.

"Sure," Jordan responded with a slight flippancy, mirrored by the subtle roll of his eyes.
"Okay. We're scheduled for five minutes for this meeting, but the president has discretion to either increase or decrease this time. Let's go, gentlemen."

Lauren finished as she pushed the door open, leading the way into the room and holding it from the inside. The bold red carpet and presidential emblem were immediately visible.

"President Reign," Lauren paused as he stood up from the chair behind the Resolute desk and walked around to the center of the room. "It's my pleasure to introduce you to Mr. Jordan Peck and Mr. Victor Rodriguez."

CHAPTER 9: THE PRESIDENT'S MEN

Lauren looked at her watch, noting the intricate yet simple details. It was a beautiful piece, gifted to her by her family when she completed college. Her right hand gripped the black leather band as she marveled at its minimalist, understated elegance. It occurred to her that this watch was symbolic; her life had been far less nuanced and ambiguous before entering politics. Now, the many shades of gray in the multifarious nature of her work meant there was less right and wrong—more so the least-worst course of action or the best that could be achieved.

She sighed. It was just after eleven-thirty. She had to meet those two idiot cops who went rogue and took out that school shooter. The last thing she needed today. The president would be amused, of course; he loved the idea of these two playing Rambo in an elementary school and "saving the day." Saving the day—if you didn't factor in the forty dead kids and half a dozen school staff. Jesus, what a couple of morons. They'd get on just fine with Reign.

Lauren finalized the organization of the documents on her desk within her office, located at the end of the hallway. Deciding it was time to move, she exited the small room and walked to the end of the hallway outside the Oval Office. Within a minute or so, a member of staff entered the hall with the two cops following. Time for her stage face—what she called it when readying to perform. She was nearly always "on," but there were moments when she could let her guard down and hide her inner thoughts. There was always a photographer, a foreign dignitary, or a member of the public nearby, and her every movement was captured, reported on, and analyzed. A big breath, as if sucking in the necessary demeanor and expelling her actual personality while she performed. Professional speaking voice now on.

"Mister Peck, welcome. Officer Rodriguez, my name is Lauren Chalmers. I'm chief of staff for the president. Thank you for this meeting; it's an honor to have you here."

"Thank you, ma'am."
"The honor is all ours, ma'am."

The big one was not a bad-looking man by any means. Tall, with wide shoulders, he looked a little like he could be a poster child for the Aryan Brotherhood. Maybe he wasn't a racist bigot with large hands and a small brain—she hadn't quite decided yet. In any case, the president would like him. He looked like the kind of idiot who would support Reign's politics without questioning things with too much critical thought. With his military background and being a cop, she was fairly confident there was going to be a photo op with the president shortly. And he was big and powerful-looking. That was the kind of thing the president liked: big, powerful men. This guy was going to impress him. Ex-military, ex-cop, American hero, white.

The other cop was a problem. With a name like Rodriguez, it was obvious he was going to be Latino before they met, but he looked really Latino. Considerably shorter than his partner, with dark olive skin and deep brown eyes that conveyed a sense of empathy missing from the cold stare of his offsider. Framed by thick black eyebrows, his sharply trimmed mustache was almost the same color as the suit he wore. The president was not going to like this. Not one bit. Hopefully, he was one of the Mexicans the president took a liking to, which of course meant he was smart enough to agree with the administration's position on immigration—despite it being very likely he was an immigrant, or at least his parents were.

Did he have an accent? She couldn't tell from the brief interaction. Please don't have an accent. The only way this could be worse was if he walked in with an oversized sombrero, accompanied by a mariachi band, shouting, Hola, amigo!

Lauren laid down the rules to the two cops. The big one, Peck, had an attitude about him. He'd been dismissed from the police force for failing to cooperate with the investigation into what happened in that gym. It was an intense controversy; in the usually divided states of America, there was a rare majority consensus that he was a bit of a hero—with an unusually small number of protesters for a white cop shooting a black kid. Of course, this kid did murder a lot of children with automatic weapons, but these days, there were always enough people on all sides of the spectrum to protest any cause. Even the shooter's parents sided with the cop on this one, though they were smart enough to betray him for their own sake.

Maybe it was fair that he was disenchanted. Until recently, he'd made a career out of serving, and now he was left with nothing. The president didn't like it—"a very big disgrace," he told Lauren. Hopefully, Reign wouldn't get too excited and fire someone just to promote this big ape to be the new Secretary of Homeland Security. No, that couldn't happen; the formal process and justification would be too drawn out to hold the president's attention. Lauren shuddered as she realized she had actually gone through the thought process of assessing this option.

She opened the door and gestured for the men to enter. The president stood up from his chair behind the Resolute Desk.

"Hello, officers, it's an honor to meet both of you. I want to personally thank you for your tremendous bravery and your resolute action in ending the terrible acts of that coward at the school."

There were vigorous handshakes and "thank you, sir" all around. Good. He hadn't flinched when he met the Mexican; he must have considered Rodriguez one of the good ones. The White House photographer flashed away, moving around the room to capture the meeting from different angles.

"Officers, please have a seat." The three men sat. The president wasn't one for small talk.
"Alright, tell me what really happened that day. Not the non-news version, not the bureaucrat nonsense—your version. The real story. I wanna hear it."

There was a moment of silence; it wasn't clear who was supposed to take the lead. Peck had a distance to him, sitting in a gaze as if his mind was somewhere else. His partner realized his lack of presence and took point as the seconds of silence increased the awkwardness of the room.
"Mr. President. Sir, Officer Peck and I arrived on the scene approximately fifteen minutes after the shooter had entered the school. We were barricaded outside the entrance, and the commander on the ground wasn't letting any officers inside because we didn't know where the shooter was. There was an understanding that he—the shooter, that is—had a high position and had taken shots at other officers, who retreated."

The president shook his head. "Unbelievable. Just disgraceful. Total failure. And you two—real heroes, by the way—went in anyway? No hesitation?"

"Yes, sir. But I don't think we're heroes. We just wanted to save as many kids as we could. We didn't know what the situation was inside, just that, you know, someone had to go in."

The president held a focused gaze on Rodriguez as he spoke. Lauren watched from her position at the side of the room. It was a gaze that suggested intense focus, with a stoic dash of slight anger to convey strength of character. But she suspected it was a cover for the distance between his alleged intellect and the actuality of his cognitive abilities. When Rodriguez finished answering the rhetorical question, the president moved on to Peck.

"Tell me, Officer Peck, what happened when you went into that gym? You went in, you saved the day. That's what heroes do, okay? Real heroes, not these softies who wait around for someone else to act."

Peck was silent for a few seconds before speaking slowly. There was something very off about this guy, like he wasn't all there, his mind turning slower than it should.

"We went into the gym. We held our weapons on the shooter. We got the kids out of the gym. When the room was clear, he reached for his rifle, and I had the pleasure of putting that son of a bitch down."

The president was gleefully amused, a huge smile spreading across his face. He loved it. Lauren, on the other hand, was taken aback by the anger and succinctness of Peck's response.

The president though, he was impressed.

"Officer Peck, that criminal you took out... and he's one of the worst, most disgusting criminals this country has ever seen. And let me tell you, the only person who is more of a traitor than him is my predecessor. You've done this country a tremendous service, absolutely tremendous, by taking that guy down. God knows our legal system is a joke, total disaster. You saved the families, you saved this nation, and you saved us all from a very, very costly mess in the courts. And let me tell you boys—I've had a few legal problems myself, it's good you've kept this guy out of the courts wasting time, very efficient."

The president sat nodding his head for a moment, as if he

strongly agreed with himself. He continued.

"Now, Officer Peck, let me tell you—you're a great man, a really great man. And believe me, we are so lucky to have someone like you working in law enforcement. Not everyone gets to do what you do. Not everyone can handle it. But you? You're exceptional."

Lauren noticed the slightly dejected look on Rodriguez's face, but he seemed smart enough to play it cool.

"Thank you, sir. But I've been dismissed from the force because of that day," Peck responded.
Reign furrowed his brow. His arms moved outward with palms slightly upturned.

"Dismissed? What? An absolute disgrace! You should get a medal, not be fired. I'll tell you, this country—our country —needs less losers and more men like you, okay? Men who act, not sit around while the bureaucrats, the politicians, the weaklings, just talk, talk, talk. They're scared, you're not."
He emphasized "bureaucrats" and "politicians," using a mockingly sarcastic and dismissive tone for this point. Lauren wondered why he was talking about losers in a meeting about a school shooting, but she blanked her mind for her own sanity before he continued.

"No. I'm going to see to it personally that this brave officer is not only going to get his job back, but you're also going to get a promotion. Hell, I'm going to create a position to correct this... this injustice. That was a very big, very bad mistake those traitors made in firing you."

Peck nodded; he was becoming ever so slightly more responsive to Reign but was otherwise impassive. She didn't know what he was thinking behind those cold and distant eyes, but he seemed to respond to praise, unless there was something far more complex simmering beneath the surface.

Next to him, Rodriguez shifted in his seat, looking uneasy.

Lauren's silent interrogation met his eyes, and she felt a slight twinge of sympathy for the man. He was well out of his depth in this situation, yet he seemed more conscientious than the other one, probably aware of the ethical quagmire they were about to wade into.

"Sir. Thank you, Mr. President," Peck said. "I appreciate you having my back."

The president, with a smug smile across his face, clapped his hands together as if he had just resolved a minor, inconsequential decision. He pointed to Lauren as if his index finger were a pistol.

"Miss Chalmers, let's get some photos for the press release. We'll get an interview lined up with a real news channel, someone who can conduct a proper interview. We're gonna show the public what real heroes are."

Lauren felt her stomach drop. She had already presumed the president would turn this meeting into a media spectacle, removing the complexities and moral ambiguities from the equation and simplifying the narrative into good versus bad, with the truth perhaps only partially represented. She thought back to her meeting with Darius Green a few days ago. She had a bad feeling the president was going to do something very dangerous.

As the meeting concluded and the men were escorted from the Oval Office, Lauren lingered back for a moment.

"Mr. President? I think we should be cautious with the presentation of these men. There may be some backlash to celebrating their heroism in the face of such a tragedy. I mean, we've made no progress on gun control; this is a highly divisive issue."

The president waved his hand dismissively.

"The American people love a hero and love to hate a bad guy. We're just giving them what they want. These men are heroes, especially Peck. I'm going to find him a job—a big job, something important. Very important."

Lauren's stomach twisted, a mix of unease and something more unsettling—an instinctual worry for Peck that she couldn't shake.

CHAPTER 10: NOVAMED

It was a moment frozen in time, frozen in her memory—back in second grade. Amidst the voracious consumption of R.L. Stine's books, a crush on Aladdin despite him being a bit too cartoonish, and the proliferation of slap bracelets, eight-year-old Lauren Chalmers sat rigidly at her desk, gripped by a deep fear of Mrs. Whitmore's draconian rule. It was hard, at eight, to gauge the age of anyone who wasn't a child—someone older than her but not yet a grandma. In any case, it seemed Mrs. Whitmore had spent a fair number of years committed to expanding her waistline, portly and comfortable in her routines.

Mia—Lauren couldn't recall her last name—was sweet, with the façade of innocence masking an acerbic sense of humor and a natural talent for the visual arts. She sat beside Lauren in the back row of the classroom.

Mrs. Whitmore had her back to the class, scribbling something on the board, when Mia, silently and discretely, passed a folded piece of paper into Lauren's hand under the desk. With some trepidation, Lauren unfolded the paper to reveal Mia's latest masterpiece: a caricature of Mrs. Whitmore, exaggerated as a beach ball with tiny arms and legs. The caption read: "No running in the hallways. Rolling OK."

Lauren stifled a laugh, quickly folding the drawing back along its creases. But then her gaze met Madison Clarke's, who glared at her with fury. Madison was an uptight little witch, always striving for the top—student council president, no doubt, just as soon as she was eligible.

"Tell Mrs. Whitmore!" Madison hissed from the seat directly in front of Lauren.

Lauren shook her head, mouthing 'no' silently. She wasn't about to betray Mia.

And then, the most unfortunate part of the whole incident occurred. Another teacher appeared at the door, briefly distracting Mrs. Whitmore. Without an adult in control of the room, Madison dropped any pretense of politeness and launched into a tirade.

"Lauren, show Mrs. Whitmore what you drew about her!" Madison demanded, her voice sharp.
"No way, Madison!" Lauren replied firmly. Mia was her friend, after all, and friends don't betray their friends. There was nothing to gain from turning in Mia's harmless doodle. Madison just had it out for her.

"You tell Mrs. Whitmore, or I'll tell her you drew it, and you'll never be my friend. It's your choice," Madison threatened, her voice low and menacing.

Mia remained frozen in her seat, wide-eyed and unsure, her lips slightly parted. She shrank back, sinking deeper into her chair.

Just then, Mrs. Whitmore returned to the room, swinging the door open with more vigor than one might expect from a woman of her age, as if hoping to catch some nefarious action underway.
Madison's hand shot up like a rocket.

"Mrs. Whitmore! Excuse me, Mrs. Whitmore! Lauren has something she needs to tell you!" Madison announced loudly, with all the drama of a Broadway performer.

Lauren turned slightly to Mia, noticing the subtle shaking of her head from side to side, her eyes bulging further open than before.

"Well? What is it, Miss Chalmers?" Mrs. Whitmore dared of her.

Lauren sat frozen for what felt like minutes on end. The eyes of every other student in the classroom were burning into her, and each pupil turned to face her.

"Miss Chalmers, patience may be a virtue, but I am not a saint, so please, articulate yourself without further wasting the class's time."

Lauren took a deep breath. "Mrs. Whitmore..." Her little heart was beating hard and fast; she could hear it in her ears, consciously aware that her voice was trembling in pitch, even with just four syllables.

"Mrs. Whitmore, Madison drew an offensive drawing of you and said she was going to blame me for it. She handed it to me, and I took it without knowing what it was."

"Bring it to me, Miss Chalmers."

Lauren stood slowly, her legs feeling weak. The distance between the back row of desks and the front of the classroom felt stretched out like several hundred yards. She placed the unflattering drawing, still folded, onto Mrs. Whitmore's desk and took a step backward as if it were a ceremonial offering.

Mrs. Whitmore unfolded the page, studying it intensely for a moment. Her face was motionless, although Lauren noted her substantial chest rising and falling in rapid movement, as if she were struggling to fully inhale and exhale. It was also difficult not to notice the older woman's nostrils flaring, involuntarily, it would seem. Her eyes moved up and down between the crude drawing and the inscription scrawled below: "By Madison."

"Miss Clarke. You will attend the principal's office and provide this drawing. Please ask Principal Hawthorne to call your

mother and inform her of your flourishing career as an artist."
"Miss! I didn't draw it, it was Mia, I swear!"

"Get out, Madison," Mrs. Whitmore barked at her, as the child scurried out of her seat, beginning to cry as she left the classroom.

"Return to your seat, Miss Chalmers, and I suggest you avoid taking possession of any further commissioned or otherwise provided artworks, if I were you."

Lauren returned to her seat, Mia turning just slightly and mouthing "thank you" after making sure the teacher had her back turned. There was a strange mix of adrenaline and guilt intoxicating her senses in the moments that followed. She hadn't fully processed what happened during the rest of the lesson, but there was one thing she knew for sure: sometimes, you had to do the wrong thing for the right reasons.

Thirty years later, on a mild December day, Lauren found herself reliving that day in second grade as she waited outside this particular office door. Her Secret Service protection agents stood twenty feet away on either side of her position in the hall, constantly surveying. Not that there was much to survey —it was quiet in the hallway.

Nowadays, she was unaccustomed to waiting. She was an important woman doing important work, no matter how twisted that path sometimes seemed. When she was alone, she had a bad habit of reflecting upon decisions she had made in the past. Decisions that were always the best choice at the time, with the options available.

Just like that day in second grade—when the world first revealed its quiet unfairness upon the innocence of a child. There wasn't always a right choice, only the one that was least wrong. Madison never spoke to her again, the silence a lingering reminder of consequence. By high school, life had pulled them onto separate paths—and maybe, just maybe, Lauren was grateful for that.

Now, there was a different kind of principal—President Reign, who operated the administration as if it were a school full of delinquents and misbehavior must be punished. He would not take kindly to an unfavorable drawing of his physique. He was, in a way, like a sergeant-at-arms and president, while also being the school bully who, after expelling someone, would ridicule them. This had never sat quite right in Lauren's eyes. She resented Madison Clarke as an eight-year-old for attempting to yield power over her, and she vowed never to be in that situation again.

President Reign had a habit of excessively promoting those he found useful—until he didn't. He relished their downfall just as much. This was really an illusion of how important they actually were. Reign also immensely enjoyed the unceremonious firing of people who came to disagree with him—which was quite often. One moment you could be part of the inner circle; the next, you could find yourself blasted across the media, ridiculed, and bearing the full ire of the unquestioning devotees of the president.

The problem here today was that there were few people in the world capable of designing the technology she had been dispatched to discuss, and Darius Greene was one of them.
Unlike the brash, larger-than-life tech moguls she typically dealt with, Greene was quiet, deliberate, and seemingly uninterested in the theatrics of wealth and power. A former biomedical engineer turned entrepreneur, he had built NovaMed as a non-profit with a vision of solving problems within the medical field. And for reasons unbeknownst to Lauren, Reign had developed a sudden infatuation with the company. She had been sent today on a private jet across the country to San Francisco on behalf of the White House to meet with Darius Greene in order to seek a showcasing of their tech.

She was given her brief to go in, give the proposal to Greene, at which point Reign would take over and call him directly.

Before arriving this morning, she had expected a sterile, ultra-modern headquarters—something clinical, all glass and steel. Instead, the NovaMed campus looked like a research hospital tucked into a large warehouse space adjoining the main building. It was all very calming and decidedly un-tech-like. The whole operation felt focused and pure.

Lauren sat in the lobby, watching a sleek recessed screen display footage of a drone prototype hovering silently across an open field, maneuvering with meticulous precision. Unlike military drones, this one had a smooth, white design, resembling a futuristic paramedic in flight. Instead of weapons, its arms carried a compact medical response unit: defibrillators, trauma kits, and robotic hands that had the dexterity to perform such work.

The receptionist, an older woman with a calming presence, smiled at her. "Mr. Greene will see you now."

Lauren stood, adjusting her blazer, nodding as a gesture of gratitude, and followed the other woman the short distance up the hallway, readying herself for introductions. Reaching the CEO's office, the receptionist knocked upon her boss's door and entered immediately without waiting, holding the door open for Lauren.

Darius Greene's office was unassuming, filled with books, models of prosthetic limbs, and framed photographs of field medics using his technology in war zones. He sat behind a simple desk, wearing a dark blue sweater instead of the usual Silicon Valley uniform of ironic T-shirts and startup bravado. He was younger than she was—maybe a few years, early thirties. His skin had a warm olive tone, slightly darker than her own, but his features were refined—sharp cheekbones, a strong jawline, and dark eyes that gave little away.

It hadn't occurred to her that Greene might be of Middle Eastern descent. She scolded herself for noticing it—then immediately wondered how Reign would react. He wasn't going to like this. It was the kind of oversight her work was often plagued with. The romanticized image of precision and power, both in the White House and in the might of the nation, was starkly contrasted by the reality of constant mistakes, errors, and gross negligence—made no better by the cesspit of adulterous relationships and dangerous liaisons.

He stood as she entered, extending his hand. His grip was gentle but firm.

"Ms. Chalmers," he said softly, smoothing an invisible crease on his sleeve, his thumb grazing the silver band on his right hand—engraved with Arabic script Lauren couldn't quite make out—before extending a hand. "Thank you for coming. I'm so sorry to keep you waiting."

Lauren took a seat. "Mr. Greene, I appreciate you making the time. The president wanted me to speak with you personally."

Darius nodded, folding his hands. "Well, you have my undivided focus and attention. It is, of course, an honor to be noticed by the president for the work that we are doing here."

Lauren cleared her throat. "Your work is remarkable. The way NovaMed deploys autonomous medical response units— drones, remotely controlled droids—into high-risk areas, it's... well, it's exactly the kind of innovation that could save lives in situations where first responders can't arrive quickly enough."

Darius exhaled slowly, as if bracing himself. "Ms. Chalmers, forgive my directness here, and of course, I mean to cause no offense to you."

Lauren hesitated, then leaned forward. "Of course, Mr. Greene, likewise I come here today with nothing but good intentions."

Darius studied her for a long moment. "With all due respect, Ms. Chalmers, I'm concerned about why President Reign is interested in our work... It seems to me that he is not a man who cares too much about the kind of people we're trying to help here. You see... ma'am, neither I nor NovaMed have any interest in our technology or systems being used as a military device. It's quite the opposite, you see. We want to help people that no one else does."

Lauren opened her mouth to respond, but he pressed on.

"I started NovaMed because I watched too many people die waiting for help that never came. Have you ever been in a war zone, Ms. Chalmers? Ever witnessed a child die from an avoidable cause because soldiers kept fighting, under the direction of presidents and dictators and warmongers, safely from their offices thousands of miles away? If we lose direction from our core beliefs, we become something else entirely."

Lauren kept her tone measured. "I understand your concerns. President Reign has simply tasked me to request that you present some of your work to the U.S. government. We have an interest in helping further fund some of your tech."

Darius exhaled through his nose, staring at the framed photo on his desk. It showed two small children and a smiling woman, somewhere out in the country.

"This is a very dangerous line to walk, Ms. Chalmers. Forgive me, but I do find it difficult to believe for no other reason than to desire to do good, that the president and the government want to help progress medical technology that has no real financial benefit to anyone. Soldiers and refugees in war zones are not great customers, as you may know—we rely on donor funding and the returns on some proprietary devices we have created. As a matter of fact, this technology is still highly experimental, if and when it is ready for field usage."

"Darius," she softened her tone. "Support from the White House on this can be everything you never knew you needed to take your company to the next level."

Before she could respond, the phone on his desk buzzed.

"Sir," the receptionist's voice came through. "The White House is calling."

Lauren wasn't ready—he was supposed to wait until she sent a notification back to the White House.

Darius glanced at Lauren. "I suppose this is where the conversation stops being theoretical."

Lauren forced a small smile. "Mr. Greene, just listen to what the president has to say. I think this is a very important opportunity for you."

She stood and extended her hand, gently shaking his. "Thank you for your time, Mr. Greene."
He sat down gently in his chair behind his desk, sighing. He pressed the button on his phone.
"This is Darius Greene."

Lauren saw herself out of the office. The Secret Service was waiting outside the office for her, escorting her back downstairs and into a vehicle back to the airport to catch a private plane back to Washington.

In the back seat of the car, she pulled out her cell phone and opened her private Facebook account. She typed "Madison Clarke" into the search bar.

CHAPTER 11: HOME ALONE

Jordan turned the key, unlocked the door, and stepped inside, securing the lock behind him. He took several quick strides through the small foyer, moving past the entrance to the living space. Around the corner, he opened the drawer on the hall table where he kept his personal effects—his wallet, apartment keys, and mobile phone. Without thinking, his hand reached for his service weapon in its holster, only for him to realize his subconscious mistake. He cursed under his breath.

"You fuckin' idiot."

The living space was sparse. A long, three-seat couch in a dull color stretched along one side of the room, opposite a large TV mounted to the wall. In the corner sat a leather recliner—his favorite chair for when he wasn't on the couch.

Next to it was the sliding door to a small balcony. Jordan pulled the curtains back slightly and glanced out at the street below. If he were a normal person, maybe he'd enjoy sitting out there —maybe with a cold drink, chatting with a friend, or even having a meal. But open spaces made him uneasy. The thought of snipers on rooftops set his spine on edge.

He moved into the kitchen, where a small table with two chairs served as his dining area when he wasn't eating in the recliner. Dark, slightly dated cabinetry contrasted with the minimal stainless-steel appliances. The fridge was stocked with leftover takeout and beer. Jordan wasn't particularly fond of drinking, but when your mind is as full as his, you need something to dull it. A couple of beers and some sleeping pills were the only relief he could hope for these days. He wasn't hungry, so he reached for a beer.

As often happened when he was alone and with nothing to distract his mind, he thought of her again. The pain of the gut-punch and confusion had more often begun giving way to anger and frustration. She had cut off all contact. No warning, no reasoning—one moment they were together, and then, by her decision and hers alone, she was gone. Ghosted, as they say. Sometimes he felt deeply depressed, sometimes angry—mostly just immensely confused as to what he'd done wrong. Her cell phone was always off. She'd moved from her apartment—there was never any answer there. It was because of that fucking day—something about the way it played out, his actions. She would have seen him on the news. She knew. Something about it had made her instinctively, immediately decide she never wanted to see or speak to him again. He'd keep trying, though—for now and forever.

It was evening. Soon he'd have to decide whether to order dinner or reheat one of the partially eaten takeout meals already filling the fridge. He leaned toward the leftovers—the idea of a delivery driver knocking on the door filled him with discomfort. Then he changed his mind, deciding he wasn't all that hungry after all. He reached for another beer instead.

Returning to the recliner, he switched on the TV again with the remote that always sat on the right-hand arm of the chair. The same news channel, something he wasn't really watching. Then it happened again—images of the president. He jolted, lunging for the remote to shut the TV off. He didn't want to see that shit.

He sat in silence, staring at the now-blank screen. He took a long swig from the bottle, then set it aside. The beer had lost its appeal. After sitting in that state—caught between boredom and the urge to distract himself—he decided to shower.

Loosening the black tie he'd worn earlier that day to meet

the president, he placed it back in the wardrobe. He lifted the collar of his dress shirt and sniffed it. The shirt would need laundering. The pants, however, would live to fight another day and were folded and returned to the cupboard, along with the shined black shoes he'd worn.

In the compact bathroom, Jordan stopped in front of the oversized mirror that stretched from the vanity to the ceiling. His body had regressed since that day, and he struggled to find the motivation to continue his workouts. Suddenly, a vivid image flashed into his mind: the small gym at the police station. Inside the door frame, taped to the wall above the light switch, was a poster produced by the Philly Police Physical Association. It showed an incarcerated Black man with an overdeveloped muscular physique standing beside a bench press station. In bold, capitalized letters at the top, it read: "HAVE YOU WORKED OUT TODAY?" At the bottom: "Because he has."

Jordan hadn't worked out recently. He wondered what difference it would've made that day in the gym when he shot that skinny little Black kid in the head.

No. Fuck you, Peck.

The thought hit him like a slap. *Don't.* Plenty of good men in his platoon. On the force. Black, white, brown—like Vic. It didn't matter. It never mattered when bullets flew. Fought the same. Died the same.

He thought about the letters from white supremacists. Somehow, they'd agreed on calling him "The White Knight," along with other titles: *American Hero, The Guardian, Protector of the Innocent.* They used racial slurs with a kind of stupid creativity and defended his use of deadly force as though he'd handed out a speeding ticket instead of a bullet. Their lust for violence was sickening—surpassed only by their obsession with conspiracy theories about the shooting.

In contrast were the threats—vitriolic messages from the Black Lives Matter camp. They were fewer in number but just as intense and fanatical.

The least common were messages from people actually concerned for him. A handful of cards and emails offering thoughts and prayers for what he must've gone through. Witnessing a school massacre.

A sudden surge of panic hit him. He rushed into the kitchen. The cabinet beneath the sink was jammed, and it took effort to pry it open. He reached in and patted around until he felt it—the cell phone he had hidden there. Relief.

"Fucking destroy it, man," he said aloud.

He should, of course. The contents were not in his favor. He'd nearly done it a dozen times—smashed it, tossed it off a bridge, buried it. But something always stopped him. Maybe it was the millions of people who would be proven wrong. In some twisted way, he enjoyed the power of controlling the narrative. It was the only power he had left.

Jordan composed himself, turned, and locked the bathroom door before turning on the shower.
He stood under the water for some time. Instinct told him five minutes had passed—it was muscle memory from years of timed showers.

"Fuck you," he muttered.

He stepped further into the stream, letting the hot water pour over him, but it brought no relief. His mind raced, spiraling through disjointed thoughts, trying to latch onto anything that made sense. His body was here, but his mind was somewhere else. Somewhere dark.

Images flashed: the president, that woman—his chief of staff or whatever she was—his past. The weight of what he'd seen and done hung over him like a suffocating cloud. He couldn't escape it. He tried, but the thoughts wouldn't stop. The day's events replayed over and over—the meeting, the tension, the faces of those who cheered him and those who cursed him. There was no escape. Not from the public. Not from himself.

He thought of her again. Lauren. He couldn't stop. Her presence, her confidence. The way she carried herself—so assured, so composed—and yet something about her unsettled him. Maybe it was the control she wielded. Over others. Over him.

He imagined her—the deliberate grace in her movements, the precision in her speech. Maybe it was the way her long legs met the gentle curve of her hips, the slim waist, the way her clothing clung to her figure.

The image lingered. He could almost feel her gaze, cool and assessing. A sudden warmth spread through his chest, then his stomach. His hands clenched. His body reacted. It wasn't just her—it was what she represented. Control. Power. Something to feel, anything to fill the void.

She looked nothing like Emily. But maybe a change was as good as a holiday.

The water drummed against his skin as he closed his eyes, trying to banish the thought. But it stayed, growing stronger. His pulse quickened—a mix of anger, confusion, and something he couldn't name.

"No," he whispered.

His grip on the showerhead tightened. The line between fantasy and reality blurred until he couldn't tell them apart. He tried to shake it. He had to. He was a cop, damn it—not some broken vet with a warped mind. But the thoughts clung to him like shadows. They weren't about Lauren—not really. They were about control. About power. About feeling something— anything—other than this hollow ache.

His hand tightened into a fist. He opened his eyes. His chest heaved. Memories of violence flashed—the choices he'd made, the screams of kids, the cold steel of his weapon. His body ached with the weight of the past.

"No," he said again, voice rough.

His mind drifted back to the day. Vic was okay. It was a cordial position. Vic—the asshole—was a good man who too often let his morals get in the way of doing the wrong thing for the right reasons. And the president... what the fuck was that about? He was just like Jordan imagined—only weirder in person. The surreal feeling of seeing someone you'd only ever watched on TV. Jordan didn't know if the president would really get his job back. He didn't know the rules of politics or media. It would probably be forgotten in a few days, and he'd fade back into insignificance.

Then there was that Lauren woman. Uptight bitch. Still, he had to admit—she was attractive. That long-legged, lean frame, the immaculate style, those sleek glasses framing her flawless skin. That resting bitch face. The power she carried in that slim little frame. Yeah, he could see why the president kept her close. She wasn't traditionally beautiful, but the power? That was something.

As his erection faded, he emerged from the fantasy. He'd spent enough time in the shower. He turned off the water, stepped out, and toweled himself dry—careful not to look in the mirror. He hated the mirror these days.

He threw on a sweatshirt and track pants from the wardrobe. Suddenly, he felt like another beer. Grabbing a six-pack from the fridge, he felt sufficiently resourced to return to his recliner. He remembered he needed his phone, grunted softly, and retrieved it from the hallway table before settling back into the chair.

He opened the dialer and entered her number. She wouldn't answer—she never did anymore. They were on a break. But he knew she listened. Even if it did nothing for her, it gave him peace. One day, she'd come back to him. It was inevitable. It wasn't her fault—they were taking a break because of him. He made poor decisions. There were consequences.

There was no dial tone. The call went straight to voicemail. She never answered anymore.
"Hi, this is Emily. I'm not here at the moment, but please leave me a message, and I'll call back!"
Her voice—sweet and energetic—made his chest tighten. It reminded him of the days when he could call her just to hear her laugh. To hear her say everything would be okay. He pictured her with that bouncy blonde hair, always smiling— even on the days she was just as lost as he was. They weren't together anymore, and it was all his fault, but soon he was going to make it right. They'd be together again.

"Hey, Em... it's me again," he muttered into the phone, the words heavy. "I just wanted to call and tell you about my day. You probably saw it on the news... I met the president."

Jordan took a sip from his beer. He had so much to tell her.

CHAPTER 12: AND THEN, THERE WERE TWO.

It had now been almost six months since a young Black kid walked into Hope Valley Elementary School and murdered 45 people. Of course, the only reason to mention that he was Black was because the president had certainly taken offense to it. There were more questions now than there had been at the time, and even more opinions—on the news, from commentators, and in that cesspit of the worst of humanity: social media. More vitriol was authored in a minute than a person could read in a lifetime. Violence continued, inevitably. There had been no incidents as devastating as Hope Valley, but still, the loss of life persisted. Almost every week, there was another incident involving a gun somewhere in an American school.

Back at the White House, just down the hall from the Oval Office, Lauren sat at her desk, the ever-increasing feeling of dread pressing against her chest. A blend of adrenaline, fear, and something that hovered just shy of panic clouded her ability to function. Somewhere between solving the problem of violence and making it worse, a tangent had emerged—one that could birth something far more insidious.

Of course, he had failed to recognize the limits of his own stupidity—and had now exceeded them. Gratuitous and profound absurdity, eclipsed only by the grandiosity of his self-belief that he was, in fact, making the country great.

Lauren shuddered at the memory of campaign slogans she'd worked on five years ago with his buddy from New York—

Hammond. What was his first name again? The stress she was under made accessing memory harder. Occasionally, she would try a mind-clearing trick, running through the alphabet and prompting names with each letter to trigger recall.

A… Allen, Alex, Alfred… Alfredo? No, not an A.

She moved forward through the letters, and by the time she reached "U," it was clear the trick wasn't working. There were notes and records, of course—more documents generated during the party's tenure than any human could reasonably read.

It didn't matter what the guy's name was. It was just a nagging annoyance.

President Reign: He's going to REIGN hell on unemployment, taxes, and crime!

Let it Reign!

And of course, her least favorite of all:

We're gonna make it Reign!

Wanker.

She smiled faintly, her mind drifting back to her semester in England. It was a popular insult there, hurled at politicians, athletes, or mates at a bar. There, at least, it was understood that politicians weren't to be taken too seriously. Of course, their prime minister wasn't preparing to unleash robotic, armed sentinels to patrol elementary schools.

Reign was now in his second term as president—despite the popular opinion that he was wholly incapable of holding the office. His appeal to the everyday American had gotten him there. A background in East Coast real estate and a string of flashy business ventures had sold the image of a savvy entrepreneur with a firm grasp of business and economics.

Despite his lack of experience or political acumen, President Reign had become a sensation—and not for any positive reason. He was an enigma: his words often nonsensical, his policies erratic, but his presence undeniable. People had grown used to him—his brash, bold approach that flew in the face of the establishment.

When he spoke, it was always grandiose. Always about the "big win," and how he alone could fix problems no one else dared to touch. His speeches were peppered with declarations of *"Believe me!"* and *"This is gonna be huge!"*—always followed by dramatic pauses. It was, as many had described it, "politics as entertainment."

What worried Lauren most, however, was the direction he was heading. Once an idea lodged itself in his brain, he would pursue it obsessively—regardless of the consequences. The program's details were troubling. Convoluted. Confusing. His usual approach: applying a solution far simpler than the problem required. But that was just one part of her role. She was still, first and foremost, the person who solved problems.

She had covered up most of the president's more problematic actions. His penchant for sexual misconduct—hardly unique among politicians—was a regular issue. On numerous occasions, she had overseen the drafting of non-disclosure agreements and arranged payments for young women— women who perhaps knew better, but were strategically enterprising with their bodies.

Reign's real talent, however, was playing the long game. He had a knack for placing people in roles that would eventually benefit him. Sometimes, it was hard to tell whether it was genius or idiocy. In many ways, he resembled a godfather—not just of politics, but of business and the judiciary. One day, you might find yourself called upon to return a favor.

A meeting with the president was scheduled in thirty minutes, and 'Big Mac' would be arriving soon. 'Big Mac' was, of course, the nickname for John McMann, given by those who'd served beside him in the White House trenches. He and Reign shared a deep self-admiration—and, notably, a love for the burger that inspired the nickname. Everyone knew McMann ate at least one every day. It had become part of his lore and only served to further endear him to the president.

He was former military, of course. That was practically a prerequisite for someone like McMann to build the empire he had—bonding with his mercenaries through shared experience. He had served in special operations and reportedly achieved great things, though their legitimacy was often questioned abroad. Now, he was CEO of Warlord Peacecorp, a private military company contracted to provide security for the government and other interested organizations.

He was, without question, the absolute worst person to be heading the program. Even setting aside the alleged war crimes, abuse of power, undue political influence, and his well-documented lack of ethics, he was a raging megalomaniac—narcissistic, manipulative, and dangerous. His only redeeming quality was that even the UFAA thought twice before crossing him. McMann was the kind of man whose enemies had a tendency to disappear—or die—under suspicious circumstances.
But of course, conflict between them was inevitable.

Her phone rang, snapping her from her thoughts. It was a White House staffer. She picked up the Bluetooth earpiece she had removed earlier to give her ear a break. Once it was back in place, she pressed the button to answer.

"Hi there, this is Lauren Chalmers?"

"Ma'am, uh—sorry, Mr. McMann has arrived. Can we take him

to the president now? Wait... Mr. McMann, could you please wait a moment? Sorry, Miss Chalmers—he's on his way. He's just walked through."

Lauren exhaled heavily as she hung up. She knew she had only a few seconds to spare. Summoning all the motivation she could, she rushed into the hallway to intercept McMann.

"Lauren, I'm here for the meeting," he said, eyeing her up and down without bothering to hide his scrutiny. No pleasantries, no greeting, no ceremony. He didn't care for such things—and neither did Lauren.

He strode down the hall, Lauren trailing two steps behind as his long, determined strides closed the distance to the Oval Office. She couldn't help but notice his grotesque, overly developed musculature bulging against his clothes. It had to be artificially enhanced, she thought. The man was well into his fifties, yet he looked like a bloated bodybuilder.

A wave of disgust washed over her—at his powerful frame, and the contempt he clearly felt toward her. A flicker of fear caught in her chest when her mind wandered to darker places. She imagined him shoving her into a recess, overpowering her, forcing himself onto her. There was no way she could fight back—he was probably three times her body weight. She felt a deep sympathy for any woman he had likely abused, and a profound pity for his poor wife, trapped in his shadow.

He lumbered toward the Oval Office door, knocking with the unshakable confidence of a man who believed his power to be absolute.

Lauren silently hoped, for her own sake, that the president wasn't in a compromising position—and that his pants, at the very least, were on. She winced as a memory flashed through her mind: the meeting with the ambassador to Uruguay.

The ambassador had come to discuss trade agreements and

tourism initiatives aimed at encouraging more Americans to visit her country. Lauren had entered the Oval Office first— only to find Reign asleep at his desk, pants unzipped, and his member proudly on display. His personal laptop was open in front of him, playing... whatever it was playing.

Lauren had practically tackled the ambassador out of the doorway, as if saving a child from the path of an oncoming car.

"Please, ma'am, I'm so sorry—could you wait just a moment? The president might be having a medical episode!" She'd slammed the laptop shut without daring to look at the screen. She was too terrified to know.

Now, she let out a quiet breath of relief. Reign was seated at his desk, staring blankly at the wall—a position she could only hope was an improvement. If anyone asked, he'd claim he was mentally preparing for the meeting. Lauren suspected he was thinking about golf.

Reign quickly sprang to his feet, moving around the desk and shaking McMann's hand with exaggerated enthusiasm.

"Big Doouggg!"

"John, it's great to see you. We've got some very important business to discuss today. You've done some really tremendous work. Very great work. Let's dive into the details of this program."

He maintained the vigorous handshake, his eyes locked with McMann's in an unbroken stare. There was an unmistakable mutual appreciation—a camaraderie forged through shared ego and power. Lauren noted that both men were large, with broad frames and similar height—but McMann, undeniably, was the more physically imposing. His muscles strained visibly beneath his shirt, a stark contrast to Reign's softer, less defined build.

This was often the dynamic among politicians and power

brokers: large men could use their size to intimidate, unless they met another neanderthal of equal magnitude. In those cases, they often forged unlikely alliances.

Reign returned to his seat behind the Resolute Desk, while McMann settled across from him. Lauren moved to the corner of the room, pulled her phone from her right pocket, and opened a document to take notes for the meeting.

McMann noticed—and immediately took issue with it.

"Hey! Hey, darling," he said, raising a hand in protest. "No need for that, okay? I'll have one of my team provide a summary of the key points after we're done. Sound good?"

Lauren glanced at the president. He nodded solemnly, a silent agreement passing between them. With slight hesitation, she locked her phone and returned it to her pocket.

McMann clapped his hands together loudly, his enthusiasm almost jarring given the gravity of the discussion ahead.

"Right! Doug, we've made some serious progress with the program. A great deal of research is complete, and we have a solid understanding of how to make it all work. We've also been busy acquiring some strategic locations for future deployment."

"Good, that's very good news. Any issues with land acquisition for the sites?" Reign asked.

"Doug, look, we've done the smart thing here. We're not building these sites on top of someone's penthouse on Fifth Avenue, are we? A lot of these sites are—how can I put this? —well, if we hand out a couple of casino chips on the reserve, or offer a new truck and a bottle of moonshine down South, everyone's happy."

"Absolutely. A great outcome for everyone involved, John. My thoughts are, we're actually improving these areas in the process. It's an honor for these people to contribute to making this country great. Win-win situation. Smart move, John. Very smart."

"Thank you, Mr. President. Now, let's talk about two problems here. First, the CEO from Novamed isn't exactly being patriotic with his level of cooperation—and that's not even the biggest issue. The CEO, Darren…"

Lauren interjected, "Mr. McMann, the CEO's name is Darius Greene."

McMann's expression darkened slightly, clearly displeased by the interruption. "Yeah, whatever. Darius, then. Doug—Mr. Greene—well, he's not exactly *green*, if you catch my drift. In fact, he's more along the lines of… let's just say he doesn't appreciate bacon as much as we do. Bit of a diversity hire, if you know what I mean. Kinda looks like he should be selling falafel balls out of some food truck downtown."

"Great, you're telling me he's a homosexual?"

"No, Doug. No. Well… he might be. Yeah, probably actually. Actually, he does look like he smokes a bit of sausage. But that's not the biggest problem. My team's research into Darren suggests he might be a little too fond of, well… jihading, if you catch my drift. I just don't think it's a good look."

"Damn it, John—you're telling me we almost went into business with the Nation of Islam on a national security project?"

"Yes, Doug. Well—not exactly the Nation of Islam. They're a Black nationalist movement. This guy's more of a… well, look, I just think it's a problem. We might need to outsource this to someone a little more patriotic, if you know what I mean."

The president leaned back in his chair, a slight frown creasing his forehead. "That's a very good point you've raised there.

I get it—we need the best people and the best team. But... presentation is important. We need to think about how we present this. Do you think we need someone else to be the face of the program?"

McMann rocked his head forward and back in thought.

"Same difference, I suppose. We could risk being progressive— though I really don't think your supporters will like the about-face. But... if this thing goes south, we might need someone to take responsibility. You know—let's cover our six on this. Thing is, Darren's only part of the equation. He's providing the hardware we're retrofitting. I mean, this guy originally designed the tech for medical and rescue support, both domestically and in conflict zones overseas. Damned if I know how he thought he'd make any money out of it!"

Reign and McMann both laughed boisterously. From her corner, Lauren felt physically heartbroken by the casual dismissal of Darius's work—and by the potential solution McMann had suggested: letting the man shoulder the blame if something went wrong.

Of course something would go wrong.

"Alright," McMann continued. "Let's run this by my guy in PR and see what he thinks. I've got someone on the team—Doug, we've got Connor Hammond. Buddy of yours from New York, I think?"

Connor! The name jolted into Lauren's mind. Perhaps it had been mentioned in a briefing or memo, during one of her dazed moments in the office. Quite the charmer, she recalled. Reign was clearly fond of him as well.

"Of course I know him. Great guy. Really terrific. One of the best. And I'll tell you, I really like him. He's got tremendous energy, a fantastic mind, and he's done some amazing things. Believe me—I've known him a long time, and he's always been a winner. So yeah, I know him, and I like him a lot."

"Great. I'll take this issue to him and see what he recommends regarding Aladdin over at Novamed," McMann declared, effectively wrapping up the point.

"Tell me about your team," Reign said, leaning forward. "Let's get into the details. How exactly is this program going to work?"

Still seated in her corner, Lauren sat in a daze, staring blankly ahead, her mouth slightly open.
"Right, well Doug, we've got some of the best men on this program—but I've gotta be real with you—we need more. I mean, we've got the idea, and the bones of the program are solid, but we need something to take it to the next level. Let me be blunt, Doug: there's a missing piece to this puzzle. Once the operation is up and running, it's going to change the world. But there's a gap between what we *can* do and what we *need* to do."

"We need more talent on the project? More money? What is it?" Reign's eyes flickered with curiosity. Lauren watched him closely, noting—as always—that his supposed business success came not from skill, but from striking deals with other rich men and spending their money while holding tightly to his own.

"Doug, your idea is great. But we don't know how to make it *work*. We can make it *look* like it works—but in real-world application, it might not perform the way we'd like."

He paused—his attention now fully shifted to Lauren.

"Doug, can we get the woman out of the room? I don't like the way she's looking at me. Feels awfully un-American, that disapproving glare. Hey, sweet cheeks, mind if the big boys talk business in private for a minute?"

"Mr. President?" Lauren asked, her voice quiet, uncertain.

"Go on, Lauren. We'll discuss anything relevant to you later, once the details are worked out," Reign said, dismissing her with a wave of his hand.

"Of course, sir," she replied, gathering her things.

Lauren rose and exited the room, a wave of deep embarrassment crashing over her. She was a woman skilled in repressing emotion, in masking her thoughts—but now, with tears threatening to rise, she quickened her pace, disappearing from view before anyone could see her face. Crying would be career suicide. There was no way she'd give someone like McMann the satisfaction.
As the door closed behind her, she caught a final parting shot from McMann, his voice slathered in smirking contempt.

"Fuckin' 'Me Too' movement, Doug. Used to be only one reason to have a woman like that around the office. Can't even have a decent affair anymore without a lawsuit."

She couldn't hear Reign's reply, but she knew him well enough to guess. Fortunately, he'd never crossed that line with her—he was smart enough to know that without her, he wouldn't be half the president he imagined himself to be.

Back in her office down the hall, Lauren opened the bottom drawer of her desk and pulled out her packet of Xanax. With a bottle of water she kept on hand, she swallowed two tablets, leaned back in her chair, and closed her eyes, waiting for the medication to take hold.

"I hate Big Macs," she muttered to no one in particular.

She focused on her breathing. Slowly in. Hold. Then exhale. Again and again.

About twenty minutes later—though she hadn't checked the time when she was kicked out of the meeting—McMann came barreling down the hallway. A White House staffer scrambled out of his way as he passed. He spotted Lauren through the open door and, without breaking stride, called out:

"See you later, cupcake!"

His voice was loud, smug, and deliberately obnoxious. He didn't pause for a response.

Lauren shrank into her seat, retreating deeper into her mind. She thought of him as a repugnant beast—his demeanor execrable, entirely devoid of diplomatic tact or emotional intelligence. And yet, he was revered by the president and countless supporters. She would have to work with him, of course.

She closed her eyes again and let herself drift, the creeping indifference brought on by the Xanax washing over her, softening the sharp edges of her rage and humiliation.

As Lauren closed the door behind her, McMann leaned forward, barely able to contain himself.

"Fuckin' 'Me Too' movement, Doug. Used to be only one reason to have a woman like that around the office—can't even have a decent affair anymore without a lawsuit."

Reign's face twisted with frustration. "Tell me about it. How the hell are we supposed to run the country with all this bullshit? National security, the economy... and now we've got to worry about some woman's feelings."

McMann let out a dry chuckle, his tone dripping with disdain. "Well, hell, Doug, you've had your share of giving interns and the ambitious a chance to 'serve their country,' right? Maybe show her what *real work* looks like. She looks like she could use a bit of your *leadership.*"

He made a crude motion with his hands—his lewd gesture unmistakable.

"Might loosen her up a little, don't you think?"

The two men laughed raucously, their mouths flapping like ventriloquist dummies, all teeth and grotesque joy. Reign slapped his knee and leaned back in his chair, guffawing as if it were the funniest thing he'd heard in years.

"Seriously though, Doug. The legs and ass on that woman—*hmm-hmm*. They go all the way up, don't they? Not much going on in the titty department, but a nice little package otherwise. That cute, angry face she's always pulling. She's got that librarian thing going—but you *know* she's into some kinky shit. How the hell do you get anything done around here?"

"I'm very productive, John. Fixed the economy, immigration, taxes... I just spend forty-five minutes a day staring at that ass, then handle the country in the remaining fifteen."

"Damn, I'd love to grab a piece on the way out. You think that'd be a problem?"

The president paused, a thoughtful look crossing his face.

"You know, John, you wouldn't think it looking at her—I've got some real doozies on my team, believe me. A LOT of incompetence around here. You wouldn't know it, but she's actually a pretty solid asset. She gets things done. Sure, she's a woman, and she spends too much time worrying about her feelings—emotional, it's tough. But let me tell you, she does a better job than a lot of the men in the White House. That's the truth."

"Fair call, Doug. I'll leave her be. But if it ever comes up, and there's an opportunity—you give me a call. I'll make all her dreams come true for about an hour or two. You know what I mean?"

"I know exactly what you mean, John. I definitely do. Listen, how about we hash out a few more details on this program? I could go for a burger. Want me to order something in for you?"

"That's alright. I've gotta get going. But let's wrap this up first. That boy in San Francisco—he's not cooperating. We've made several attempts to negotiate, even offered to buy the tech off him. He's got some bullshit problem with using medical drones to save lives."

"Right. So what are our options here?" Reign asked, leaning forward.

"Look, there are a few—but none of them are as clean as just getting him to sell us the rights," McMann replied, his voice steady but edged with frustration. "We could invoke the Defense Production Act and force the son of a bitch to manufacture the tech for us. Problem is, the company's worthless. They've only got a couple of prototypes, and they're nowhere near scale. They'd have outsourced production anyway."

"What about government funding?" Reign asked, his brow furrowed.

"Sure. We could squeeze Novamed by the balls. Legally bind them to develop the tech for us. But same issue—the company isn't big enough to pull it off. And the CEO? No spine. That's not a good option. He'll fight us every step of the way."

McMann leaned back, arms crossed.

"That leaves us with eminent domain. We seize the tech, claim it's vital to national security, and throw them a few bucks for their trouble. It's messy, sure. But we're doing something that's never been done before. This isn't just commandeering a weapon—we'd have to prove it's necessary to save lives. Big ask."

"Sounds like that's the play then, John. We're just gonna seize the technology if they don't want to contribute to making America safer for our children." Reign's eyes narrowed, focused. "Once we have it—can you make it do what we need it to do? You've got the capabilities?"

"It's not obvious yet," McMann admitted, rubbing his chin. "Still a lot of testing, research, and configuration needed. But here's the thing, Doug—we're building a *deterrent.* We're building a *symbol.* It doesn't have to work perfectly. People just have to believe that it *does.*"
He leaned in, his voice lower now.

"No one's gonna rob my house if they know I'm inside with a big-ass gun pointed at their head. That's what we're building— a gun pointed at the head of any punk who thinks he can walk into a school and shoot innocent people. Not on *my* fuckin' watch."

"Hear, hear, John," Reign said, raising an imaginary glass.

McMann's expression softened for a moment, before leaning in again, his tone more serious. "Mr. President, I don't want to be the guy who disappoints you—and I'll be honest, I'm disappointed in myself."

"What is it, John? You can tell your president. I'm going to make all your problems go away."
McMann hesitated, eyes narrowing. "There are kinks in the program. Issues we can't fix. We've had engineers, scientists, military brass all looking at it. We need more. Something else. We don't know how to bring it all together."

Reign waved a dismissive hand. "You're telling me there are *kinks* in the program? Come on. This is a symbol, not a perfect system. The best ideas don't always work the way we think they should—but they make a hell of a statement. And *that's* what we're doing. We're making a *statement.* A big one."

He leaned back, his voice steady, but firm.

"I hear you. I get it. You're frustrated. But listen to me, John—

you don't have to worry. I know *exactly* who we need for this. Xavier Wolfe."

McMann raised an eyebrow. "Xavier Wolfe?"

"Yeah," Reign grinned, confidence radiating from him. "This guy—he's the genius of the century. If you've got a problem, and you need it solved, it's Xavier. He'll get it done. I'll call him. We'll have this thing running smoother than you've ever seen. Don't worry, John. I've got this under control.

You're gonna be just fine."

"You're absolutely right, Doug."

Reign leaned forward, his voice sharpening. "Forget Novamed. We take the tech. And we get better people on the project. Xavier Wolfe—he's the guy. No whining. No bureaucratic bullshit. He's one of us. The man builds rockets, cars, flamethrowers... and best of all? He *owns* social media."
McMann chuckled, nodding with approval. "He's absolutely the best guy for the job. No one else can pull this off. Bring him in."

Reign slammed his fist on the desk, his enthusiasm peaking.

"America's gonna be so safe, you won't even believe it."

CHAPTER 13: A WOLFE IN A SHEEP'S WOOL SUIT.

The fluorescent lights buzzed overhead, garishly lighting the empty McDonald's counter. The crew—mostly teenagers and young adults sharply dressed in uniform—milled around their stations, unsure what to do with a full lunch shift's worth of staff and no customers. They kept busy wiping down already-clean benchtops and rearranging napkins and condiment sachets with a kind of ritualistic diligence.

An ambitious young man attempted to breach the staff entry door, dustpan and broom in hand, trying to clean the dining area. A Secret Service agent abruptly stopped him, raising his hand like a stop sign and pointing him firmly back toward the kitchen.

Around a dozen agents stood guard in the dining area—impassive, suited, earpieced. Outside, there were more. Large black SUVs blocked the drive-thru and customer parking lot from view.
In the distance, a fryer popped faintly as an old fry floated to the surface, eagerly awaiting the next deployment of baskets into the vat.

As if from nowhere, Xavier Wolfe sauntered in through the employee entrance, trailing the unmistakable scent of sandalwood cologne and self-importance. He didn't so much walk as glide—his movements effortless but calibrated, as though optimized to exude just the right amount of arrogance while appearing totally unaware of it.

At forty-eight, Wolfe looked younger than he should, but he had access to every anti-aging regimen and biohacking experiment known to man. His jet-black hair was brushed back meticulously, each strand aligned with almost mechanical precision, gleaming unnaturally under the fluorescent light. The slim-fit blazer he wore wasn't just tailored—it was engineered, every line a testament to his obsession with control.

"Well," he said, his voice smooth, almost musical, "I have to admit, this is... very humble."
He exhaled through his nose, a soft chuckle escaping as his gaze swept the room. "Feels very real, you know? Salt of the earth. Authentic."

His eyes flicked to a teenage employee wiping down an already spotless counter. "It's important to stay grounded. I eat here all the time."

He was lying. Xavier Wolfe definitely did not eat McDonald's all the time.

He strode toward the counter, running a single finger along the surface as if expecting to discover some profound insight about fast-food economics. "You can tell a lot about a civilization by its McDonald's. Efficiency. Scaling. Nutrient optimization."

He nodded, approvingly, as though the entire global supply chain were his personal invention.
Looking between the last remaining register on the counter and the row of self-service screens behind it, he smirked. "That register is like China. Most of their technology is obsolete."

Then, turning back to his captive audience behind the counter, he clapped his hands together. "Anyway! Let's talk disruption. I assume we can order? I'll take, uh..."

He squinted at the menu as if deciphering alien script.

"A Big Mac. No bun. Extra sauce. Actually… just give me a cup of the sauce."

The employees stare. Xavier Wolfe does not. His gaze sweeps the room, looking everywhere *except* at the person he's speaking to—analyzing, inspecting, muttering incoherently to himself about perceived inefficiencies in design and function.

A smaller man behind him, dressed in a charcoal suit, thrusts a steaming cup of coffee into his hand. It's in a plain white mug—not a Styrofoam cup. Wolfe doesn't drink from those. He takes the cup without looking, his attention already elsewhere, scanning the faces of the agents stationed at every exit and corner.

His mind is always multitasking—calculating probabilities, running simulations. Right now, he's wondering how long he'll be stuck here before something interesting happens.

"Mr. Wolfe, you're early," one of the agents says, stepping forward with a clipboard.

Wolfe barely acknowledges him, his gaze fixed on the golden arches outside the window. Beyond them, civilians mill about, peering curiously at the spectacle they aren't allowed to enter.

"Of course I'm early," Wolfe replies, finally turning to the agent. His smile is razor-sharp, slicing through the tension in the room. "Punctuality is for people who don't value their time. I arrive when things need to get done."

He gestures vaguely toward the plastic booths and sticky tabletops.

"Which, I assume, is why we're here instead of the Oval Office? To *get things done*?"

His assistant coughs lightly—a polite reminder that Wolfe tends to monologue. Xavier waves him off, takes a sip of the coffee, then grimaces.

"Terrible," he mutters, setting the cup down on a tray meant for Happy Meals. "I knew this would be terrible."

The convoy arrives like a thunderclap.

Black SUVs with tinted windows screech to a halt in staggered formation, engines growling as if daring anyone to come closer. The first vehicle spits out Secret Service agents, their movements sharp and practiced, weapons visible but not raised. They fan out in perfect synchronization, scanning every corner of the block with cold efficiency.

Pedestrians on the sidewalk freeze mid-step, clutching phones and coffee cups, eyes wide with confusion and awe.

"Move back! Now!" an agent barks at a small crowd forming near the hastily erected barricades across the McDonald's parking lot.

A mother holding her toddler stumbles backward, nearly tripping over the curb. The golden arches gleam behind her, mocking the chaos.

President Reign steps out next, his polished shoes striking the asphalt with authority, his towering frame commanding attention. His red tie flutters slightly in the breeze as he adjusts his jacket and strides toward the entrance. Agents swarm around him, forming a human wall that shifts with his every step. He waves and grins broadly without really looking at anyone in particular.

"Is this really necessary?" someone mutters from the crowd, their voice swallowed by the low hum of another approaching engine.

McMann's arrival is louder. Brasher.

His convoy—three matte-black trucks bearing the Warlord Peacecorp insignia—rolls up like an invading army. Men in tactical gear disembark, helmets gleaming under the midday sun, rifles slung across their chests. Their movements are less polished than the Secret Service, but no less intimidating.

One of them scans the perimeter with a pair of binoculars —unnecessarily. The Secret Service has already covered every possible threat vector.

"Clear," another calls out, nodding toward McMann's vehicle.

The door opens, revealing McMann's hulking frame. He steps out without hesitation, boots crunching against the pavement, broad shoulders squared like he's expecting a fight. His eyes sweep the scene—agents, civilians, Wolfe's private security already inside—before narrowing slightly. He grunts something inaudible and marches toward the restaurant.

"Sir, we've secured the interior," one of his men informs him as they fall into formation at his sides.
McMann doesn't respond. He just keeps walking.

The convoy arrives like a thunderclap. Black SUVs with tinted windows screech to a halt in staggered formation, engines growling as if daring anyone to come closer. The first vehicle spits out Secret Service agents, their movements sharp and practiced, weapons visible but not raised. They fan out in perfect synchronization, scanning every corner of the block with cold efficiency. Pedestrians on the sidewalk freeze mid-step, clutching phones and coffee cups, eyes wide with confusion and awe.

"Move back! Now!" an agent barks at a small crowd forming near the barricades hastily erected across the McDonald's parking lot. A mother holding her toddler stumbles backward, nearly tripping over the curb. The golden arches gleam behind her, mocking the chaos.

President Reign steps out next, his polished shoes striking the asphalt with authority, his towering frame demanding attention. His red tie flutters slightly in the breeze as he adjusts his jacket and strides toward the entrance. Agents swarm around him, forming a human wall that shifts with his every step. He glances at the gawking onlookers waving and grinning broadly without really looking at anybody in particular.

"Is this really necessary?" someone mutters from the crowd, their voice swallowed by the low hum of another approaching vehicle.

McMann's arrival was louder, brasher. His convoy—three matte-black trucks emblazoned with the Warlord Peacecorp insignia—rolled in like an invading army. Men in tactical gear disembarked, helmets glinting under the midday sun, rifles slung across their chests. Their movements were less polished than the Secret Service's, but no less intimidating. One of them scanned the perimeter with a pair of binoculars —unnecessarily, since the Secret Service had already covered every possible angle of threat.

"Clear," another calls out, nodding toward McMann's vehicle.

The door opened, revealing McMann's hulking figure. He stepped out without hesitation, his boots crunching against the pavement, broad shoulders squared as if expecting a fight. His eyes swept the scene—agents, civilians, Wolfe's private security detail already stationed inside—before narrowing slightly. He grunted something inaudible and marched toward the restaurant.

"Sir, we've secured the interior," one of his men informs him as they flank his sides. He doesn't respond, just keeps walking.

Inside, Wolfe watches through the smudged glass doors, sipping water from a branded McDonald's cup. His private security team lingers awkwardly near the counter, where a bewildered teenage cashier is held hostage by the unrelenting glare of a Secret Service agent—one who seems to take a small amount of pleasure in the teenager's discomfort.

The fryer beeps incessantly in the background, ignored by everyone until a manager suddenly snaps to attention and rushes over to press a button on the front of the unit.

"Finally," Wolfe mutters under his breath as he catches sight of McMann and Reign approaching. "Was beginning to think I'd been stood up."

Outside, regular customers continue to pile up. Someone bangs on the locked doors of an SUV blocking the restaurant's entrance. Two Secret Service agents advance toward the man, who promptly turns and walks away. Others stand nearby, snapping photos of the absurd spectacle.

A man in a suit and tie argues with an agent stationed between two SUVs parked out front.

"Come on, I just want a damn sandwich!" he shouts, waving his briefcase for emphasis.

The agent doesn't blink.

"Area's closed. Move along," comes the clipped, final reply.

"Closed? It's a McDonald's, not the Pentagon!" the man shoots back—but the glare he receives shuts him up fast.

A homeless woman nearby shakes her head, muttering incoherently about government conspiracies while rummaging through her cart. Across the street, a group of college students livestreams the scene, their hashtags already trending.

"**McDictatorship**," one of them jokes, earning a few chuckles.

"**More like McAssholes**," another adds, tilting their phone for a better angle.

As Reign and McMann finally enter the restaurant, the air inside shifts.

The fryers beep again—almost mockingly—their rhythm slicing through the heavy silence.
Wolfe stands, brushing nonexistent crumbs off his tailored blazer, and greets them with a smirk.
"Well," he says, bounding over to the two men with his hand extended, "good to see you both. Looking forward to solving world peace—or whatever other problem you have for me."

"Oh, we're going to solve some problems today, you mark my words. This is going to be a doozy," Reign replies, sliding into a booth. His broad frame barely fits the molded plastic seat. His red tie cuts a diagonal slash across his chest, popping in color against the pale laminate table. The fluorescent lights above catch the silver streaks in his hair, making them gleam like polished steel.

"First things first—can somebody get us some burgers over here? And fries? Do you both want fries? And some sodas?"

McMann sits next to him, his hulking presence consuming the space. He skips the small talk.

"Darius Greene's proposal? It's soft. Weak. Un-American." The words fire from his mouth—venomous, deliberate.

"We need someone who understands innovation. Disruption. Someone who can think *bigger*."

Wolfe tilts his head, fingers drumming on the faux-wood tabletop. He looks relaxed, but there's something calculating in his eyes—a glint that belongs to a man who knows the price of everything, especially himself.

"Darius Greene?" Wolfe says, the name tasting dry on his tongue. "He's got some interesting ideas. Not as good as mine, obviously—but cute. Quaint."

His tone is light, almost teasing, but his posture stiffens slightly, betraying his interest. Reign adjusts his cufflinks, the presidential seal catching the light.

"You've built rockets. The world leader in electric-powered engines. Cars that drive themselves. Platforms based on truth and free speech. You're the best person on the planet to take on what we need here. You're not just a thinker, Xavier—you're a doer. That's why we're here."

"True. Yes, that's all very true. I'm listening." Wolfe nods smugly, accepting the praise as though it were inevitable. "But what is it you want me to do?"

McMann leans forward, focusing intently on Wolfe.

"We want you to take the tech we're confiscating from Novamed and make it actually fucking useful," he says, leaning back as if the concept of medical droids disgusts him. "We want you to take these droids and put fucking guns on them. Lots of guns. And make 'em fast—we need rapid deployment, not a casual Sunday stroll across the battlefield to hand out Band-Aids."

Wolfe grins, sharp and self-assured.

"Well, that does sound... uh, that does sound like a pretty interesting idea," he says, tapping his temple, as if the proposal were somehow profound. "Ah—but why, though? Why are we putting guns on these droids?"

McMann doesn't hesitate.

"President Reign here, in an act of *great* leadership, has come up with the kind of idea that makes America number one at everything. Unfortunately, right now that includes school shootings—but that's going to be a thing of the past," he declares, as if it were already an historical fact.

"Exactly," Reign cuts in, his voice playful, almost giddy with childlike enthusiasm.

"These droids this Greene fellow has—I mean, I guess it's a cute idea. Sending remote-controlled nurses to clean up after fights. But let me tell you something—by the time *we're* finished, there won't be any fights to clean up."

"What President Reign means," McMann adds, his deep-set eyes locking onto Wolfe's, "is that we're going to build a deterrent to school shootings. And if anyone is still stupid enough to try it, well—it's going to be a short little performance before one of your droids puts a sudden stop to it."
He leans in slightly.

"Of course, I think there may be some *pretty significant* tax incentives for a partner who could make this happen."

"Significant," Reign echoes, lips curling into a knowing smile.

"Of course," McMann begins, before being interrupted by the sudden appearance of the McManager, standing beside the table with a plastic tray full of menu items. A second crew member follows, balancing a tray of soft drinks.

"Hurry up," McMann snaps as the manager places the food down. The teenager trailing behind visibly trembles as she manages to deliver the sodas without spilling them. She exhales in quiet relief once the tray reaches the table, then both of them scurry off.

"Fucking McIdiots," McMann mutters, before returning to business.

"We may need a little help here and there controlling the narrative. People trust your voice. We know we can count on you to silence the trolls and the fake news."

Wolfe leans back, arms crossed. For a moment, he lets the silence settle over the table.

Across the street, safely outside the reach of the Secret Service perimeter, a young long-haired man in torn jeans holds up a cardboard sign:

KILL THE RICH.

McMann spots it instantly and erupts.

"How in the *hell* did that dirty hippy make a sign that quickly?" he growls.

He presses his earpiece and speaks flatly, without emotion.

"Someone get rid of that fucking sign. I find it offensive."

A member of McMann's security detail moves purposefully across the road. He grabs the sign in one hand, his other fist clenched. The sign-waver turns and bolts.

"Kill the Rich" Wolfe finally says, nodding slowly, as if savoring the phrase. "I like that. Has a good ring to it. I'm not sure, uh what it means, but I like it" He uncrosses his arms, spreading them wide like a man embracing a golden opportunity.

"Mr. McMann, uh… tell me, did you bring me any reading materials for this meeting? Let's say, uh… blueprints for this tech? What it is you want it to…"

McMann doesn't respond. He simply snaps his fingers in the direction of one of his team. The man quickly walks to the rear of one of the Warlord Peacecorp trucks and retrieves a briefcase.

Reign seizes the lull in conversation and grabs a Big Mac off the tray, demolishing the burger in a few quick bites. Moments later, McMann's team member returns and presents the briefcase to Wolfe.

"I thought you'd never ask," McMann says.

Xavier Wolfe's eyes ignite with a sudden spark of excitement —the dull veneer lifting to reveal a flash of focus and determination. His eyebrows twitch with anticipation as he marvels at the technical documents inside.

"Tell me, uh... I need to know—give it to me. What do you want to do, exactly? Tell me in a sentence," Wolfe blurts, already slipping into his own mind, struggling to remain anchored to the moment.

President Reign answers without missing a beat.

"Look, we've got a big problem—school shootings. Terrible. Just terrible. And nobody's done anything about it. But *I'm* doing something. We take these droids—very advanced, very tough, the best—send them in, and they handle it. Shooter shows up. Droid goes in. *Bang.* Gone. No more dead kids, no more disasters. It's gonna be tremendous. Believe me."

Wolfe keeps staring at the documents, lost in thought.

McMann leans forward, impatience simmering.

"Well, Wolfe. What do you think?"

"I need writing paper. Uh, I need... a laptop. Two laptops. We need a map of the mainland United States. Maybe a ruler. Does anyone have a ruler?"

"Get the man some fucking computers!" McMann barks.

Wolfe jumps from the table and rushes to the counter. "I need paper. Anything. And a pen."

A crew member hurriedly provides the reverse side of a few tray liners and a pen from behind the register. Wolfe darts to a clear table, slamming the makeshift paper down like it's classified intel.

"Where's a computer? Someone go to my car and get my briefcase with my laptop!"

He begins scribbling frantically, yanking his cellphone from his pocket and punching in notes and calculations.

"I need my laptop!" he yells again—just as an aide rushes forward and thrusts it into his hands.
Wolfe opens it with the glee of a child unwrapping a toy on Christmas morning. He starts typing furiously, cross-referencing documents, sketching figures and system diagrams beside him on the paper.

Back at the original table, Reign and McMann remain seated.

Reign helps himself to another burger. McMann takes a loud slurp from a massive soda, his gaze fixed on Wolfe, now working like a man possessed.

"This is beautiful," Reign says, his grin widening—*all teeth now*.

McMann doesn't say anything, but the slight incline of his head and the gleam in his eye speak volumes.

Then, Wolfe suddenly stands, eyes wild, trademark smirk fully in place.

"Now," he says, "let's talk specifics. Because if we're going to do this…we're going to do it big."

He stands to attention, posture radiating command, as he begins the presentation.
"The armed droid program requires a solution that combines speed, precision, and an unmatched ability to respond to threats instantaneously… I need a whiteboard. Uh, does anyone—did anyone bring a whiteboard?" He trails off, staring ahead.

"Somebody get the man a fuckin' whiteboard!" McMann barks, as if the fate of the nation depends on it.

Two agents burst through the 'Employees Only' door into

the kitchen, weaving through stainless steel appliances and flustered staff. They reach a staff room in the back where a whiteboard is mounted to the wall. With little effort, one agent rips it free while the other scoops up markers from the tray below. They storm back through the kitchen, restaurant employees frozen in place, wide-eyed and unsure whether to intervene or keep pretending to wipe things.

Wolfe is initially pleased as the whiteboard is set down in front of him—until a frown creeps across his face.

"I suppose this will have to do. Uh, you couldn't find a smartboard?" he grumbles, exasperated. "Anyway, we're wasting time. The board *does* matter."

One of the agents who raided the staff room begins ripping off pinned notices and photos—birthday flyers, roster sheets, an outdated COVID hygiene checklist—before wiping away the lingering marker notes with a handful of napkins.

Wolfe takes over and begins drawing a crude map of the United States.

"Now. We're going to have **448 drones**, each stationed at secure locations across the United States," he announces. "These locations are chosen with strategic precision—factoring in population density, geographical obstacles, and the optimization of response times. This ensures that no matter where... the closest drone will be within striking distance in under five minutes."

He circles clusters on the map aggressively, then glances back.

"That's how many sites we're going to need to hit that window across most of the mainland. Do we want to do Hawaii? Look, maybe the number will need refining."

He pauses, letting the weight of the idea land.

Reign nods gently, that goofy smirk etched into his face like a cartoon emperor watching fireworks.

"Now," Wolfe continues, pacing slightly. "Once an alert is triggered, the system activates its AI. Centralized control centers—maybe several, maybe just one, we'll see—receive the alert and begin the deployment process. There's inbuilt redundancy, obviously."

He waves a hand vaguely.

"Now, who controls this? Could be law enforcement. Maybe military. I'm not sure yet. We'll figure that out later."

He refocuses.

"The system performs millisecond-level calculations. Each drone's flight path is recalculated in real-time for maximum efficiency. No delays. No bottlenecks. It's about pure execution."
Wolfe's eyes gleam.

"I can build the kind of drones you need. Dual propulsion systems—rocket-assisted for long-range sprint, drone motors for precision navigation. They'll *fly* to the threat."

He leans back in his chair, grinning.

"The suits themselves? Designed using NovaMed's advanced tech. But we're not just sending in droids—we've weaponized them. Every unit is fitted with a full range of non-lethal and lethal **options**. From high-impact tasers to submachine guns, they're armed for anything."

He taps the side of his head, then points to the imaginary HUD in front of him.

"Control pod. Full remote operation via exoskeleton. Full virtual reality interface. It's going to feel just like playing a video game."

He turns to Reign and McMann, satisfaction gleaming in his

expression.

"This program will be the model of modern defense. Efficiency, precision, speed, and power—all delivered from a distance. The deterrent will be so swift, so overwhelming, that school shootings—and *any* other form of violence—will become a thing of the past."

Reign and McMann glance at one another, then back at Wolfe. Reign grins.

"Listen, Xavier—that was the best presentation. Maybe ever. Absolutely incredible. You're like the Big Mac of tech: huge, satisfying, and everybody loves your work."

He extends a hand across the table.

"So welcome to the team, buddy. Let's make history."

CHAPTER 14: A DAY AT THE PARK

It was a mild, weathered day—perfect for the plans they had made for this Saturday in October. It had been essential to schedule the date for the weekend; her calendar, of course, was immovably rigorous, and there were always Sunday evening preparations for the week ahead.

Extensive communication had already taken place between them—countless text messages that flowed easily. He had begun to wait anxiously for the buzz of his phone, eager to hear from her. Most of their conversations were lighthearted small talk, occasionally veering into deeper territory. In his opinion, they clicked extremely well.

The neighborhood bustled with vibrant energy, blending old-world industrial features with modern architecture. Boutiques, galleries, and restaurants populated the streetscape, making it a great place to spend the day—*if it weren't her home neighborhood.*

He was relieved to find parking on the street near her building. Glancing at the dashboard, he saw it was twenty to eleven—too early to approach her apartment. The convenient parking spot had thrown off his timing. He decided to wait in the car for ten minutes and exit at ten-fifty. *"Send me a text when you're outside,"* she'd told him. He'd found it unusual to schedule a time so precisely, but she had explained, *"I'm an old lady now— I like to be in my pajamas and in bed by eight o'clock."* It was, of course, a built-in safety mechanism—an escape route if things didn't go well.

As he waited, he took stock of the neighborhood. Her building was new, all clean lines and trendy textures, its sleek facade jarring against the rough red brick and old-fashioned windows of the surrounding structures. The smooth, sharp-edged concrete at its base stood in contrast to the uneven, cracked sidewalks across the street.

He surveyed the street. Narrow, lined with cars parked on both sides—all facing one direction. As a matter of habit, he always left a large gap in front of his vehicle in case a quick exit was required. Today, the space was tighter than he liked, but he could still maneuver out by nudging the smaller car ahead of him if it came to that.

The people moving through the neighborhood were eclectic in ethnicity and gender, with a noticeable skew toward young adults his age. Some wandered aimlessly; others walked with clear purpose.

About twenty feet ahead, a young woman—perhaps in her twenties or early thirties; it was hard to tell under the hijab— exited a boutique coffee shop. She was followed by a man who could presumably be her husband. As she stepped out first, he remained behind, gesturing forcefully with tightly controlled arm movements. He stood perfectly still while his chin beard bobbed as he opened his mouth to speak. A thick gold chain rested on his chest, poking out from the collar of a matching designer tracksuit. Bright white branded sneakers flashed beneath it all.

She appeared small beside him, shoulders drawn in, shrinking toward the pavement. After a moment, the pair continued down the street.

Sitting in the car, pain began to radiate in his chest. *A heart attack?* He pressed two fingers to the side of his neck. His pulse was racing—too fast. His chest began to heave, struggling to pull in air. Each breath felt poisoned, stale, useless. Panic climbed his throat.

Not now. Get it under control.

He clenched the muscles in his feet, held, then released. Then his calves—contract, release. He moved the tension upward through his body in steady progression. Slowly, his heart rate began to drop. The heart attack—if it had been one—was averted.

He opened the glove box, pulled out a small towel, and wiped the sweat from his face. Then he reached for the half-full bottle of water in the center console and took a sip.

It was time to get out of the car.

He had surprised her by gaining access to her apartment building. There was a security door downstairs, but when a neighbor entered carrying a bag of groceries, he flashed his police badge under the guise of needing to ask a resident a quick question. He was waved in without hesitation. He made a mental note to speak with her about increasing security in the building.

He knocked three times on her door.

She was surprised when she answered, expecting a neighbor —not this somewhat disarming cop. He was attractive, but beneath the surface, she sensed an uneasy darkness in him. She hadn't yet decided if she truly liked him, but she felt comfortable enough to believe she wouldn't be murdered—at least not *by* him, or a police officer.

The surprise was evident on her face.

"Jordan, oh—hi! How did you get up here?"

He smirked. "I tasered an old lady while she was bringing in her groceries. Left the security door ajar for me."

She stared for a beat, analyzing his face. Then he smirked again, and she realized it was a joke. She laughed, shaking her head.

Damn, he thought. *She was cute.* Maybe five-foot-four, with oversized blue eyes and strong blonde hair that fell just to her shoulders. Somewhere between the girl next door and a quintessential all-American cheerleader. She had a mix of innocence and latent sexuality. Jordan felt a shiver of attraction. He couldn't afford to mess this up.

"I see. Well, that seems a little excessive," she said, playing along. "But she *is* a bit annoying when you're in a hurry and she wants to talk about the most inane topics in the stairwell."

"Don't worry," he said. "She won't be bothering you any time soon, ma'am."

Emily smiled. "Just give me a couple of minutes and I'll be ready. Would you mind waiting out here?"

"No, of course not. Take your time."

Five minutes later, the door swung open. She stood in a simple white T-shirt and jeans that did nothing to obscure her petite, toned figure. The scent of her perfume struck Jordan the moment the door clicked shut, the fragrance curling in the air around him. He had no idea what it was—but it only made her more irresistible.

"Shall we?" Emily asked, tossing her keys into a front pocket. They walked side by side down the stairs and out onto the street, where Jordan's 2020 Chevy Impala was parked.

"Yes, here is my police-standard sports car." Jordan opened the front passenger door for her.

"It's quite nice! You know, as an elementary school teacher, I own a standard-issue Civic."

"I didn't know that," Jordan said deadpan. "I definitely didn't run a background check on you to make sure you weren't going to murder me on the first date."

"Wait—you didn't, did you? You *can't* do that, surely?" she asked, concern creeping into her voice.
"No," he laughed. "I'm joking. That would be illegal. I'd be investigated by IA and probably fired."
"Oh, good! I mean, I don't have anything to hide, but I'm sure there are some cops out there who are, well... less than ideal?"

"There are bad eggs, like in any job. But there are a lot of checks and balances now. Everything gets logged. I promise, I didn't run a background check on you before coming to meet you—I was just teasing."

"Very good, officer. So... where are you taking me, anyway?" Emily asked, her sweet, melodic voice lilting in that endearing way that made Jordan grin.

"You want to know? Or do you want it to be a surprise?" he asked, the grin widening.
"Oh, I want to know! I want to know everything! Confess, Officer Peck!"

She giggled at herself, and Jordan couldn't help but smile too. She was surprisingly disarming.
"Fine," he said. "But only because I'm scared of you, Miss Carson—and I don't want to get put in detention after school..."

"Oh? You sure you *don't* want that?" Emily bit her bottom lip, grimacing slightly and glancing sheepishly into the footwell. Jordan pressed on, steering past the awkwardness.

"As I was saying—here's the plan of attack for today. First, we stop at Whole Foods Market on Penn Ave to stock up on supplies. Various types of bread, delicious cheeses, sliced meats, fruits... maybe some cupcakes. I'll probably forget disposable cutlery, so your job is to remind me before we check out. After that, we head to checkpoint A: Fairmount Park."

"Oh, that's lovely. A picnic in the park."

"Right. At the park, I'll secure a spot for the picnic rug I packed in the trunk before picking you up. Then I'll lay out the feast and impress you with my culinary skill—by which I mean arranging things I bought into a visually appealing display. After lunch, we'll take a stroll. There's that Japanese garden nearby. Have you ever been?"

"No, I haven't, actually."

"Well, we could do that. And depending on how well this goes —if I haven't said anything stupid by later in the afternoon —I might see if you'd like to grab a drink at Rittenhouse Square. Maybe dinner. And at the end of the evening, I'll provide a formal escort to your front door, where I'll wish you goodnight. And if you're lucky..."

He paused, watching her reaction.

"...maybe I'll give you a goodnight kiss."

"Well, that all sounds very nice. It seems like you've put a lot of thought into today—and done your homework. You're quite romantic. It's nice... thank you for taking me out."

"You're welcome—and it's my pleasure."

They rode in silence for a moment, stopping at a red light. Emily suddenly lit up, remembering something.

"Oh! That reminds me," she exclaimed. "You should've heard some of the questions my class asked me after your active shooter presentation!"

"Oh yeah? Like what?"

"Well, one of the questions was, 'When you arrest someone and use your handcuffs, do you tickle the person for being naughty?'" She grinned. "Another one was, 'Do you get free McDonald's when you drive a police car through the drive-thru?' And there were *so many* versions of, 'Can you arrest my brother for messing up my room or not sharing snacks?'"

Jordan smiled, then launched into his reply with mock seriousness.

"Well, in order of questioning," he said, "I only tickle them if they make me chase them. Sometimes you *do* get free food at a restaurant—usually if the owner supports cops or wants a little free press by having uniforms in there. And lastly, yes—I absolutely arrest people for not cleaning their rooms. Nothing like a 24-hour hold in county for a disobedient eight-year-old who won't pick up their clothes. A couple hours in a cell with some gangbangers tends to make Mom seem *really* reasonable."

Emily laughed, her eyes sparkling.

"You're very funny. I didn't expect a policeman to have a sense of humor like you. You're quite witty."

"Yeah, thank you. I like to mix a little comedy with my police work. The perps really enjoy it. I throw in a few knock-knocks when I'm serving warrants."

"Ohhh—like a shit sandwich?" she asked, straight-faced.

"A what now? A *shit sandwich*, Emily?"

"You know... say something nice, then the shitty part, then something nice again. Like, 'Hello, sir, that's a lovely shirt. You're under arrest for murder—but hey, I really like your hair.'"
Jordan burst out laughing.

"Oh, and do you want to hear *my* police knock-knock joke?" Emily asked, trying to suppress a grin.

Jordan hesitated, amused. "Alright... who's there?"

"Warrant."
"Warrant who?"
"Warrant you expecting us, bitch? You're under arrest!"

Jordan laughed. "God, Em, you're being a bit aggressive there. The Philly Police Force is a professional organization. We hardly ever shoot suspects or beat confessions out of them anymore. But hey—let's ease up on the offensive language."

"Oh, I'm sorry, I was just pretending to be a cop," Emily said, grinning.

"No, I'm joking," he laughed. "We do that stuff all the time. Honestly, I think you'd make a great officer."

"Well, I *do* beat the children occasionally—if they get their math questions wrong," Emily replied with a wink.

Jordan laughed again, shaking his head.

"You know, Emily... I really try to be a good cop. Treat people with respect. Do the job right. Some of us are genuinely good guys. We're not all bad."

"Yeah... I believe you, Jordan," she said softly. "You seem like a good man."

After a short drive, the couple arrived at the grocery store on Pennsylvania Avenue. With some friendly deliberation, they selected a hand basket full of picnic goods—bread, cheese, meats, fruit, and cupcakes—agreeing on everything by consensus.

Just before they reached the checkout, Emily darted to the side.

"Jordan! You forgot the eating utensils!" she called. "I don't want you to think I'm not ladylike if I'm eating with my fingers!"

With supplies in hand, they returned to Jordan's Chevy and continued the journey to Fairmount Park. They found a shaded parking spot at Lemon Hill, the namesake mansion standing tall in the background.

After several hours lost in deep conversation, Emily was now far more familiar with Jordan's high school football days, a somewhat thorough overview of Philadelphia police operations, and a brief mention of his two tours in Afghanistan.

In turn, Jordan had been educated on the inner workings of Midwest high school cheerleading. Emily had grown up in Iowa and received a partial academic scholarship to Temple University in Philly. There was also talk of a possible promotion—an opportunity at another school outside the city. She was still undecided.

Jordan had teased her about never leaving school.

"I *loved* school, Jordan!" Emily grinned.

"Sure, but maybe it was a little easier for you than for some people... I mean, you're beautiful, smart, and funny. People like you. They probably *want* to be your friend."

"Oh, and it was hard for you?" she said, raising an eyebrow, her voice teasing. "Mister football player—big, strong, handsome boy. Was it difficult deciding which cheerleader to kiss?"

Jordan laughed. "Mack out? Do you mean *kiss*? And for your information, I'm a gentleman. I don't go around macking out all over the place."

"Hmm, shame. That's what I was planning to do with you later," Emily said casually—so casual, in fact, it was hard to tell whether she was joking or not.

After finishing the picnic, they consolidated the remaining

food into empty packets and tossed the waste in a nearby trash can. Then they agreed to walk along the riverbank. Emily linked her arm through Jordan's—the height difference made it a bit awkward, but they managed.

As the sun dipped toward the horizon, the day's plan continued to unfold. They returned to the car, crossed the river, and headed toward Rittenhouse Square for drinks. Afterwards, they shared dinner at a wood-fired pizza joint nearby.

When the meal was done, Jordan drove Emily the few miles back to her apartment, this time parking farther down the street. He offered to walk her to her door, and she offered no resistance.
At the base of her apartment building, she pulled her keys from her bag and opened the security door.

"You'd better escort me up to my apartment," she said with a grin. "This looks like a *very* scary neighborhood."

He followed her up the stairs, trailing slightly behind. His eyes were unconsciously drawn to the perfect proportions of her lower body, the soft taper of her waist. With each step, her T-shirt rose just slightly, offering a glimpse of skin. A surge of electricity shot through his body, landing squarely in the vicinity of his groin. He had decided that he liked her immensely. And though the temptation to push things further was strong, he held back. He didn't want to ruin the chance of a second date.

At the top of the stairs, Emily suddenly turned, raising both hands as if to stop traffic.
"You're too tall. Stop right there," she ordered.

Then, as if on cue, her hand reached up to gently pull his face down toward hers. Without hesitation, she kissed him —passionately. Her tongue was surprisingly confident for someone so petite.

She pulled away, eyes sparkling.

"Well… goodnight. See you later!"

And just like that, she turned on her heel and started walking away, leaving him momentarily stunned.

He watched her, still processing what had just happened. Then she glanced back over her shoulder, smirking.

"I'm joking," she said, her voice warm and playful. "You want to come in for a nightcap?"

More than I've ever wanted to do anything in my whole life, he thought—but kept his cool.

"Yeah. I'd love to."

CHAPTER 15: STRATEGIC SPINS, UNSTOPPABLE WINS.

To: [President Reign c/o Lauren Chalmers] Lauren.Chalmers@whitehouse.gov
CC: [Big Mac] John.McMann@WarlordPeacecorp.com
From: [Connor Hammond] Connor@AIA.com
Subject: Public Relations Advisory Report – Gunman

PRIVATE AND CONFIDENTIAL

Dear President Reign and John,

Thanks for bringing me in as a consultant on this project. You're going to change America with your vision for safer schools. It's a brilliant move on behalf of President Reign. As requested, you'll find my report attached. It's brief and as succinct as possible: I understand President Reign is a busy man who just wants the facts without hyperbole.

Stay resolute!

Connor Hammond
CEO, Apex Influence Agency –
AIA: Strategic Spins, Unstoppable Wins.

REPORT: PUBLIC RELATIONS MANAGEMENT – IMPLEMENTATION OF ARMED DRONE PROGRAM

PRIVATE AND CONFIDENTIAL
Subtitle: *A Strategic Report for the Program Chief and the President*

Introduction

Intended Audience: This report is prepared specifically for the Program Chief and the President, providing a comprehensive overview of managing public relations and communications.

Scope: Prepared in conjunction with technical advisory from Warlord Peacecorp, this report provides guidance on public relations management, excluding technical specifications outside the expertise of this firm.

Program Messaging and Narrative

The school defense program aims to utilize cutting-edge technology to combat the rising and ongoing threat of school violence perpetrated by individuals and small groups seeking to cause destruction. The purpose of this report is to outline the best approach for communicating the aims and capabilities of the drone program to the American people; reassuring the public that this program enhances constitutional freedoms rather than undermining them.

During the authoring of this report and the development of the program, a code name was created for ease of reference: **GUNMAN.**

Limitations and Concerns of Program

Given the operational limitations of the program, it is advised that public messaging focuses on deterrence. There is a possibility that the technology may not function as intended in real-life applications; therefore, a strong awareness campaign is necessary. Suggested positioning statements include:

"Don't Take Your Guns to School, Billy."

- Graphic: Bottom right; young male figure, disheveled, unkempt hair, dressed in dark clothing (potentially a trench coat), with a hunched posture expressing inner turmoil. He holds a weapon.
- Top right; Gunman stands tall, illuminated in bright white like a gallant knight, juxtaposed against the dark figure.
- Tagline: *"Don't take your guns to school, Billy; because*

Gunman is on the job."

"Gunman's Gonna Stop You."

- Initial focus groups indicate push back from conservative states. A proposed campaign will emphasize Gunman's divine endorsement.
- Concept: A rural school with pick-up trucks and yellow buses parked out front. Gunman stands at the gate, a book in one hand, a weapon in the other.
- Tagline: *"Guns for Good. Guns for God."*

"Gunman: Guardian of Innocence."

- Scene: An elementary school classroom. A wholesome young teacher stands before her students, a bright red apple on her desk.
- The blackboard features: *"A is for Apple,"* accompanied by a steaming apple pie illustration.
- In the back of the room, Gunman stands watch. A young boy turns, grins, and gives Gunman a thumbs-up. Gunman returns the gesture.
- Message: *"The children feel safe with their Guardian of Innocence watching over them."*

Further Public Communication Strategies

- **Celebrity Endorsements:** Secure high-profile figures to promote Gunman as a cultural icon. Consider national sports heroes, music stars, or even actors known for patriotic roles.
- **Merchandising:** Capitalize on back-to-school promotions. Gunman branded backpacks, lunch boxes, and school supplies can reinforce program visibility.
- **Live Demonstrations:** A halftime show at the Super Bowl could showcase Gunman's firepower and aerial capabilities. Consider reaching out to fictional pop icons like *Jaxon Cross* or *Riley Skye* for musical tie-ins.

- **Gun-Cam Subscription Service:** Create an interactive experience by offering subscribers exclusive access to live Gunman deployments. Competitions could include VIP experiences such as *"Gunman attending your birthday party."*

PR Challenges and Solutions

1. Concerns About the Origin of the Technology

- The core technology was initially developed by *Darius Greene*, a Muslim-American, for non-military applications. There may be public concerns that his original work was repurposed for surveillance and combat.
- **Solution:** Control the narrative: Frame this as *"American innovation at its finest,"* emphasizing the technological advancements rather than its origins.

2. Weaponization of Medical Technology

- The system was originally designed for emergency medical responses but was adapted for tactical security use.
- **Solution:** Highlight the humanitarian aspect: Gunman doesn't just neutralize threats, it *prevents* violence before it happens.

The Need for a Public Face

Gunman requires a strong figurehead to lead the initiative, someone who embodies the program's values and reassures the public. Ideally, this person should be:

- An all American hero
- A symbol of strength and resilience
- A beacon of hope and justice

Potential candidates include:

- A decorated veteran or retired special forces operative
- A respected former law enforcement officer

- A charismatic media personality with strong patriotic credentials

By positioning this figure as the *"face of Gunman,"* we create a unifying icon that inspires trust and support nationwide.

Final Thoughts

This program represents a transformative step in national security. With the right messaging, Gunman can become more than just a security measure; it can be a cultural force. The strategies outlined above will ensure that the American people embrace Gunman as a protector, not just a machine.

Let's make history.

Connor Hammond
CEO, Apex Influence Agency

Dear Mr. Hammond,

Thank you for your report and advisory into considerations for the implementation of the school defense program.

President Reign wishes me to advise that he found your report very thorough and some great and fantastic ideas. Also, your report was very strong, and he is pleased that you are as enthusiastic about making America as safe as he is.

Thank you again for your input into this program, it is invaluable.

Best regards,

Lauren Chalmers
Chief of Staff
Office of the President.

CHAPTER 16: AN UNWELCOME GUEST

In the liminal space between dreaming and waking, Jordan became aware of a forceful, mechanical rhythm—knocking. At first, the intrusion seemed to blend into the remnants of whatever dream had occupied his mind. But as consciousness took hold, a jolt of adrenaline snapped him fully awake.

The precision was almost metronomic—four knocks, a pause, and then the cycle resumed. Jordan raised his wrist and rotated his forearm to check his watch. Nine-thirty in the morning. For most, a perfectly acceptable time for social interaction. To Jordan, it was a deeply offensive violation.

Knock knock knock knock.

He threw the covers off his body. Only the top half of him was clothed. He hesitated between grabbing a shirt and confronting the persistent knocking. A bolt of fear surged through him now, consuming him. His hands trembled and his heart pounded so violently it nearly stole his breath.

Knock knock knock knock.

He opted against getting dressed. Instead, he opened the top drawer of the small bedside table and retrieved his Smith & Wesson M&P9. Holding the weapon with his finger off the trigger, he checked the magazine well. As he expected, it was fully loaded. Satisfied, he moved toward the door, setting the handgun down on the small hall table around the corner from the entrance.

Knock knock knock knock.

"Who is it? What do you want?" Jordan stood sideways to the door, his back against the hallway wall—right hand closest to the weapon, left hand ready to fling the door open and deliver some well-earned discipline to the tenacious percussionist outside.

"Jordan Peck, I need to speak with you. This is a matter of national security." The voice was authoritative and loud enough to dispel any notion that this was a joke.

Jordan opened the door slowly. It was okay. He exhaled, steadying his breath. The threat seemed less urgent now, replaced by curiosity. Whatever this was, it had overtaken his discomfort.

As the door opened, a hulking behemoth of a man barged inside, flanked by another man—both dressed in sharp, functional suits. Their weapons, though concealed, were betrayed by the bulges of steel under fabric.

"Peck. Do you know who the fuck I am, son?" The man's voice made no attempt at civility. He was an uninvited force of nature, unbothered by courtesy.

Jordan didn't know—but he wasn't given a chance to ask.

"I'm John McMann. CEO of Warlord Peacecorp, program director of the new school defense initiative, Master Sergeant, United States Marine Corps, retired—and all-around American patriot and hero. Listen, son, tuck in that gut, will you? I can't concentrate while it's flopping all over the place. Watson, locate this man's wardrobe and find something to hide his fat gut. And I don't mean one of the dresses he wears when no one's around. Maybe a T-shirt… extra, extra… extra-large."
The security detail moved past Jordan without acknowledgment, scanning the space for the bedroom.

McMann noticed the Smith & Wesson on the hallway table. "And son, let's put that fucking weapon away before you get hurt, will you?"

He made eye contact with his subordinate, who turned at the mention of the weapon. McMann gestured with a tilt of his head. The man seized the handgun, quickly released the magazine, and—with the barrel pointed at a safe 45-degree angle toward the kitchen—racked the slide. The chambered round ejected and landed softly on the carpet.

With that done, the subordinate disappeared down the hall. McMann, meanwhile, stared Jordan down with open disdain. The man returned, holding out a sweatshirt. McMann looked at it with contempt.

"What is that? Looks like something I'd use to mop up after I finished with your girlfriend. Get some new clothes, Peck. Class it up."

Grabbing the shirt from his colleague's outstretched hand, McMann threw it to the floor and stomped it under his boot, twisting as if extinguishing a cigarette.

"What the hell, man?" Jordan snapped, his patience clearly expiring.

"You shut the hell up... *man*. Here's the deal, you burned-out, degenerate, hippie-looking motherfucker. I'm leading the new school defense program, and it turns out the President needs a volunteer to front the initiative. Despite my better judgment —and the fact that you currently look like someone who understands school shootings—that motherfucker is you."

He locked eyes with Jordan, nostrils flaring like a bull about to charge.

"Do you have any questions, dickhead?"

"What do you mean, *front the initiative*?"

"Well, duh, what I mean, duh, dumb-dumb," McMann mocked, stumbling his words like a cruel impersonation of a disability before snapping back to form. "What I mean is: *you're gonna be fucking useful* and serve your country as the face of the new program. Gun up, Gunman."

"I have no idea what the hell you're talking about."

"I'm talking about *you* stopping being a fucking sissy, growing a pair, and becoming a national hero. You're gonna wear the suit, fly all over the goddamn country, shoot some motherfuckers, and save the day. Then you can go home to your boyfriend and do whatever it is you gays do."

"I'm not gay, McMann."

"You'll be whatever the fuck the President and I tell you to be, you worthless sack of crap."

"Yeah? And if I refuse?"

McMann's eyes bulged, nostrils flared. His grotesquely muscular body, a walking testament to chemical enhancement, rippled with unnatural mass. His biceps ballooned, triceps visibly striated, forearms webbed with angry veins. But despite the looming threat, he spoke to his colleague with eerie calm.

"Would you wait outside in the hallway, please? The grown-ups need to have a little talk. I'll buy you a lollipop later for being good."

The man nodded and stepped out. The door closed. McMann's demeanor shifted. The bravado dropped. What remained was darker—calculated and lethal.

"If you refuse, Peck, then you're looking at thirty to forty years for third-degree murder, official suppression, maybe even a human rights violation for shooting that Black kid after he surrendered in the gym."

He stared directly into Jordan's soul. His sheer physical presence faded, eclipsed by the intensity of his will. Jordan stood frozen, caught between terror and adrenaline.

"What the hell are you talking about?"

The raw innocence in his voice only enraged McMann further.

"I know everything, Peck. Poster child for mediocrity. High school quarterback who couldn't get a scholarship, too dumb for college. So...you join the Army at eighteen—what were you, E-4? Two enlistments? Because you couldn't figure out anything better? A fucking nobody. Yeah, you saw some action in Kandahar and Helmand, but your garbage shooting probably got more of your own guys killed than the enemy. You disgust me." McMann took a moment to glare into his eyes, inches away from him.

"And then, you became a cop. Even worse. The only remarkable thing you've ever done in your pitiful life was shoot an unarmed Black kid who had already surrendered. What's your strength, Peck? Disobeying simple fucking orders? How do I know? Maybe Rodriguez told me. Maybe I've got a witness. Doesn't fucking matter. I know."

Jordan didn't respond. He stared straight ahead. His face was tight with defiance, but tears streaked silently down his cheeks.

McMann dialed his tone down—barely.

"Look, Peck. Here's the SITREP. We need a friendly face for the American people to get behind. And for some reason, the President's got a hard-on for you. He thinks you're *the guy* to make everyone feel warm and fuzzy about sending a suit like this into danger zones.

"And let me tell you, you check all the boxes for someone eminently expendable if this thing goes south. If you screw it up, I'll perforate your fucking skull myself—and that's if I'm feeling unusually generous. Otherwise, enjoy thirty to life in gen pop at ADX Florence.

"So let me really emphasize how much I'm going to appreciate your cooperation. Do we understand each other?"

"You want me on this program? I don't even understand what the program is."

"No. I *don't* want you. *President Reign* wants you. But at least you figured out half the equation with that thick, ugly head of yours. And it doesn't matter what the program is. What matters is: you're going to do it. I've got real soldiers for this. But none of that matters."

McMann paused. Something had caught his eye in the kitchen —a framed photo.

He walked toward it, picking it up.

"Fuck me, Peck. Who's this little babe? Your sister?"

"Nooooo!" Jordan roared, primal and guttural.

"How the hell does a pathetic, weak-ass motherfucker like you get a woman like that? She makes me wanna...damn, I'm getting all excited here."

McMann held the photograph against his crotch and began to thrust.

Jordan crossed the room. "Don't you fuckin' touch that"

McMann swung a backhand across the face of Jordan as he approached, dropping the frame as he raised his hand, the glass smashing as it hit the tiled floor of the kitchen. He followed with a swiftly executed upper cut from his right-hand into the stomach of Jordan.

"Son, that was your first, last, and only free pass you get when it comes to my patience which let me tell you, it's done. Now you will co-operate as needed, fully with my program or I will stick my boot so far up your ass it's going to need a passport before it leaves. Do you understand me Peck?"

Jordan lay winded on the carpet of the living room, on his side he nodded, pain compromising his ability to answer.

"DO YOU FUCKING UNDERSTAND ME PECK?"

"I do. Yes" Jordan wheezed an answer.

"Good now if I want to hear you speak again, I will take my dick out of your mouth."
McMann reached into his pocket and retrieved his phone. After mashing about on the screen, he raised the handset to his ear and spoke.

"Yeah. Chalmers. Peck is onboard, tell President Reign. We'll commence the training program now".

CHAPTER 17: VIC, THE RAT.

The door to his apartment slammed shut, and the emptiness left behind by the intruders settled in, thick and suffocating. Jordan groaned in pain—anger and a deep sense of betrayal gnawing at him. He rolled across the floor, winded from McMann's attack, struggling to get to his feet.

He staggered around the apartment, his chest heaving, until he found his cell phone, still charging in his bedroom. His hands, shaking with rage, fumbled over the screen as he accessed his contact list. His thumb swiped through it in a blind, frantic fury before he pressed the phone to his ear. The dial tone rang—twice, three times. His heart pounded so intensely he thought it might kill him. Four cycles of the dial tone before the call was answered.

"Hey, Jordy, man. What's happening?"

"You motherfucker, how could you do this to me?" Jordan's voice was a sharp bark of fury. "What the hell, man?"

"What are you talking about?" Vic's voice feigned either confusion or the act of someone who had rehearsed the response.

"You fucking ratted me out for shooting him?!" Jordan spat, his voice rising.

"Shooting who? What? Jordy, calm down. I don't think we should be talking about this over the phone—"

"It's too late. They know! They've got me, Vic! You fucker! You fuckin' Judas! Why? Why did you do this to me?" The words erupted between his gritted teeth.

"Jordy, I swear I didn't do anything. I never told anybody nothin'..." Vic's tone sounded sincere, but something about it felt off.

"Then how the fuck do they know? How do they know what happened that day?" Jordan demanded.

"I don't know, Jordy, but it wasn't me. I swear on my life—I didn't rat on you."

"Then why the fuck is some government prick in my apartment, signing me up for some bullshit mission? He attacked me! He knew everything!" Jordan's voice cracked with desperation.
"Okay, man, okay, look. I don't know. Let's just meet up somewhere and work it out."

"No. I don't know if I can trust you anymore, Vic. You were supposed to be my partner! You don't fucking do this shit!" Jordan shouted, his fury mounting with each word.

"I didn't, Jordy, I swear! Let's just meet up—"

"No! I can't trust you anymore. Stay the fuck away from me!" Jordan's voice was guttural, a sound born of betrayal and disbelief.

"Jordy, I..." Vic's voice trailed off, but Jordan didn't wait. His thumb slammed the screen, violently ending the call.

He crumpled to the floor, shaking and sobbing uncontrollably. Then, just as suddenly, he jerked upright. Any discomfort evaporated, replaced by a surge of purpose. He leapt to his feet and rushed into the kitchen, flinging open the cabinet beneath the sink. He ripped the bottom shelf free with a powerful motion, his hand floundering helplessly in the empty void.

It wasn't there.

He tore the shelf out completely, exposing the bare floor. The phone was gone. His mind spun with the implications. He stumbled back to his feet, hunched over the sink, and retched violently into it. His stomach emptied repeatedly until there was nothing left but air. He collapsed onto the cold tile floor, barely noticing the chill against his bare skin.

Outside, in a black SUV, McMann's employee sat with a laptop and a set of headphones.

"Sir, he just called Rodriguez. Accused him of reporting him to the government for shooting someone. It got pretty heated... Is he talking about that black kid at the massacre?"

"Jesus. What a fucking moron," McMann muttered, his voice calm and detached. "Keep this conversation between us, or you won't have to worry about your NDA. I'll make sure you can't talk at all with my boot in your mouth. Got it?"

"Yes, sir."

"Good. Keep monitoring his communications and keep me updated."

CHAPTER 18: AN INCONVENIENT FOURTH.

It was McMann again. God, she hated her cell phone. She was now at a point in her career where every notification on the damned device made her anxious. She could screen him, but the oaf would likely continue calling or reach another aide within the White House to get whatever it was he wanted. She sighed with desperation and accepted the call.

"Mr. McMann, how can I help you?" She adopted her most refined and authoritative tone—in the way that many professional women alter their voices for a role, like a newsreader lowering her pitch to let the boys know she was fully capable in her role.

"Chalmers, meeting with the president in an hour. I'm bringing in special counsel, that Harrison asshole. Clear his schedule, will you? It's non-negotiable." He barked down the line.

"Mr. McMann, I'll have to check with the president and our team to see if we can clear any time on the schedule..."

"Chalmers, listen. I'll be there in an hour—it's already scheduled. Probably wouldn't hurt if you could appear too. You'll probably have some homework after the meeting anyway, and I don't have time to fuck around explaining the situation multiple times. Alright? See you in an hour."

He ended the call.

It would be far easier to just facilitate the meeting than deal with McMann not getting his way. Lauren walked down the hallway to the Oval Office. He wasn't there. She returned to her office and used her landline to call an aide.

"Emergency meeting with John McMann and legal counsel at 12 p.m. Can you please flag as urgent and alert President Reign's phone?"

She put down the receiver. Moments later her cell phone buzzed: *Meeting confirmed, 12 p.m.: Oval Office.*

Lauren arrived slightly before twelve and took her seat in the Oval Office. Shortly after twelve, McMann barged through the door, followed by a middle-aged man in an uninspiring suit —slightly pudgy, with the gleam of slickness that most used car salesmen and all lawyers impart. Harrison was the lead White House counsel; he was, of course, often involved in daily business and well known to both Lauren and the president. Reign liked him because he was a yes-man. Reign would dream up something legally ambiguous, and Harrison would take it back to legal and make it work.
McMann, of course—as usual, lacking in decorum—began without any introductions and launched straight into business. The lawyer scrambled to find a seat.

"Doug, look, we've got a big problem here. The scanning technology—we need to be able to quickly identify any potential perps carrying a weapon. I've got an idea, but it's not gonna sound very appetizing when I tell you..."

"John, let me tell you—you're a tremendous patriot. Everyone's talking about it. People are saying you're a hero. What you're doing—unbelievable. It's going to make our education system so safe, so great, the best in the world, believe me. No one will do it like you. It's going to be huge."
McMann shrugged, slightly nodding that he already knew that.

"Alright. Are you familiar with GFSZA? You know, the Gun-Free

School Zone?"

"Yes, you can't have a firearm within a thousand feet of a designated school zone. So what's the problem here? We don't want criminals with guns anywhere near schools."

"Doug, the problem is—on deployment, we need to find the school shooters immediately. So, we've got some tech—we're talking big fuck-off scanning capabilities: millimeter wave scanners, infrared, terahertz imaging, radar—all kinds of shit on these things. It's all linked up to AI and machine learning. The problem is the fucking Fourth Amendment."

"I don't follow. What's the problem? Which one is the Fourth again?"

"Illegal searches without cause. Doug, with the program, we could've ended the Hope Valley massacre within minutes— saving God knows how many lives. The problem is people and their fucking rights."

"Yes. Some of those amendments are a real pain in the ass for me too. So, what are you saying? We can't search for an active shooter because it might violate someone's rights?"

"Exactly. We could face shutdown of our scanning tech because it can quickly assess and search for weapons among a large crowd. We're talking about legal challenges. Look— I've got this fellow from legal; Harrison here is a senior advisor on national security law," McMann explained, pointing to Harrison, who looked like he'd rather be anywhere else at that moment. "Alright, Beaumont—you tell Mr. President your concerns, and we'll explain why you're being a crybaby."

Harrison cleared his throat. He seemed as nervous as a man about to advise the president on how to violate at least one constitutional amendment should be.

"Mr. President, we have two clear constitutional issues here with this program, and they're doozies. We're talking about the Second and the Fourth Amendments—that is, the right to bear arms and the rights of people not to be subject to illegal searches."

Reign interrupted. "How does this relate to the Second?"

"Well, Mr. President, this technology can—with incredible reliability—detect weapons within a large geographical area, within the thousand-foot radius of the GFSZ. The problem is, effectively, we can't search people without cause. Even though it is illegal to possess a firearm within a thousand feet, we can't enforce that unless we have reasonable cause to search everyone. That then brings up an issue with the Second—the right to bear arms."

"So, what you're telling me here is that it's only illegal to have a gun in the gun-free zone *if* we know that you have a gun?" Reign scolded the counselor.

"Well, yes—and as you can imagine, there's going to be a lot of critical response to this. Not the least of all will be the UFAA."

"Fuck the UFAA, Doug. Nobody here is scared of the UFAA. Except obviously Harrison, and probably Chalmers. Hey, Chalmers—you scared of Dickhead Garrison?" McMann exploded.

"No, sir. I don't believe that is relevant to the discussion here, but I would advise against alienating the membership of the UFAA," Lauren offered calmly.

"Listen, I've been saying it for months: we're gonna make schools safe again. We're gonna do it. Nobody's gonna do it like I am. Trust me—nobody. What's the plan here? Just tell me— let's make it happen."

Harrison took up the mantle again.

"Sir, the most straightforward path here is an executive order.

It's going to involve an alteration to the Gun-Free School Zone Act. Effectively, it means that within the zone, you are subject to a search of your person via non-contact scanning and assessment. I think it needs to be very clear that this is to determine if individuals are in violation of the act and will be subject to prosecution."

"That's taking it easy on the criminals anyway, Doug. Why don't we add in the use of authorized lethal force for any person found to be in possession of a firearm within the GFSZ?"

"Mr. McMann, please—you cannot be serious suggesting we can just shoot anybody with a weapon on them within a thousand feet of a school?" Harrison sounded terrified.

"Could we do that? I think that's showing a tremendous commitment to law and order, and I am very passionate about law and order," Reign mused to the room.

Harrison pleaded. "Mr. President... no. There is no way in the world we could sign an executive order to authorize lethal force on top of what is at this moment a Fourth Amendment violation. It would be disastrous. All you would achieve is the fastest objection and injunction in the history of law—no, sir... please don't consider that as an option."

"Fine. But for the record, I thought that was a tremendous idea. Shows great leadership from me. I want the criminals to know that if you want to use violence against innocent children, we will use *more* violence against you. And you won't like it. You won't like it one bit," Reign conceded.

"Maybe there's another way," Harrison offered. "Potentially, we could use a legal framework that circumvents the normal procedural constraints when the nation faces an imminent, high-stakes threat. In a situation like an active shooter scenario within a school zone, we could activate a national emergency exception under exigent circumstances. This would allow for the immediate deployment of surveillance and intervention without the usual requirements for probable cause or a warrant. This loophole would essentially function as an extension of emergency powers, akin to those invoked during a declared state of emergency but specifically tailored to address exigent law enforcement needs. To ensure its legality, we'd frame it as a targeted emergency powers clause— a temporary suspension of certain constitutional protections —granting the deployment of drones and other rapid-response measures under the pretext of preserving public safety. The public and legal framework would have to be structured in a way that prioritizes the urgency of the threat, while safeguarding against overreach. This would allow us to act swiftly, before the normal legal process can intervene."

President Reign sat back in his chair, musing for a moment, chin slightly elevated.

"You know, this is exactly what I'm talking about. Legal loopholes—believe me, I love 'em. You get to cut through all the red tape, get things done faster. People are tired of waiting, and *I'm* tired of seeing these school shootings happening, day after day. You want results? This is how we get results. Let me tell you, I've been saying this for years—when there's a crisis, when lives are at stake, you don't waste time with paperwork. You hit 'em hard and fast. We'll make sure the laws can work for us, not against us. And believe me, we'll do it legally—even if doing it legally means we have to make it legal. So, if that's what it takes to protect our kids—let's do it. It's time to be tough. It's time to win."

Lauren couldn't stop herself from speaking any longer.

"Sir, I fear that we've moved off target for this program. We're talking as if violent criminals are targeting schools for opportunistic acts of benefit—they're not. These are predominantly young people with mental health issues, bullying, abuse—whatever the cause. They're sometimes seeking retribution or infamy. Sometimes they're just very mentally unwell. I fear we are pursuing the wrong path here, taking offensive measures as if we're defending against attacks. Surely, we could consider gun control or mental health initiatives to work on this problem…"

"Shut up, Chalmers," McMann yelled, his face red with anger, pointing an extended index finger across the room. "If you don't love guns, you don't love America. All we're talking about here is if some fucking geek that can't get pussy wants to bring daddy's guns to school that we are going to shoot the shit out of them. It's that simple."

Lauren dropped her gaze to the ground. She couldn't believe she found herself in the same situation again—within the same room, and the same man reducing her. She focused hard to push away the tears welling in her eyes. It was futile. She felt the moisture gathering. McMann scoffed.

"Yeah, I thought so."

Reign, oblivious to the awkwardness of the situation, pressed on.

"OK, Counsellor Harrison. What will happen when we sign the executive order?"

"Implementing this through an executive order is going to face significant legal challenges. As we covered, there are two very serious amendment issues—just the Fourth alone could cause insurmountable problems."

"Yes, it is a big problem. John, this program—it *can* work without the search functions, but you're saying it's necessary?"

"Yeah, I am. You go back and watch the footage of the Hope Valley shit-show. People running around crazy, hundreds of cops hiding out front of the school. There shouldn't be one person inside that complex with a weapon who doesn't want to die. We could have had it scanned and identified within a couple of feet the location of that piece of shit kid – otherwise we're talking about clearing each room of a very large, disjointed and complex system of buildings".

"It's non-negotiable then – we're going to enact this executive order. Counselor, what do you think will happen?"

"Well, you'll sign the order at which point you can either go with full publicity or take a more nuanced approach – it either case I'd expect it to garner considerable media attention, the clandestine approach would probably not go down very well with the public. In any case as usual the order will be published in the federal register."

"No. I want full publicity on this, we'll be doing a full presentation on the program and the need for this order".

"Sir that's entirely up to yourself – I merely provide legal counsel and not advice on how to be the president. From there we could potentially expect several legal challenges from individuals, organizations, maybe even states. I would expect a considerable volume of lawsuits to be filed; these will be in the district court of course. Likely there will be a consolidation of all the cases, perhaps a few lead plaintiffs, I'd expect the UFAA to want a front row seat on this. Your opponents will seek an injunction to stop the executive order – that's going to end up in a federal district court. Now I think that this issue is going to be way too big for them to issue the injunction so it's going to end up in federal court. It's going to end up in the federal court anyway, the only uncertain aspect is whether the district will have the balls to issue an injunction, in which case you'll go to the court of appeals".

"Doug, that's good news. You've got some friends on the bench there. It's going to end up going your way". McMann offered to the discussion.

"Yes, that's right. You know I have a lot of support on the bench, some really great people who understand what it takes to make our country the greatest on the planet. John, how far are we from realistically launching the program?"

"Six months, maybe five—we're finalizing the machine learning and AI. Peck is currently undergoing extensive training to perform his role."

"Good, that's very good. No point signing this executive order so far out, then, is there? It should be done at the same time we reveal the program—shut up some of the critics when we save lives. What do you think, Harrison?"

"I agree, sir. There's no point issuing an executive order that can't even be used. The best justification for the order will come from a successful deployment of the program."

"Alright, listen up. In six months, when we roll out the biggest, most incredible commitment to safety—seriously, people are gonna love it, they're gonna be crying, hugging their kids, thanking me—we slip in the executive order. No one's even gonna care. They'll be too busy cheering for America. That's how we do it. That's how you win. Alright, get it drafted. Have it ready to go," the President announced.

"Good work, Doug. Really great work," McMann grunted, as if he were on a football field and ready to slap the president on the ass.

"And thanks to you too, Harrison. I guess for your absolutely enlightening legal analysis."

"Thank you, sir," Harrison replied.

"Yeah, great, thank you. Now fuck off, will you?" he said as they exited.

With McMann and Harrison out of the room, Lauren gathered

herself. "Thank you, sir. I'll be in my office."

"Lauren?"

"Yes, Mr. President?"

"You've been doing some really tremendous work. And I get it; you've got concerns. Everybody's got concerns. But let me tell you something, making America great? It's not for the weak. Gotta be tough. Gotta be willing to do what needs to be done. And you? You're tough. I like that."

"Thank you, sir."

Lauren's shoulders slumped as she replied, letting the weight she bore collapse around her. It was a rare compliment, and she was caught off guard. But only for a moment.

"Lauren, get Captain Evans on the line for me, will you? Remember the guy that stood around while all the children were being shot?"

It took a moment to organize the call. Two of the White House aides scrambled to track down the captain at his station, and soon enough, the full weight of the Office of the President bore down on a lowly police captain from Philadelphia.

"Evans... You know, I was just thinking about leadership. Real leadership. The kind that steps up, takes charge, does something when kids are getting shot up in elementary schools. And then I thought of you, standing there, doing absolutely nothing. Just incredible. A masterclass in what not to do. I mean, what were you waiting for? The shooter to run out of bullets? Let's be honest, you blew it. But don't worry, I'm a solutions guy. I fix things. So, I'm going to outsource your job to someone who knows what the hell they're doing. Hey, you know what I'm gonna do..."

As soon as Reign mentioned outsourcing, Lauren caught his eye and mouthed that she was heading back to her office.

Hearing a police captain get flayed alive by the president wasn't something she needed to stick around for.

By the time she sat down at her desk, her phone buzzed with a notification, another post from the POTUSA account.

Soon, we will never again deal with the kind of gross incompetence shown by 'CAPTAIN' Evans at Hope Valley Elementary. Worst police officer ever. Change is coming. I'm going to REIGN hell on school violence.

CHAPTER 19: THE COLD CALL.

"Miss Chalmers? Madam?" The voice grew louder. "Lauren?" A gentle touch on her shoulder brought her back.

She had dozed off—or perhaps just slipped into a moment of oblivion. It was probably the cocktail of pills she'd been taking regularly: anti-anxiety medication that numbed her, followed by a dose of sleeping tablets. She'd gotten into the habit of taking them before leaving work, to knock herself out before getting home.

"I'm sorry to disturb you, ma'am, but your transport has arrived." The young White House aide looked visibly uncomfortable as he delivered the news. It was fine. She wanted to go home. Badly.

A black sedan waited at the gate, the driver standing by while two men in sleek black suits stood outside. Her security detail shadowed her movements beyond the White House grounds. One of the men scanned the area outside the gates, his movements mechanical, as though following some pre-programmed routine.

The second man held the rear door of the sedan open for her. "Hello, ma'am," he greeted, his mouth curving into the faintest of smiles. Most of these men were devoid of personality, but this one had something different about him—though she couldn't quite place it. Perhaps he was flirting? The kind of men she spent most of her days around didn't bother with flirtation, they were more in the vein of harassment.

After she climbed inside, he closed the door and walked around the back of the vehicle to take his place in the rear.

The sedan pulled away, heading east along Pennsylvania Avenue toward her apartment in Capitol Hill. Lauren allowed herself to relax slightly. The promise of slipping off her shoes and taking a long, hot shower at home offered some fleeting comfort.

It had been two days since her meeting with McMann and the lawyer. The tension was palpable now. The storm was coming —it was only a matter of time before everything exploded. There were no secrets in politics, and the White House was about as tight on leaks as the Titanic at the bottom of the Atlantic.

Her phone vibrated inside her handbag; the ringtone muffled within its confines. She dug it out and glanced at the screen.

"Alicia Turner, UFAA Lob."

Lauren didn't need to look up the name. It was part of her job to know everyone she dealt with—names, titles, positions. Alicia Turner was a political lobbyist for the United Firearms Advocates Association, but Lauren knew her as much more than that. Turner was a hardline enforcer: part watchdog, part pit bull. The kind of woman who believed guns were the solution, never the problem. If this were a schoolyard, she'd be the one organizing her boyfriend to beat up the weaker kids who dared question her authority.

She glanced at the security man next to her. He subtly elongated his torso and raised his chin, clearly trying to intrude on her privacy. His lips pulled back into an exaggerated grimace; his eyes wide in mock disgust.

Lauren suppressed a laugh, snorting softly. She quickly covered it with a measured breath, composing herself.

"Hello. Lauren Chalmers speaking."

"Lauren. It's Alicia Turner, from the United Firearms Advocates Association."

"Oh, Alicia, hi. How are you?" Lauren's tone was neutral, but her nose involuntarily wrinkled as she said it.

"Not that great. Lauren, I think we need to talk about President Reign. We're hearing a lot of chatter about tightening gun restrictions and some nonsense about illegal weapon searches for law-abiding citizens under the guise of school safety. Richard, of course, is justifiably worried."

"Oh? I'm not sure what you've heard, and of course, I can't confirm the contents of confidential discussions that—"

"Oh, come on, Lauren." Turner interrupted, her voice thick with irritation. "We're hearing about some kind of—God, I don't even know what to call it—just that he's creating some insane gun control program using constitutional violations and technology. I'm hearing stories about robots with guns. It's exactly the kind of ridiculous rhetoric that Reign will probably try to implement!"

"Alicia, I can assure you, your intel is so far removed from fact, I'm not sure how to respond to it."

"You can respond by taking some notes. The UFAA is vehemently opposed to any measures that strip rights from gun owners. We'll fight you on this, and you better believe it. We oppose using dangerous technology to endanger the lives of children in our schools."

"Okay, Alicia. I'll make a note of your concerns."

"Oh no, Lauren. I'm not done. Our position is that you need to get firearms into the hands of our educators, school security staff, and good people. We cannot strip away the Second. We need more guns in the hands of people and more God in this country."

There was a brief silence. Lauren rubbed her eyes, trying to focus as her chest rose and fell quickly in irritation.

"You know what I think, Alicia? I think the UFAA is worried that this program may actually work to reduce school shootings in this country. You are aware that no other country on this planet experiences school violence as frequently or as severely as we do? You think it's fine to practice active shooter drills with children between lessons on learning to read and do math? And your solution is to add more guns to the equation and ask schoolteachers—people who went into education to teach, not to be armed security guards?"

Lauren's words were sharp, her voice steady despite the rush of adrenaline coursing through her. As she spoke, her hand trembled slightly, but she clenched her jaw, ready for a retort.

The security man sitting next to her held up his phone, proudly showing off a text message he'd written on the screen:

"U.nited F.ucking A.ssholes of America!!"

Lauren shot him a look, her eyes flicking to his face. If she were to be honest, he wasn't what she'd consider attractive —slightly shorter than the others, his features ordinary. But something about his presence intrigued her.

Before she could process that thought, Alicia's voice cut through again.

"Wake up, Lauren. It's the Second Amendment, not the second suggestion, not the second option when the bad guy starts shooting at you and you want to defend yourself with good intentions and a Black Lives Matter T-shirt."

"Oh, God, you're out of your mind," Lauren replied, her voice dripping with disbelief.

"Oh, right, I'm the crazy one. Coming from the chief of staff for the worst president since Clinton. Why don't you give him a call and ask him what he thinks about lack of judgment?"

Lauren's heart hammered in her chest; the stakes of the conversation finally hit home. She needed to reel it back in.

"Would you like to know what I really think, Alicia? I think your duplicitous little club of pro-gun nut jobs fail to condone these shootings because, honestly—and stop me if I'm wrong here, Alicia—what you and Garrison really profiteer from is every time one of these events happens. When we talk about gun control, your memberships skyrocket, your donations flood in, and you validate the existence of your nonsensical organization. You thrive on the fear these shootings create, because every time it happens, you get to ramp up your rhetoric."

"You sanctimonious little bitch, Lauren—you want to try your luck at the next election without the support of the UFAA? You're alienating your core voter base. Who the hell do you think votes for Reign? Huh? People who love guns, the Second Amendment, and America. You want to go to war with the goddamn UFAA? Huh?"

The mention of a potential war with the UFAA hit her hard. Fear gripped her, knowing she'd crossed a line.

"Alicia, look, of course, we don't want to work against you. You're right; our voter base is strongly represented by the UFAA." Lauren spoke calmly now, her tone soothing. She looked out the window, the Capitol Building's neoclassical dome rising in the distance. Its beauty felt like a distant thing, separate from the ugly conversation she was entrenched in.

"You're goddamn right, Lauren. I'll be in touch. Oh, and another thing—go eat something. You look terrible on TV."

The phone line went dead.

"She sounds nice."

The voice from beside her startled Lauren. The security officer, his face blank and expressionless, had spoken.

Lauren narrowed her eyes. "Do you realize how grossly inappropriate it is for a member of my security detail to comment on official presidential business?" she asked, her voice stern.

The officer shifted in his seat, a nervous glint in his eyes. "Yes, ma'am. Very inappropriate."
Lauren pressed her lips into a thin line. "Consider yourself lucky I don't report you to your superior."

The officer immediately straightened up. "Yes, ma'am. Sorry, ma'am. It won't happen again for the rest of the ride home."

Lauren tilted her head slightly, the faint hint of a smile playing at her lips. For the first time in a long while, she found herself drawn to this man's unusual demeanor. A small spark of admiration flickered in her eyes, though she quickly concealed it.

CHAPTER 20: TRAINING MONTAGE

Of all the assets, infrastructure, and real estate owned by Warlord Peacecorp, the *pièce de résistance*—at least from McMann's point of view, which was always inevitably correct—was the state-of-the-art headquarters of the program.

It was discreetly subdued, exceedingly so by the usual standards of John McMann, who much preferred sheer physical domination and grotesque displays of power. The fact was, the facility didn't need to be that large. Considering all the launch sites spread across the United States, the real estate assets were vast, with each site covering around ten thousand square feet. Some were worthless plots of land, others situated in urban locations. A few were even built atop high-rise buildings.

The cost was irrelevant—if they never had to launch and reload a site, the expense didn't matter. If Teddy were here instead of that pussy Reign, he'd be awfully proud of him. He was going to talk loudly and carry a big stick. A big stick that he was going to shove up the ass of anyone who didn't love freedom and care about the children.

Everything was controlled from this single base of operations, ironically one that did not house a launch site. There was no point; the facility's location was irrelevant to the program's deployment. It could be anywhere in America. So it came to be that the center for the school defense program was positioned in Omaha, Nebraska, in a brand-new, state-of-the-art building occupying just over a hundred thousand square feet.

It housed the control room, operation center, accommodations for staff—including that idiot Peck—a cafeteria with a decent offering of American cuisine, training areas, and meeting rooms. In McMann's humble opinion, it was the most beautiful piece of art he had ever seen. And if there was one thing the world needed, it was beautiful art.

Of course, he didn't give a damn about Omaha or the entire state of Nebraska, for that matter. Nevertheless, it offered some advantages. The city had acted awfully pleased to welcome the headquarters, not that it mattered; the federal government could do whatever it wanted. He didn't concern himself with trivial matters like building permits or local taxes.

When the options had been presented to McMann, he had, unfortunately, found himself agreeing with Omaha's top ranking. Sure, it was geographically centralized—which didn't matter since everything was done remotely and via virtual reality—but it made the concept of centralized control easier for simpletons to grasp. Infrastructure was favorable, with telecommunications networks and transportation hubs as good as anywhere else.

The city had a decent tech industry and wasn't infested with West Coast hippies. And while he had access to the federal government's checkbook, McMann wasn't about to get fleeced on San Francisco real estate or compete with big tech for labor. No, he would offer this backwater a shot at the big stage. At least there was an Air Force base nearby, offering him a high-speed ticket in and out, and they could provide security if any cowboys tried to interfere. Not that he needed their security—the program itself could fuck up anyone who wanted to make trouble.

Peck was housed in private quarters within the headquarters' accommodation section. It was well-appointed, on par with a decent four-star hotel. The program's launch was now just under six months away, and by God, if that sack of shit didn't meet the training requirements, McMann was going to be very disappointed. Although not surprised. McMann was hopeful that he would fail.

Peck was transferred in early February. McMann had sent an agent to escort him from his Philadelphia apartment to the airport. He had been informed that Peck had the audacity to question the mode of transport. "Why the private plane? We could have taken a commercial flight," he had allegedly asked in a dubious tone. Don't be a little bitch, Peck. You're working on behalf of the U.S. government now, and if there's one thing we don't want to hear about, it's your prudence toward fucking frugality and responsible fiscal management. McMann really couldn't stand the guy—Peck, the monosyllabic moron. As soon as he failed the training program, McMann was going to personally transfer him to Gitmo or maybe another black site he had access to.

The first night was spent in a budget hotel about ten miles from the site. Not that the budget aspect was important —McMann just didn't care about Peck's comfort. A new chaperone took over after the flight and arrival at the accommodation. Dinner was outsourced to a delivery service, and Peck had opted for a large pepperoni pizza and some kind of cinnamon-based dessert from a ubiquitous pizza chain. His request for a six-pack of Buds was summarily denied. Fun time is over, son.

Apparently, Peck had trouble sleeping that first night. McMann, however, slept like a baby every night—usually after discharging a respectable-sized wad into some intern or employee who understood the value of networking. Otherwise, it was an escort, and on really rare occasions, like her birthday, his wife. Yes, a good ramming from John Junior was a great experience, something that nearly everyone could enjoy.

And he was going to give Peck a good ramming—metaphorically, of course. Though, he had been known to deliver a good turkey slap to junior associates within Warlord who had fucked things up. "Who's a dickhead?" he would gleefully yell while slapping his member onto the forehead of an insubordinate lackey—always with an audience. Everyone laughed. It was a great team-building exercise for the boys.

From his office, McMann was buzzed by the front desk—Jordan Peck had arrived. He fumed for a moment before barging down the hall and into the reception area. "Peck!" His name bounced off the hard surfaces, booming like a megaphone. "About time you arrived. Let's get down to business, son. Follow me." He had seemingly appeared out of nowhere, walking fast with large strides.

"Always walk as if you have somewhere important to be, Peck. From now on, you always have somewhere important to be—so act like it." Jordan struggled to keep pace despite the age difference—McMann was at least twenty years his senior but artificially augmented with a cocktail of performance-enhancing drugs. Nothing wrong with a little supplementation to keep up.

"Yes, sir." McMann wasn't sure yet whether Peck would conveniently have an accident during training and be replaced by someone far better suited, but he was trying to keep an open mind. "Let's do the tour, son. You're gonna dump your bag in your dorm, we'll tour the facilities, and this afternoon, you start your training to become a goddamn certified American hero." He stopped mid-stride. "And Peck..." He turned and locked eyes with him.

"Yes, sir?" Jordan responded, forcing himself to sound neutral.

"If you fail this training, you will cease to exist. I will fucking erase you, and nobody will even remember you existed. So, absolutely no pressure—just do your best. But if you fail me, your existence will serve no purpose to anyone. I will fuck you like a cheap, crack-addicted hooker with no regard for whether she has AIDS. You understand me?" By the time he finished speaking, he was growling.

Oh yes, sir. Peck was in for a rigorous training program. Completely unnecessary for what was essentially a desk job requiring about as much exertion as playing video games, but this was for public perception. He needed to look the part. America needed a hero, and he was going to look like one. A real-life Captain America.

Besides, there was the marketing aspect—the action figures, lunch boxes, maybe even a video game.

Nothing said American hero quite like a large man who used physical violence to solve problems.

Anyway, as a half-assed high school footballer, Peck had done some weightlifting in the past. Right now, though, his body was flabby, unconditioned, and lacked any definition. Not under McMann's watch. He was going to be Peck by name and by nature, with pecs so big they made other men question their sexual orientation. He started on a full-body workout program: heavy sets on every major muscle group—deadlifts, squats, bench press, overhead press, barbell rows, and his personal favorite, weighted chins. McMann had employed a former Marine drill sergeant turned bodybuilder. It was his job to fix Peck's physique—make it appear the way America wanted its action heroes to look. Bigger was always better.

Specialized meals were brought in for Peck; there were to be no cheeseburgers. Big, fuck-off-sized portions of sweet potatoes, rice, enormous chunks of steak, and some greens. Three big meals a day and a couple of protein shakes in between.

After the mandatory two-hour gym sessions every other day, it was time for training with the simulation. Peck was surprisingly adept at this, with a natural talent, and his proficiency developed quickly. McMann was surprised—he wasn't nearly as stupid as he had given him credit for.

During the afternoon, it was time to train the mind. McMann had engaged several practitioners of questionable ethical standing to take part in the program. As the president had stated, "What may raise questions today will provide answers tomorrow," and "the means will justify the results."

The president, first and foremost a businessman, was also quite fond of pointing out that sometimes forcing an outcome was "just business," which even McMann—with all his empathetic shortcomings and lack of human decency— understood to mean a willingness to exonerate yourself from any moral ambiguity. Of course, McMann couldn't care less about ethics in business or war. After all, there was a cause even more important than doing business: national security. The only thing that exceeded both was doing business for national security. Yes sir, the annals of history would record John McMann as the moment America said no more.

He knew very well that the cause required Jordan Peck to conform to the goals of the program, and that's why he needed a hard reset of his brain. The full gauntlet of psychological conditioning was required.

There was stress inoculation training, whereby the simulation would gradually increase the level of intensity and consequence. Desensitization to reduce his emotional responses involved repeatedly showing crime scene photos with an audio track of screaming, crying children, automatic gunfire, and explosions booming loudly. Some images included an armed perpetrator hidden among the carnage, others did not; the training required Peck to instantaneously locate the shooter within three seconds. If he failed, a loud gunshot would explode through the headphones he wore. Over time, he stopped showing any visual response to the stimuli. It seemed to be working.

McMann's favorite part of the psychological training was behavioral modeling, the segment that truly fired up his patriotic enthusiasm. This part of the training involved juxtaposing images of school shooters with iconic American heroes, both real and fictional. The first image showed a weak, hunched, and disheveled loner struggling to hold his rifle. Then, in sharp contrast, the training would cut to responses from legendary figures of American toughness. It might show Dirty Harry after a shooter was incapacitated, asking, "Do you feel lucky, punk?" or John McClane quipping, "Yippee-ki-yay, motherfucker." Sometimes it was John Wayne reminding Jordan, "A man's got to have a code, a creed to live by, no matter his job."

McMann made a mental note to ask why they hadn't included anything from Schwarzenegger—at least a line from *The Terminator*, even if Arnold had become a bit of a pussy in recent years.

In addition to fictional American heroes, there was the presidential edition of the training as well. Lincoln would tell Peck, "The best way to predict your future is to create it," or Roosevelt would offer strength: "We have nothing to fear but fear itself." Even MacArthur was included, telling the Filipinos, "I'll be back."

It was all McMann could do to hold back from getting a rock-hard American erection when he oversaw these sessions.

Yes, it was all proceeding very well—much better than McMann would have given Peck credit for. That idiot was actually exceeding the requirements of his training. He just needed to be broken down and reassembled into the kind of man the program required. McMann was filled with patriotic fervor and a lustful yearning to fuck something up. God damn it, he felt good—euphoric enthusiasm for the program surged through his veins.

Around three months in, McMann decided that Peck needed more pecs. Sure, he looked quite healthy by then—his waist was trim, his body lean, with a level of toning that might be considered aesthetically pleasing. But this wasn't a holiday at the lake. America didn't need a guy who could carry groceries up two flights of stairs without puffing. America needed a superhero. Nothing wrong with a little vitamin 'S' supplementation.

Initially, McMann was worried the cycle would be implemented too late into the training for the grand reveal. Fortunately, with no previous exposure to the juice and the finest stack prescribed by a fantastic doctor, the results were astronomical. Astronomical muscle growth and development, finished off with a bit of Winstrol to flush any water retention.

Wide, powerful shoulders and lats tapered to a chiseled midsection. The cephalic vein was prominently pronounced down each bicep. The triceps popped—three full heads, the lateral forming a perfect horseshoe. His lower body was equally powerful, developed through punishing deadlifts and squats. The abs were important, the kind of people who undertook school shootings never had six packs.

Yes, John McMann didn't care much for homosexuals and their nonsense, but it was a fine-looking ass that was going to fill out the uniform he'd wear.

About the time the cycle began, there was a progress meeting with the president at the White House. That uptight little bitch Chalmers took issue with the supplement program, and this infuriated McMann.

"John, I really must object to this course of development in the program. It's entirely unethical, and not least of all, unnecessary," she had whined.

Not being a soldier—and a woman, no less—meant that of course she couldn't understand why it was necessary. Any real man knew you could never have too much power. There would never be a time you didn't wish your biceps—or your dick— were bigger.

Yes, she was a real bitch, that one. After the meeting, he told Reign they should get a chief of staff with a penis so they could sort business without all the talk about feelings.

Anyway, he disregarded Chalmers' input and pushed on. The result was glorious. He had done it. He was going to solve a lot of problems for this country with this program, and he'd be remembered in history for his great effort, vision, and brilliance. Yes, he could see his name up there in history already: Ben Franklin, George Washington, Dwight D. Eisenhower, Douglas MacArthur... and John McMann.

He was in good company among his peers.

All this protecting America and the kids was making him very hungry. He was going to get himself a burger.

CHAPTER 21: THE PRESIDENTIAL SEAL OF APPROVAL

Jordan found himself going through the familiar process of entering the White House again. It was much later than his first visit—well into the evening, with the August heat still hanging heavy in the air.

McMann had provided him with a sharply tailored charcoal suit for the occasion. It was custom fitted to accommodate his now impressively imposing physique—an upgrade from the cheap suits he'd once worn sparingly in his private life. The white dress shirt, crisp and clean, was paired with belted dress pants. The high-quality cotton felt soft against his skin, a stark contrast to the rough, harsh fabrics of the government-issued uniforms he had worn earlier in life.

Jordan found his hand wrapped around his watch face, head bowed. It had been a gift from Emily, on his birthday. They'd only been dating for six months at that point, but she'd spent at least an entire week's salary on the timepiece. In that moment, he'd realized how deeply he loved her—and that he was going to marry her one day. A stab of torment pierced his stomach, and he wished she hadn't cut him out of her life.

The security checks were less intrusive than his first visit. Jordan's career had taken an upward turn recently, placing him into the ranks of national importance. The Secret Service agents nodded stoically as he passed, addressing him as "sir" so often the syllable began to lose meaning.

There were fewer aides and staff scurrying around the White House interior this time. It didn't take long before he was escorted to the door of the Oval Office once again, an aide knocking and awaiting the President's response before entering.

"Please come in, Mr. Peck. The President is ready to see you," the aide informed him before stepping aside.

A few steps inside, Jordan instinctively saluted the Commander in Chief. Come to think of it, he wasn't sure whether he was technically still a member of the military—or even exactly what branch of the government he worked under. He supposed he worked for McMann, who in turn was a private defense contractor.

It wasn't immensely important for Peck to fully understand these arrangements. At this stage, he wasn't being paid as handsomely as he was to do anything other than look good and hang out at the operations center, engaging in something akin to playing video games all day.

Jordan immediately noticed the shift in President Reign. His eyes widened and focused intently on him as he stood in the middle of the room. The President rose and came to him, vigorously shaking his hand with as much strength as a man in his later years could muster.

"Now that's what I'm talking about," Reign said, his trademark pompous grin twisting with a hint of something insidious.

"You've always had the size, but now you've got the kind of look that says 'don't mess with me.' You know, we don't want someone doing the kind of important work—and this is very important, the stuff you're going to be doing for this country —we don't want some DEI hire here. We need a good quality American man to face this program and get results."

"Thank you, sir." Jordan wasn't quite sure how else to respond.

The president continued standing close, directly in front of Jordan. Awkwardness enveloping them before Reign walked around him and locked the door to the Oval Office before returning to stand obscenely close once again.

"I can't believe how much you've changed. You've got the build for it now. Doesn't hurt to have the looks to go with the muscle, does it? You know, it's important we have the best people for the job, and I think you could be a real asset."

"Thank you again, Sir..."

Jordan had undergone extensive stress training in recent months, specifically designed to reduce his susceptibility to unwanted reactions to stimuli or stress in the field. He had worked to desensitize himself to violence and the harsh realities of battle. But this... this was different. His heart began to beat harder, its rhythm quickening and growing louder in a crescendo of panic. He felt his skin flush, not from the heat of the room but from the weight of what was happening.

Reign stepped forward, his face inches away from Jordan's. The faint smell of fast food lingered in the air, an odd, almost surreal detail that clashed with the gravity of the moment.

"When I'm closing a deal, sometimes I just have to grab them by the balls, you know what I mean, Jordan?" Reign's voice was low, insistent. There was an arrogance to it, but something else, too—something more sinister.

Jordan froze. His mind scrambled to process the words, to understand the situation. Was this really happening? His pulse thudded in his ears, drowning out the rest of the world. Sweat began to bead at the back of his neck, a cold sweat. His breath came quick and shallow. His body fought to stay composed, but the panic was overwhelming, seizing control.

Reign reached forward. Jordan's body stiffened, his muscles

locking in place. Reign's hands were uninvited, and Jordan felt his pants begin to loosen, his belt shifting, the fabric moving against his skin. But his mind... his mind was still stuck in disbelief.

The president's words were like a slap, stinging Jordan with their casual cruelty. "I can do anything I want, did you know that?"

It wasn't just the words. It was the way Reign moved, like he was in control of everything, like Jordan was no longer a person but something to be used. Jordan felt detached from himself, like his body wasn't his own. His hands shook at his sides, immobile.

He couldn't bring himself to fight, to stop it, to scream.

"I can do anything I want," Reign repeated, a twisted satisfaction in his voice.

Jordan's head swirled. It couldn't be real. He was still in control of his body. He should move.

Don't just stand there. It was happening too fast, too violently. A mix of confusion, shame, and rage churned inside him, but his legs wouldn't move. His brain refused to process it in a coherent way. It was a haze, an overwhelming fog of panic. Jordan was a large, powerful man—he could kill the president with a sudden blow if he wished—but he couldn't. He just stood there, suspended.

Minutes stretched on, each second like an eternity, but Jordan couldn't tear himself away. His mind screamed for him to leave, but his body remained paralyzed, frozen in place. Every instinct he had screamed for escape, but his muscles refused to obey.

Finally, with a slow exhale, Reign stepped back, releasing him from the suffocating proximity. "I have some important business to attend to," he said with a dismissive wave. "You might want to put your pants back on before you leave."

Jordan stood there for what felt like a lifetime, his hands still trembling at his sides. He was vaguely aware of the president's hand reaching out to shake his once again, a meaningless gesture that felt like a mockery.

"Thanks for coming in," Reign said, his tone as casual as if nothing had happened.

Jordan didn't know how he managed to move, but his legs finally found their strength. He quickly adjusted his clothing, his hands shaking the entire time. He didn't dare look at Reign again as he walked out of the room, the door clicking softly behind him.

The hallway outside felt surreal, like he was in a different world. His heart was still racing, his mind a chaotic blur. What had just happened? What was he supposed to do now?

"Mr. Peck?" A soft voice broke through his haze, and Jordan looked up to see a female aide standing a few feet away. Her gaze lingered on him, a quiet understanding in her eyes —the kind that said she knew. Without a word, she stepped closer, her hand hovering near his elbow. "Come on, Mr. Peck," she said, her tone gentle, almost as if she were speaking to someone broken. "I'll get you to your ride."
"

CHAPTER 22: MEET MY FRIEND: GUNMAN

Lauren found herself wondering how she ended up backstage at what resembled a music concert. In a way, it was—though the musical performers were merely a supplementary part of the main event.

The President, hyperbolic in his cryptic announcements on social media, had claimed today would be one of the greatest days in American history. He had relentlessly heaped praise on himself and his administration while simultaneously ridiculing his opponents. Rumors had swirled, of course—some with minor factual elements. After all, the White House and the administration were even more porous to leaks than WikiLeaks itself. Ironically, this time, most of the news reports were far off the mark. The UFAA was the closest, probably due to the level of craziness inherent in the organization—where no idea seemed too far-fetched. Richard Garrison would be in a rage within the hour; he would either come straight at her tonight or launch a defensive attack using social and traditional media tomorrow.

She walked toward the large, heavy black curtain that hung between the backstage area and the exposed outdoor stage. Agent Mason, standing with his back against a solid wall of the structure, followed her every movement with his gaze. Peeking out from the far edge, she looked up over the high-rise buildings and bright signage toward the sky. It was gorgeous weather for the event. The dark clouds that had menaced the tops of the buildings had dispersed. August in New York always carried the risk of rain. From the President's notes for his presentation, she knew he would reference the clearing skies as a sign that God himself supported this program—but she wasn't sure if he believed that. Or in God at all. He did, however, believe that his constituents believed in God, and therefore, by extension, so did he.

She pulled her head back behind the curtain, aware of the huge crowds and media outside. Always conscious that she could be photographed at any moment, the thought of being caught with her head ungraciously outstretched like an ostrich—ridiculed on social media or a political news program—was one she couldn't shake. She still remembered Alicia Turner's comment about her appearance on TV, even though it had been months ago. Yet, the spectacle outside the curtain intoxicated her senses, and she found herself standing there for several minutes, her head still peeking out.

Lauren found herself, as she often did, begrudgingly impressed by the audacity of President Reign. Times Square was a spectacular backdrop for the reveal of the Gunman program. The stage stood at the triangular tip of the area, near the convergence of Seventh Avenue and Broadway. The bright lights of the billboards illuminated the assembly, their giant screens periodically synchronizing to display the message *"We're Making America Safe"* in bold white lettering against a blue background.

Lauren was unsure how that had come about. There had been some discussion about commandeering all the billboards, but the private ownership structure made it very difficult. There must have been financial compensation—or some motivation given to the owners. He probably signed an executive order that would be repealed immediately—but not before the show was over. She dreaded to think about it.

The vacant open stage stood ready in place, already set with microphones and musical equipment. The powerful sound system rumbled far below its capacity, blasting mostly rock music by artists sympathetic to the President. A dazzling cacophony of sound and a chaotic collage of gaudy, mesmerizing lights overwhelmed her senses. An eager sea of people spread out along Broadway and Seventh, occupying the closed streets in a commitment exceeded only by New Year's Eve. Most didn't even know why they were here—only that they'd been promised a front-row seat to history.

Say what you will about Reign—people doubted him constantly—but he was brilliant at times, engaging and disarming, even though he often sounded ludicrous in his statements. Eventually, you just gave in to him.

"This is a good thing for America, Lauren," she muttered to nobody, wondering if she should just give in to him.

She revisited a conversation she had had with Mason a couple of weeks earlier. He had been adamant that the secret to Reign's success was his lack of both cognitive and emotional intelligence. His scope of emotions? Angry president, sad president, hungry president. Mason had argued that this absence of nuance in his feelings granted him the freedom to operate without a full understanding of right and wrong.

"I disagree," she had refuted. "The man has been on this planet for almost seven decades, living a varied life full of vast experiences and meeting all kinds of people. While he may struggle to articulate the depth of his emotions and uses extensive intensifiers in his language, the intricacy of emotion is not limited to those with the ability to express them."

At the time, she'd been confident in that argument. Now, watching the stage, she wasn't so sure. If Reign truly grasped the depth of human emotion, wouldn't he have changed, even slightly? Wouldn't he have developed a conscience? Or was Mason right? Had he been carried this far in life by sheer force of will, oblivious to the moral weight of his actions?

Suddenly, her train of thought was interrupted. Across the backstage area, amid the scurrying of stagehands and production crew, Lauren made the mistake of locking eyes with Blaze Richboy. He was a repugnant little bastard of a hillbilly, whose career was built on a talentless fusion of Southern-influenced rock, rap, and country—each genre debased under his touch. He'd managed to gather a fan base of people who lived in homes with wheels and didn't finish high school, a fact he proudly flaunted with his self-styled moniker, which seemed designed to remind everyone of his financial success. Despite his millions, Blaze looked like he still lived in a trailer, his dirty, scraggly mullet flowing backward from under a trucker cap. His scrawny body suggested he hadn't seen much in the way of nutrition or physical activity. Swaggering across the temporary wooden stage floor, he caught her attention.

"How are you doin', sweetheart? Ever shaken hands with a platinum artist before?" he boasted.

He was taller than she had imagined—and surprisingly not as foul-smelling as she expected.

"Mr. Richboy, nice to meet you. I'm Lauren Chalmers, Chief of Staff and Assistant to President Reign," she said, extending her hand. She quickly pulled it back after the brief shake, careful to avoid lingering too long, not wanting to give the wrong impression.

"Wooo hoooo, baby! That's a mighty fine job you got there," he drawled.

"Thank you, Mr. Richboy. It's a very important position, and an honor to serve the President," she responded, trying to keep the conversation professional, not wanting to digress into any tangents about his after-show plans or the kind of people who'd end up in his trailer.

"Ma'am, no need for the mister. Just call me Blaze, Missy Lauren."

She studied his face closely, wondering if this was all an act —or if he genuinely was a bona fide redneck. Either way, she couldn't care less. The thought of escaping this conversation was all she wanted.

"Very well, Blaze. Are you ready for your performance? You'll be playing during a visual presentation on the screens. I'm sure your fans will be really engaged by your role in the exhibition," she said, extending her arm to wrap up the exchange with a handshake.

"Anything for guns and America, hell yeah, girl!" he hollered with all the enthusiasm of someone with a shallow understanding of politics.

Lauren's phone buzzed, and for once, she welcomed the persistent vibration in her pocket.

"Excuse me, Blaze. I'll speak with you later." He nodded with an unsettling smirk—a leeriness that made her feel strangely vulnerable.

Her eyes darted to where Mason stood, his gaze locked on Blaze with simmering anger. The musician noticed and gave a jerky nod in Mason's direction before swaggering off toward the performer accommodations.

Returning to her phone, Lauren accepted the call from an aide. The background noise was deafening, the rotor blades of a helicopter roaring over the line.

"Ma'am, the President is scheduled to arrive in thirty minutes," the voice shouted over the noise.

"Thank you, confirmed," Lauren replied, her voice cutting through the chaos.

She scanned the bustling scene, her eyes landing on the event manager. She strode toward him, placing a hand on his arm to get his attention.

"The President is en route, thirty minutes."

He nodded, his expression serious, and immediately grabbed the walkie-talkie clipped to his hip. It was go time, and exactly thirty minutes he arrived.

Above the commotion and the dazzling lights of Times Square, the thunderous arrival of Marine One, with its decoy trailing, cut through the air with an almost aggressive show of power. The crowd below craned their necks, pointing at the sky, their eyes locked on the helicopters as they sliced through the air. The deep, resonant hum of the rotors drowned out the sounds of the city.

Even Lauren, seasoned and cynical from years in public service, couldn't help but feel a flicker of patriotic fervor. The sheer spectacle, the thundering force of the helicopters cutting through the skyline, was impressive—almost majestic. It was a breathtaking display of control and authority, unnecessary and dangerously close to reckless if anything were to go wrong. But then, that was President Reign's vision —bold, brash, and undeniably audacious. Lauren grudgingly acknowledged a sliver of respect for him, for his unrelenting confidence.

The aircraft banked slightly over Central Park before beginning its controlled descent onto a makeshift landing pad, the accompanying choppers continuing their flight off over the city.The area was flanked by black SUVs and a few high-powered sedans, all guarded by the Secret Service. NYPD cruisers formed a protective circle around the perimeter. Moments later, President Reign bounded out of the helicopter, greeted by a crisp salute from a Marine in full dress uniform —navy blue coat with red trim, gold buttons, and gleaming black dress shoes. Reign returned the salute with a flourish, then marched toward the nearest black SUV, flanked by an ever-present swarm of agents who seemed to materialize out of nowhere.

He made his way to the vehicle, but the memory of the security briefing lingered. Concerns had been raised about the vulnerability of such a public landing.

"No," Reign had dismissed them with a wave. "Central Park is a huge part of New York. It will make a statement. Everyone will see it, and it will be great." Of course, he didn't worry about logistics. After all, it wasn't his job to personally secure two highly public, open-air spaces.

Security was an imposing presence on the ground. In addition to the usual Secret Service agents, uniformed military personnel in full tactical gear—bulletproof vests, helmets, and M4 carbines—formed a tight perimeter, a jarring contrast to the usually peaceful serenity of Central Park. Squad cars from the NYPD lined the roadways outside, while sniper units were strategically positioned around the area. In the hours before, undercover units had quietly staked out the park, scanning the crowd, their efforts augmented by drones and helicopters conducting overhead surveillance. Of course, the public remained unaware of the President's exact mode of transport, adding to the shock and awe of the spectacle as the helicopters flew in.

The motorcade quickly fell into formation as the vehicles switched positions, deliberately confusing any attempts to pinpoint which one carried the President. It was a planned maneuver designed to add an element of uncertainty. The entire process would take exactly ten minutes from the moment the helicopter landed.

The NYPD had already secured the streets and set up blockades, clearing a path to Central Park. The black SUVs, flanked by two squad cars abreast, advanced with precision, cutting through the city as if on cue.

It was time for the show to begin.

At that moment, all the giant billboards in Times Square flickered and dimmed in perfect synchronization, drawing the attention of the thousands gathered. The sudden contrast to the usual flashing lights and noise caused a brief ripple of confusion before giving way to a moment of quiet anticipation. Then, on the massive screens, an image of the American flag waving in the breeze appeared. The crowd erupted into cheers, whistles, and thunderous applause, the sound reverberating through the square.

The first notes of "The Star-Spangled Banner" sounded from a lone trumpet, its hauntingly patriotic tones filling the air with solemnity. The crowd instantly fell silent, hands over their hearts, hats clutched in respect as uniformed NYPD officers stood at attention in salute.

As the anthem reached its grand crescendo and drew to a close, the crowd erupted in unrestrained enthusiasm. The heavy beat of rock music blasted through the speakers, the bass drum thundering with such force that it vibrated the chest cavities of those near the giant subwoofers. Stage lights flashed to life, and the screens shifted to the bold message: "We're Making America Safe Again."

A lone figure emerged from behind the curtains, confidently stepping up to the fixed microphone on a small podium in the center of the stage.

"Goooood evening, New York City and the United States of America!" he bellowed, his voice booming over the crowd's wild cheers, a man with confidence and belief as if Jesus himself had chosen this moment for his second coming.

"My name is Sterling O'Connor," he said, feigning modesty. "But of course, you already knew that!" The crowd responded with uproarious laughter and cheers.

"Ladies, gentlemen, boys, and girls – I'm not forgetting anyone here, am I? No? Fellow Americans, tonight is history. You are here to not only witness, but to be a part of history. Your children's children will know that their granddaddy or grandma was here tonight, at what will be remembered alongside other great moments in American history: The Gettysburg Address, MLK's dream, the moon landing... and now, in a few moments, the man I personally consider to be the greatest president this country has ever had..."

O'Connor paused, nodding to the crowd as their rapturous ovation erupted, drowning out his words until it subsided.

"The greatest president this country has ever had, and he's going to be here on stage in just a few moments."
A wave of reverent affirmation swept through the crowd as they nodded solemnly and clapped fervently.
Backstage, Lauren moved toward Mason. "They don't even know what they're applauding," she sighed, her voice tinged with despair.

"Maybe Reign is going to bring back the Nazi movement; that hasn't been done for a while?" Mason suggested, a wicked grin tugging at the corners of his mouth.

Lauren shot him a glare, the kind reserved for a recalcitrant schoolboy. Mason knew full well what the presentation was about. Back on stage, the crowd had quieted, now hungry for more from O'Connor.

"Now, folks, we have a problem in our nation," he began, pausing for effect as the audience hung on his words, eagerly anticipating a solution. "Violence in our schools. I'm here tonight to tell you that our president, President Reign—the greatest president this nation has ever elected—is going to end violence in our schools."

A wave of roaring applause erupted, forcing another dramatic pause. Backstage, Mason grumbled under his breath, "This is going to go on for hours if we applaud every time Sterile

O'Conman waffles around with his pandering rhetoric."

On stage, O'Connor continued.

"President Reign is here tonight to act against this crisis. Let me tell you folks, as of right now—because school's out for the day—but come the first school bell tomorrow, there's not going to be another massacre ever again in America!"

"That's right, folks!" O'Connor shouted over the applause. "Now listen, President Reign has worked extremely hard against all the challenges that the Bureaucratic Collective has thrown at him. I'm talking about the demon-crats here—make no mistake. They've tried to procrastinate, delay this program, and been more concerned about political correctness and canceling it before they even knew what it was. Folks, President Reign has disregarded and cast aside the objections of the Woke-O-Crats, and he has solved school shootings. I mean, if it were up to them, we'd all be here celebrating the rights of school shooters, making sure we don't misgender them, respecting their uniqueness and their right to commit murders. You know, if it were up to them, we'd still be on the first page of developing this program because we'd still be debating the gender-neutral pronouns to call it. But not President Reign, no sir. President Reign has, in an incredibly short period of time, conceptualized, developed, and implemented this program. Let me tell you, you're going to love it. Fellow Americans, I present to you the President of the United States of America, Mr. Douglas Reign!"

The pounding, syncopated rhythm of "Eye of the Tiger" blasted through the sound system, building toward a crashing crescendo of cymbals and distorted power chords. The stage lights swirled and flashed in time with the music. The crowd reached a euphoric frenzy, enthusiasm reaching its peak as President Reign burst onto the stage, walking to every corner, waving to the audience with his right hand extended and raised. It wasn't until the first chorus of the song had ended that the crowd's excitement began to ebb, and the music faded out.

"I love New York!" The crowd erupted in exhilaration once again.

"This is probably the biggest turnout, the greatest number of attendees for any presidential announcement, up until this point in history. What an amazing crowd you are. I think this is the best-looking crowd I've ever addressed, am I right?" The crowd enthusiastically agreed.

"Now, folks, I came here tonight to talk about something incredibly important—very important. On November 24th of last year, there was a terrible tragedy—just awful. If you don't know about it, let me fill you in. A really bad person, the worst kind of person, went into an elementary school in Hope Valley, Pennsylvania, just outside Philadelphia. This terrible individual, this very bad guy, did something horrendous—killed a great number of people, I think it was 45 people in total? A lot of people, including children and educators. But —and this is very important—the only reason this tragedy wasn't even worse was because of a very brave police officer, Officer Jordan Peck. He's a true American hero, folks."

Reign paused, allowing the audience to show their appreciation for Peck, then continued.

"Let me tell you, Jordan Peck is a really great man. Probably one of the best law enforcement officers in American history. If you agree with me, and I think you do, you're going to love my presentation tonight. Do you all agree that Jordan Peck is a great American and a great law enforcement professional?"

There was solemnness to the applause this time, with many in the crowd placing their hands over their hearts.

"On November 25th—the day after this very bad person did those terrible things, I went on TV and I told the nation, enough is enough. That's right, I said I was going to put an end to this madness—our babies getting shot and, God forbid, worse things happening. I promised that I was going to fix this problem, that I was going to make America safe again!"

"I'm going to tell you a secret because this is a truly great audience tonight, and I think you deserve to hear it. A lot of people, really a lot, said, 'Reign, you can't say that!'" Reign adopted a higher-pitched, nasal tone, exaggerating the way his critics might sound. He waved his hands around with his elbows bent and pulled close to his torso, emphasizing the mockery with dramatic, exaggerated gestures.

"What about my political opposition? They'd rather we just let these truly bad, violent individuals carry out their school shootings. They say things like, 'Oh, you know, when the police were called, they misgendered the shooter and didn't use their preferred pronoun.' That's right, folks. 'We have to respect the rights of the bad guys—what about the murderers' feelings? Let's focus on affirmative action while there's another dozen massacres in elementary schools.' Would you believe it?"

The crowd murmured, a majority shaking their heads, expressions of rage filling their faces.

"Before I went on TV, I was told by many people—many cowardly politicians, some lawmakers, and even some people in my own administration—that by solving gun violence in our schools, I was going to upset a few people. Let me just say, some of those people... they're no longer in my administration. Do you know what happened? I gave them the 'Reign Check,' and I think we're all familiar with that. The Reign Check: DCM edition. Don't come Monday—your employment has been canceled."

The crowd hollered in vindication, cheering in celebration of the defeat of the program's detractors. Reign stood at the podium, his arms slightly bent and outreached, palms facing upward.

"What are you going to do? What can you do?" he mouthed as the crowd cheered.

"America is on a path to redemption. There's been some very bad mismanagement of our country over recent years—very terrible. Some of the worst politicians we've had in a long time. These bad people have let violence run rampant in our schools. But that was before. Now, America no longer has a problem. I'm about to unveil our new school defense program and let me tell you—you're going to be impressed. You're going to be so happy to see that no child, no educator, no law enforcement hero—nobody—is going to be shot or killed in our schools anymore".

He paused for a moment, looking about the crowd. Like a stand up comic, holding his timing to deliver punchlines. The crowd humming with energy as the bright lights of Times Square threw devilish colors about.

"Well... maybe one person. Let me say this: if you're planning on bringing a gun into any of our schools, well, you'd better have your funeral arrangements sorted out."
"You know, politicians... they do a lot of empty talking, but not much action. I think maybe you'd like to see what I'm talking about. What do you say?"

The billboards and advertisements dimmed in unison, the lights of the surrounding buildings switching off. The sudden darkness stunned the audience, leaving them momentarily dazed. A lone snare drum began its relentless tap—each bar of three beats ending with a rapid drum roll, over and over—slowly increasing in intensity, becoming more insistent with each measure.

After several bars, the screens flickered to life, showcasing the imagery of an American eagle soaring high against a bright blue sky. Anticipation began to build in the audience as they looked about, unsure of what was about to unfold.
President Reign, finally stepping forward at the podium, spoke again with gravitas. "Ladies and gentlemen, boys and girls, if you look to the skies, you will witness history in the making."

A murmur of excitement rippled through the crowd. Then, the powerful strains of *Semper Fidelis* surged from the sound system, the brass instrumentation sweeping over Times Square in a wave of authority and grandeur. The crowd looked up, their eyes tracking the sky as a rocket shot overhead, its boosters detaching and free-falling for a moment before catching flight.

A brief, muffled pop echoed as the rocket exploded in a flash of light, glowing fragments disintegrating as they dissipated into the sky.

The drone descended smoothly, its flight precise and calculated, hovering thirty feet above the crowd. The robotic combat suit attached beneath it became visible in the air, gleaming with a menacing promise. It glided closer to the stage, just above the heads of the audience, then tilted sharply upward with a controlled, powerful movement, its motors whirring with intensity.

Inches above the stage floor, the suit detached with a mechanical click—the autonomous combat system now standing at attention directly next to President Reign. The suit was an arsenal in itself—equipped with enough firepower to overthrow a small country, adorned with high-powered rifles and long-weapons mounted on its back.

Without a word, the suit raised its arm in a sharp salute

to the president, then pivoted ninety degrees to face the crowd. The audience erupted into cheers and applause, a wave of exhilaration washing over them as the suit stood—a formidable symbol of strength and security at Reign's side.

"So, does everyone like my new suit?" Reign asked, grinning. "Folks, let me tell you something—"

what you're seeing here is incredible. Absolutely amazing. This is the future, right here, folks. And, of course, it's American-made, American-designed, and believe me, it's the best you can buy. The absolute best. No other country in the world could build a suit or a program like this. It's state-of-the-art. It's going to change everything. This suit, and this program—it's going to make our children safe."

Reign paused for emphasis, his voice lowering a touch. "And let me tell you, I know a lot about suits. But this one? This is something special. Something incredible."

He waved a hand dismissively as if addressing a thought in his head. "Now, I know some of you might be wondering, 'But, Mr. President, how's one of the most advanced semi-autonomous, remotely controlled armed robotic law enforcement suits going to work?' Well, I'll let you in on a little secret. You're a very great crowd, and you deserve to know. You see, I'm all about transparency; very serious about it. Now, let me tell you something. Months ago, after the terrible tragedy in Hope Valley, I came up with this program. Not too long ago. I'm not your typical career politician. You know the ones I'm talking about, if it were up to them, this program would take decades to develop. They'd hold summit after summit on carbon emissions of drones, focusing on renewable energy, hoping the suits would run on windmills. And don't even get me started on their diversity initiatives, or their endless debates on what color the suits should be. Very sad."

Reign shook his head in mock despair, gesturing with both hands as if to illustrate the sheer absurdity of it all.

"I'm going to tell you why my program will end school violence in America," he continued, shifting his tone to one of confident finality. "Did you all see that suit launch from the rocket?" The crowd roared. "That rocket system is the most advanced of its kind—American-designed, of course. Now let me tell you how it works. And let me tell you something else: there will be no more bullets flying toward our beautiful babies."

He leaned into the microphone, urgency sharpening his voice. "Here's how it's going to work. If you bring a weapon onto school property in this country, we're not just sending a regular law enforcement officer. No. You're going to get this guy right here." He pointed to the robotic suit standing beside him. "I present to you, the American people, of the greatest country on Earth: the Gunman—Safe Schools Defense Program. If you launch an attack on any school in this country, we will send Gunman, and he will gun you down."

"When I heard about what happened in Hope Valley, I said, no. You know what? No more. I'm going to end this. Let me tell you how. This suit—right here—is the most advanced of its kind. Nobody else has anything like this. This isn't some pipe dream. This suit is launched strategically and arrives on site within five minutes. That's five minutes, at worst, anywhere in America."

He paused for emphasis, pacing slightly as he gestured to the crowd.

"When I heard about the bad guy in Hope Valley, I didn't hold some affirmative action summit or waste time trying to cancel somebody. No. I made a plan. I took action. The only thing I'm canceling is school shootings. I'm giving them the Reign Check. And no, I'm not talking about sitting around and making plans—I bought up four hundred and forty-eight drone launch sites across mainland America. That's action."

He pointed to the sky, as if picturing the launch sites in orbit. "That means we've got hundreds of these suits, ready to launch anywhere in the United States the moment someone threatens a school. If a criminal—one of these really bad guys—sets foot on a campus, Gunman will be there. And he'll apprehend the shooter. And by 'apprehend,' I mean with a vengeance."

A ripple of excitement passed through the crowd. Reign leaned in again, his tone growing more intense.

"Does everyone remember the brave police officer who stormed Hope Valley Elementary and terminated the violent criminal behind those atrocities? That man—that great American hero—is Jordan Peck. And in a moment, I'm going to bring him out here. You know, the socialists, the left-wing extremists, they wanted to put this hero in jail. That's right —they tried to persecute him. The man who saved dozens of lives! But I'll tell you something: Officer Peck is getting a Reign Check. He's getting a promotion!"

The crowd erupted. Reign raised a hand to calm them, a triumphant grin spreading across his face.

"These suits—four hundred and forty-eight of them—are built and stationed in launch sites all across the country. But they need heroes to operate them. From a central command center, located in Omaha... that's in Nebraska, a really great little city in a fantastic state. I gave their economy a little boost—while solving gun violence in schools."

He gestured with both hands, broad and theatrical. "In Omaha, we've built the nerve center of the Gunman School Defense Program. From here, the best, most highly trained operators this nation has ever seen will respond to school shooting threats in under five minutes. And folks, that's the worst-case scenario. In most cases? Two minutes. Like a drive-thru—quick, easy, and with tremendous speed. Faster than Congresswoman Sinclair would destroy the economy if she ever got elected in November."

Reign let the applause hang in the air for a moment before raising his hand, silencing the crowd with a dramatic gesture. The energy in Times Square was electric, the weight of the moment palpable.

"Now, folks, I told you this man right here is the real deal. A true hero. Jordan Peck, the man who walked into Hope Valley Elementary and faced down that violent criminal. He didn't hesitate. He didn't wait for someone else to step in. He did what needed to be done. And now, he's here with us today—stronger, more focused than ever before—ready to make sure this never happens again."

Reign turned to Jordan, placing a hand on his shoulder in a show of camaraderie.

"Jordan, we're all so proud of you. The bravery you showed that day saved countless lives. You stepped up when others were frozen in fear, and that's what makes you a true American hero. And now, as part of this new program, you're going to lead the charge. You're going to be the face of the Gunman Program."

Jordan nodded stoically, his expression unreadable as he stood next to Reign. His muscular frame, accentuated by the sleek tactical suit, radiated a quiet strength that matched the raw power of the robotic suit standing beside him. He was every bit the embodiment of the idealized protector Reign was promoting—unflinching, unstoppable, a symbol of American might.

"Together," Reign continued, his voice rising, "we're going to make sure our schools are safe. And it starts with this—the Gunman Program. With Jordan leading the way, and these suits ready to deploy at a moment's notice, we'll bring peace back to our children's classrooms. No more waiting. No more fear. We're taking back control."

The crowd erupted into another wave of cheers, their applause deafening, as Jordan stood tall, his salute still held strong. He didn't speak, didn't move—just let the moment wash over him. The intense focus in his eyes suggested he was already thinking about the weight of the responsibility now resting on his shoulders.

Reign soaked in the cheers, his grin widening. He leaned in closer to the mic, as if letting everyone in on a secret. "And folks, let me tell you something else... Jordan Peck isn't just any hero. He's our hero. The hero of the future."

With that, the crowd went wild once again, chanting Jordan's name as the two men, the suit, and the energized crowd stood together in solidarity, united by a shared purpose.

"Ladies and gentlemen, thank you for being here today. This is a moment of great significance—not just for us, but for every child and every school across this great nation. Our schools are the heart of our future, and we have a solemn duty to ensure they are safe and secure. Today, I am honored to stand with someone who embodies courage, dedication, and a relentless commitment to justice. Jordan Peck is not just a hero; he is a beacon of hope and strength.

Jordan, you've served our country with unwavering resolve, and now, we're joining forces to make an unbreakable pledge. Together, we will protect our schools. We will ensure that every child can learn and grow up in an environment free from fear. We will commit resources, implement advanced technologies, and work tirelessly to keep our educational institutions secure.
So, Jordan, do you pledge, here and now, to stand with me and every parent, teacher, and student in our unwavering commitment to the safety of our schools?"

Jordan paused for a moment—whether for dramatic effect or not—before stepping forward to the microphone.

"Absolutely, Mr. President. I pledge to use every resource, every skill, and every ounce of my dedication to safeguarding our schools. We will work together to ensure that our educational institutions are places of learning and growth, not fear."

Finishing his pledge, Jordan took a step back, allowing Reign access to the microphone once more.

"Folks, you can see what's happening here. Only under a Reign administration would we see something this incredible. I would say it's unbelievable, except there's nothing unbelievable about American ingenuity, our strength, and the courage to stop gun violence within our schools. Let's give Officer Peck—Gunman—let's give Gunman the respect he deserves."

The crowd applauded, many standing in salute toward the stage, facing Reign, Jordan, and the robotic suit. Jordan and the android walked slowly backward, waving to the crowd— the suit controlled remotely, its movements mechanical, the pneumatic systems sliding in and out as they powered the limbs. President Reign was left alone again on stage.

"Some of you might be wondering, how's this going to work? How are we going to know there's a threat in our schools? How are we going to know there's an active shooter? You might be wondering... and I'm going to tell you. It's the most advanced, wonderful technology.

Every single educator in an educational institution will have access to an app on their cellphone. Now this app, folks— you've never seen anything like it. No other country in the world gives their educators access to technology like this. What this application will do is serve as a silent alarm to dispatch Gunman. And let me tell you, that's a silent alarm that will trigger a very loud response.

Any teacher who hears, sees, or senses a threat in their school —we'll be just a couple of minutes away. Additionally, the principal will have a direct line to the control center, and of course, law enforcement will still have the authority to take charge. Police will also be able to request a dispatch of the system through the control center, which remains fully accessible to them."

The crowd clapped again—this time with a more respectful, refined applause. An overwhelming consensus of agreement was evident.

"Now folks, I have to tell you—I can't take all the credit for this. Though, you know, I had a big hand in it. A very big hand. But there's a guy—you know him, everybody knows him—Xavier Wolfe. Tech genius. Visionary. American hero. The best. They call him the smartest guy, maybe ever—I don't know, but I hear it a lot. And let me tell you—he's the man who made all this technology happen. Made it work. The suits, the propulsion, all of it—very complicated stuff, folks. The most technical you've ever seen. And he did it. So, let's bring him out, let's give him a big, big hand."

The crowd welcomed Xavier Wolfe to the stage. He pranced about, walking from one side to the other with the over-excitement of a small child. Awkwardly extending his arm, waving stiffly, he approached the microphone.

"I could stand up here all night, folks, but you know what? I think we've covered a lot, and you're going to love what's coming next. This is big, it's historic, and we're making it happen right here. But I'll tell you what—Sterling O'Connor, the best, right? He's doing an amazing job tonight. So, let me hand it over to Sterling. He's going to keep this incredible event rolling. Sterling, get up here!"

Sterling O'Connor bounded back onto the stage with the energy of a late-night television host, vaulting to the microphone.

"Ladies and gentlemen, those of you watching at home —probably the entire nation—let's give it up for your commander-in-chief, President Douglas Reign, and the new hall monitor for school safety across America... Officer Jordan

Peck!"

With the crowd roaring, O'Connor hollered over the noise. "Let's get some music out here to celebrate! Ladies and gentlemen, one of the finest American musicians and performers alive today—Mr. Blaze Richboy!"

Blaze Richboy, in all his mullet-haired glory, burst onto the stage, accompanied by his band of equally disheveled-looking rednecks. They took their positions at their respective instruments—already provisioned on stage—and with Blaze holding a cordless microphone, they launched into a medley of their songs as fireworks exploded from rooftops around Times Square. The innumerable screens showed close-ups of the band, flashing between scenes of the crowd.

Their performance featured extensive references to firearms, including selections from their catalogue: *"Shoot First, Ask for Freedom Later," "Ammo for America,"* and the crowd favorite, *"Shootin' Our Way to Peace."*

With the musical number complete, the band exited the stage after a lengthy farewell by Blaze, who continued to walk around flashing thumbs-up gestures and firing imaginary rounds with finger guns into the air. Once clear, O'Connor returned once more.

"Wow, that was absolutely patriotic, passionate, and appropriate. Give it up, ladies and gentlemen—Blaze Richboy! Now, we have one more special guest here tonight to give a few more details on the program and some changes to make America safe again. Everyone, I'd like to introduce your former heavyweight champion of the world... Mr. Tiiiiitan Rooooourke!"

Backstage, Titan Rourke walked past Lauren before stepping onto the stage. He acknowledged her with a simple "Ma'am," already acquainted after she had brokered the deal. He was being paid a neat million dollars for his part in the performance. Lauren wondered if being hit that many times in the head meant he didn't fully grasp what he was about to do.

"Mr. Titan Rourke... Sir..." O'Connor joked, feigning fear. "Titanium Titan, as we know you... What do you think about the Gunman?"

Rourke paused. Backstage, Lauren mentally crossed her fingers in an attempt to telepathically assist him in remembering his lines.

"Sterling, he is gonna knock out anyone that wants to bring a gun into a school." As he delivered the line, he stepped back and shadowboxed a couple of quick jabs, dangerously close to the innocent podium holding the mic. "There's just one thing I got to tell you, Sterling," he added. "Mr. President Reign, we just have to make a little change to some laws. Now it's just gotta be —no one is gonna be able to have a gun anywhere within 2,000 feet of a school."

"That doesn't seem to be a big deal, Titan, does it?" O'Connor offered.

"It's no big deal. If you want to be a champion, you don't take your guns to school. And if someone does have a gun, you just gonna stand back and let Gunman go in and sort it out. If you is in there holding a gun and Gunman is on the job, he's going to knock you out. It's going to be a knockout combo."

"Right, so no guns within two thousand feet of a school—just to avoid Gunman thinking you mean harm to the children. Perfectly reasonable. I think there was an executive order released just to clarify that information. So thank you, Titan. Everyone—Mr. Titan Rourke, former heavyweight champion. And folks, I'd say he's still got it. Let's not argue with the man."

Let's not argue with the man" Rourke turned and walked from the stage without looking backwards to acknowledge the slightly subdued cheering and applause from the audience.

"Thank you, Mr. President. When President Reign approached me—personally, I might add—he said, 'Xavier, I need the best. The most advanced technology. The future.' And I said, 'Mr. President, say no more.' I took the challenge. I revolutionized it. Total game-changer. Nobody thought it could be done—except me. And now, thanks to my brilliant team, we've delivered the most cutting-edge security force in American history."

He paused for effect, lifting his chin slightly as if preparing to deliver a profound, historic conclusion.

"President Reign, it will be glorious—you, leading an army of white men, protecting the nation."

A murmur rippled through the crowd—some hesitant laughter, scattered applause, and a few audible gasps. President Reign, standing just behind Wolfe, clapped loudly, his grin stretched a little too tight. Lauren behind the curtains of the stage just buried her face into her hands, wishing to disappear into them.

"Well!" Reign boomed, stepping forward, his voice slicing through the awkward tension. "That was... something! Big, big thinking, folks. Big ideas. A true visionary!" He gave Wolfe a firm pat on the back, physically nudging him away from the mic with practiced finesse.

Wolfe, still grinning, gave a stiff thumbs-up, then tried to pivot. "And with that... let's take a look at what the future really looks like."

He gestured toward the massive screens behind them.

"Alright, folks—let's take a look at the screens around us for a little presentation we like to call *Gunman in Action*."

The screens lit up, rapidly cycling through a dramatic montage. Footage of the Gunman suit in high-intensity training simulations appeared—firing at targets with unerring precision. Close-quarters takedowns. Long-range strikes using precision rifles. The artificial intelligence embedded within the suit calculated every variable in real time: wind speed, distance, temperature, humidity, altitude, bullet drop, the Coriolis effect, and spin drift. Every shot fired accounted for dozens of environmental factors with cold, inhuman precision.

Long-range terminations were its specialty. It didn't need cover. It didn't need concealment. It simply calculated, aimed, and eliminated.

Backstage Lauren couldn't see the screens but could hear the music blaring from the powerful speaker system. She whispered in Mason's ear. "This is the monstrosity that Reign commissioned from Richboy and that Clay Maverick moron, you know the country music singer who's always talking about the good ol' days and how real men carry guns?"

Mason looked confused. "Can't say I know any of his songs", he responded. "Well, consider yourself lucky, you know what they called it? Guardians of the Hall, and that's not even the worst part, wait till the rap part, he's got Chike Craaazy to feature to garner a wider appeal... they're going to stream this song for royalties". Lauren informed him, defeated in tone.

"Kind of catchy!" Mason quipped as he bopped his head along to the beat. Lauren rolled her eyes at him as the song played on. She looked very forward to the moment she could take her next Xanax.

In the heart of this land, we make our stand,
With iron in our grip and freedom in hand,
Guardians of the hall, we're here to fight,
Protectin' the children, keepin' 'em safe at night!

Rockets flyin' high, got no fear at all,

It's America, baby, answerin' the call.
You can't take our freedom, we stand real tall,
Defendin' the schools, like we saved 'em all!"

CHAPTER 23: THE UFAA WON'T STAND FOR IT

Richard Garrison was livid, pacing the confined space of his office like a caged animal. His entire body trembled with fury, each step landing with a heavy stomp, as if he were sidestepping an opponent on the football field.

It was 9 p.m. in Texas, an hour behind New York, where Reign had just finished presenting the Gunman program. The spectacle had been a disaster. Nothing good could come from such an egregious attack on civil liberties and reckless abandonment of the Constitution. Alicia would be there soon. She was calmer than he was and would have a rational plan.

The knock on the door, though expected, startled him. Consumed by rage, his thoughts were a tangled mess. He stormed over and flung it open.

"Hello, Alicia. Come in, will you?" he said through gritted teeth. "What the hell did I just see on television? Did you have any idea what that goddamn moron Reign was up to?"

Alicia shook her head in disbelief. "I had no idea. I didn't even know we had this kind of technology. Our intel from the White House was focused on the gun-free zone…" She trailed off, exasperated.

"Alicia, he signed an executive order authorizing searches on any person within two thousand feet of an educational institution. What the hell are we going to do to fight this? He'll just keep reissuing it or amending it to keep it alive. How do we shut it down legally?"

Garrison reached into his bottom drawer and pulled out an emergency bottle of whiskey and two glasses. His hands trembled slightly as he poured an oversized shot into each, handing one to Alicia.

"Well, first thing—we're filing a lawsuit to contest the order. Our grounds? A gross violation of the Second and Fourth Amendments. Hopefully, we can get it stopped. But Richard, this could be a big fight. The order might stand while we challenge it, and Reign... he's got that Supreme Court stacked."

Garrison slammed his empty glass onto the desk. "Damn it, Alicia, let's just get it moving. This is the biggest threat to freedom I've ever goddamn seen. We're going to mobilize everything and everyone against Reign. I'll give him a goddamn *Reign-check*, out of office! And what in tarnation is this app? How the hell are we supposed to arm teachers if they think they can just use an app instead of learning how to shoot?"

"It's a big problem, Richard," Alicia said, shaking her head. "We don't want people lulled into a false sense of security, thinking law enforcement will swoop in like superheroes and save the day. That's not how this works."

"Just get the press release out tonight, won't you, darlin'? We can't look caught off guard—our members will look to us for protection. Hell, the whole damn country needs us."

Alicia nodded. "Yes, Richard. It needs to go out immediately. I'll get the team on it and have it back to you within the hour for approval." She placed her glass down. "Thanks for the drink. Next time, it'll be to celebrate."

Alicia returned to her office and sat down in front of her computer. This would be her thesis—a document of utmost importance. Her country needed her.

She toiled for nearly an hour, hunting for the right words.

Words to protect America. Words to appease Richard. Her mind buzzed with fury. Her fingers pounded the keys, bouncing angrily off the space bar. Delete. Retype. Again and again.

Who the hell did Reign think he was, stomping all over the Bill of Rights? He was worse than the radical far-left. Maybe he really *was* a communist. She wanted to write that into the press release, but she knew it had to be airtight. That bitch Lauren Chalmers—cozying up to Reign—she was probably behind this. Alicia knew Lauren had blocked her calls.

Alicia smirked as she typed out a text: *You looked like absolute trash on TV. Never going to get a man looking like that.*

Eventually, satisfied with her work, she sent the press release to Garrison for final approval.

United Firearm Advocates Association (UFAA) Press Release Title: UFAA Condemns Overreach of Executive Order and Gunman Program

The United Firearm Advocates Association (UFAA) strongly condemns the recent executive order authorizing the use of the Gunman drones and suits to conduct indiscriminate scans of individuals within two thousand feet of educational institutions. This invasive measure represents a severe overreach of governmental power and a direct assault on our fundamental civil liberties.

In addition to our concerns about privacy rights, we are alarmed by the implications of the Gunman program itself. This program, which integrates advanced surveillance technology into a militarized enforcement system, threatens to erode the protections enshrined in the Second Amendment. The introduction of such technology undermines the necessity and legitimacy of civilian firearms, which are vital for self-defense and maintaining a balance of power.

The UFAA is calling for immediate legal action to challenge both the executive order and the Gunman program. We are mobilizing our network of legal experts, civil rights activists, and concerned citizens to launch a comprehensive campaign aimed at halting these measures. Our legal teams will file lawsuits contesting the order and program on constitutional grounds, particularly regarding unreasonable searches and infringement on the right to bear arms.

Furthermore, we urge the public to remain vigilant and voice their opposition to these intrusive measures. It is essential that we come together to protect our democratic freedoms and ensure that technological advancements do not come at the expense of our personal liberties and constitutional rights.

The UFAA will continue to advocate for policies that uphold the values of transparency, accountability, and respect for individual rights. We stand firm in our commitment to defending the Constitution and safeguarding the freedoms of all Americans.

For further information or to get involved, please visit our website at [UFAAwebsite.org] or contact our press office at [UFAAcontact@org].

About UFAA:
The United Firearm Advocates Association (UFAA) is a leading advocacy organization dedicated to protecting civil liberties and promoting democratic values related to firearm ownership. We work to ensure that government actions remain within the bounds of the Constitution and that individual freedoms are upheld.

CHAPTER 24:
CONSTRUCTIVE CRITICISM

In the month since Reign had unveiled the Gunman program in a dazzling Times Square presentation, the onslaught had been relentless. Lauren sat perched on the edge of her sofa, knees pressed tightly together, hands clenched, savoring a fleeting moment of solitude before her Secret Service escort arrived to whisk her back into the chaos of the White House.

Reign, as usual, had managed to dodge most of the pressure. Lauren had become his shield, absorbing the brunt of attacks from the UFAA, the press, civil libertarians, fellow politicians, and anyone else with a hotline to the White House and a bone to pick with Reign's ego. There was an unspoken rule in the administration: the President was only to be presented with positive feedback. When the Vice President once asked if he could offer "constructive feedback," Reign's response had been swift: "No, you can't."

A knock at the door jolted her from her thoughts. She stood quickly and opened it to find Mason, on her security detail when he wasn't expected today.

"Hello, Ms. Chalmers," he greeted with a faintly knowing smile.

"Agent Foster," she replied, surprised. "I wasn't expecting you today."

"Well, Agent Sanchez called in sick this morning," he said lightly. "And I figured I'm your favorite federal agent."

Lauren raised a skeptical eyebrow, but the corner of her mouth twitched. Behind Mason, the second agent stood silently, casting curious glances at their exchange. They descended via elevator and made their way to the White House in silence.

Within the grand entrance, Reign had installed a display —a Gunman suit, though without functioning weapons or payload, positioned like a monument. It was part statue, part art installation, part declaration of dominance. Operational for ceremonial purposes, it could be piloted from the control center for press events or visiting dignitaries.

In her office, Lauren reviewed notes for the day's meeting, once again questioning how she had ended up carrying the weight of the administration's most controversial program. Before she was ready, she was summoned to the Oval Office.

She entered and took her usual seat near the back. John McMann, Reign's ever-present shadow, was already seated beside the President's desk.

"Lauren, good morning," Reign greeted her, his tone as flat as his expression.

"Good morning, Mr. President. Mr. McMann," she replied formally.

"Chalmers," McMann acknowledged tersely, as though her very presence annoyed him.

Reign leaned back in his chair. "So, Lauren, where are we today? What's the latest on the lawsuits and the usual nonsense?"

Lauren took a breath. "As expected, lawsuits are pouring in from various organizations and individuals. The UFAA is the most vocal, of course. The suits are being consolidated and will eventually be heard by the Supreme Court. For now, the executive order holds, but this is going to be a battle. Frankly, Mr. President, the issue is that Gunman remains unproven.

People doubt the program's real-world effectiveness, and the opposition is seizing on that."

McMann smirked. "Of course they're crying. School shooters are cowards. Basement-dwelling losers. All they can do is go after kids and teachers. What's that word they use online? Incels!" He laughed. "Imagine not getting any action in high school! What a waste of time going!"

Lauren straightened, unsure why incels were a topic in the Oval Office. "That may be true, but we've poured billions into this program. If it's grounded, the fallout will be catastrophic. The public needs assurance that this isn't just a fantasy project."

McMann waved her off. "Relax, sweetie. Here's what's going to happen: some lunatic's going to go full psycho at a school. We deploy Gunman, save the day, and bam—instant success. Everyone's talking about what a genius move it was. Right, Mr. President?"

Reign spread his hands. "Absolutely, John! This program is already a tremendous success. The best, really. We've solved the problem without even firing a single shot! But let me tell you, when Gunman goes live—and it will go live—it's going to be the greatest day in American history. Huge! People will love it. The haters? They'll look so dumb. So stupid. Trust me, nobody knows how to win like I do."

Lauren's jaw clenched. "Mr. President, the lawsuits are just one issue. There's also growing concern about certain clauses in the bill—clauses that grant sweeping powers to deploy this technology more broadly."

McMann chuckled. "Oh, that. Yeah, some reporter's poking around, asking for clarification. I told Homeland Security to keep an eye on her. You know how it is—always the same types stirring the pot."

Lauren sat up straighter. "What clauses, Mr. McMann? What reporter?"

McMann shrugged. "How the hell should I know? Something about executive authority to deploy defense tech for national security. Honestly, Chalmers, I'm not a lawyer."

"I'm aware you're not a lawyer, Mr. McMann. What was the reporter's name?"

McMann exhaled. "Jesus, Chalmers. Stay calm. Nadia Al-Farouk. If you ask me, she should Al-Fuck-Off. Real interesting background, if you know what I mean."

Reign clapped his hands once. "John, you're right as usual. We don't need people nitpicking and stirring up trouble. Flexibility is important. Very important. Sometimes you've got to think big. Take bold action. Solve problems before they even start. And let's be honest, the people love it. Absolutely love it."

Lauren's stomach turned. She had flagged those clauses during the drafting process, but her concerns were brushed aside. "Mr. President, a little transparency might alleviate public concerns."

Reign wagged a finger. "Transparency? That's for losers. The world doesn't need to know every little thing we do to make them feel safe. Bend a couple of constitutional rights, stop a whole pandemic of violence. Most folks don't want to know how the magician pulls off the trick—they just want the magic. The more the media knows, the more they twist it. That's how you lose control of the narrative. You get me? Let's get that reporter's name to DHS. See if they can get her off our back."

"Mr. President, we've made unprecedented attacks on the Constitution in pursuit of your vision. The amount of maneuvering required to make this legal—if it doesn't work within the limits of the Constitution, that's not a constitutional problem. That's a warning." Her voice cracked as the emotion finally slipped through.

McMann stared at her, his eyes flickering between disbelief and rage. Reign, meanwhile, brushed it off like they were discussing something as trivial as sandwich toppings.

"Lauren—the Bill of Rights, the Constitution—these guys were losers. I mean, in the good old days of America, and I'm talking the seventies and eighties, we could actually get shit done. But now? Every decade adds more rules, more red tape. Honestly, the Constitution should be more of a... guideline. You get me?"

"Doug, you're spot on," McMann chimed in. "Seriously, Chalmers, you're like the walking, talking Constitution, and we're the good guys just trying to fix the country. And here you are—more worried about people's rights than their lives. You ever tried making an omelet without breaking a few eggs? Because you're acting like you want us to do it without a frying pan, a stove, or a fucking kitchen."

Lauren opened her mouth to respond, but Reign leaned back in his chair, grinning like a man who'd just won a bet no one else knew was happening.

"And hey, Lauren, tell me—your brother still keeping busy? Bet he's got some big projects. Maybe I should take a peek. See how things are going."

A chill crept up Lauren's spine. "He's well, Mr. President. Thank you for asking. I don't know what he's working on at the moment."

Reign's smirk deepened. "Great stuff. Really great."

CHAPTER 25: THE RISE OF GUNMAN

For the past five weeks, Jordan had followed the same routine. At precisely 4:30 a.m., he rose, drank black coffee with toast and a protein shake, then hit the gym—most mornings, at least. Afterwards, he checked in with the onsite physician, who monitored his blood pressure and blood sugar. Once a month, a full panel of blood tests was conducted. The doctor also managed his regimen of supplements and vitamins, ensuring he operated at peak physical and mental performance.

Not that it really mattered. In truth, piloting the suit was no more demanding than playing a video game. There were millions of American teenagers who could do it more effortlessly than he could—his reflexes had long since peaked. But Jordan was a symbol. And there weren't many gamers out there with pecs like his.

He stood in front of the full-length mirror in his dorm, taking in his reflection before heading out for duty. He was a tank now. Whatever McMann was supplying, it was working. Powerful. Even without the suit, he could kick ass.

He wondered if Emily had seen him in the media. It was likely that one of the kids in her class had some kind of Gunman merchandise—whatever school she was teaching at now. He could find out if he wanted to. He had access to the resources.

The command center down the hall had the technology to locate anyone. Mostly illegally, but McMann wasn't the type to bother with things like warrants. If Jordan wanted to, he could track her down. But deep down, he knew—she had to come back to him. He couldn't force it.

He was a household name now. Sure, there were detractors, but eventually, he'd prove himself. At some point, he was going to go live in the suit. Maybe she wouldn't like the extra weight and size on him. She was only a little thing.

His appointment to the program wouldn't last forever. Eventually, someone else would take his place—hopefully without McMann seeing to it that they had an unfortunate accident along the way. If Emily didn't like the bulk, he could lose it. Slim down.

Jordan pushed the thought aside. He had to focus on his work. Lacking focus could result in an innocent civilian—or worse, a child—being killed. That wasn't going to happen. Not while he had access to the most advanced weapons system ever built.

It was 7 a.m. Time to begin active duty, which would stretch until 5 p.m. He needed to stay alert, always ready for deployment at a moment's notice. Seconds mattered, and he couldn't afford to let his guard down.

Usually, he stayed within proximity to the control room, except when he needed to use the bathroom or stretch his legs. His body had become accustomed to the rigid schedule. Every day, like clockwork, he felt the urge to empty his bowels at 1:30 p.m.—about fifteen minutes after his third post-lunch coffee.

Jordan exited the control room and walked down the bland hallway, the flickering fluorescent lights casting a cold, sterile glow on the gray linoleum floor. The men's restroom was just ahead, fifteen strides away. He entered his favorite stall, grateful for the brief solitude. It was a moment of sanctuary in a world dominated by constant surveillance and endless alertness.

Three and a half more hours. Then he could finally come off

duty.

At 1:47 p.m. on a Tuesday afternoon in late September, the alert sirens blared through the hallways, ripping through the sterility and silence. The piercing sound shattered the calm. Jordan was washing up in the men's room—the furthest possible distance from the command center. His heart rate spiked. He sprinted from the bathroom, his added muscle mass shifting with every step, adrenaline flooding his system. He was terrified and excited all at once.

More than anything, he was ready to feel more powerful than he had that day in Hope Valley.

"What've we got?" Jordan barked, jaw clenched and brow furrowed as he burst into the command capsule. His limbs snapped into place in the control rig—the open exoskeleton that would serve as an extension of his body.

A technician flipped the switch. "We're live. Five-second delay in play. Keep it tight, Peck."

Jordan knew what that meant. The entire process was being live-streamed to the subscribers of *The Gunman* app. Every movement, every second, would be recorded and broadcast across millions of screens worldwide.

"Active shooter reported at Lincoln High School in Boise, Idaho," a support officer reported.

"Local police are en route, ETA eight to ten minutes. We're the closest rapid response unit."

"Of course we are. Go for launch. Three, two, one," Jordan said, voice steady as the operator across the room confirmed with the secondary switch.

Jordan's jaw clenched as he slammed his hand onto the launch button, initiating the sequence. Within seconds, the control suit snapped around him. The helmet's visual display lit up with a full 360-degree view. Immersive audio filled his ears.

His arms and legs locked into the command interface, which mirrored his movements with precision—though the suit itself was about to operate 850 miles away.

The main view screen flickered to life, showing the live feed from the suit. Tactical officers leaned forward, eyes glued to the screen as the Gunman drone launched into the air from the deployment site just outside Boise. Fully immersed in the cutting-edge virtual reality system, Jordan felt as if he were physically inside the drone.

The simulation was so vivid he could almost feel the rocket-assisted propulsion as the drone blasted skyward. The engines roared through his headset, vibrating in his chest. Electric motors hummed, guiding the flight with pinpoint accuracy.

The drone climbed quickly, streaking across the sky. In just over a minute, it reached Lincoln High School. Jordan's heart raced. He let out a quiet exhale of anticipation.

As the drone neared its target, the boosters disengaged. The electric motors took over, gliding the suit to a controlled descent. The VR interface fed Jordan real-time tactical data. He activated the suit's sensor suite: millimeter-wave radar penetrated walls, thermal imaging tracked heat signatures. The onboard AI rapidly processed the data, identifying the shooter based on stance, movement, and weapon profile.

"I've got him," Jordan said. His voice was steady. "Lone shooter, looks like a rifle. East wing, near the cafeteria. Multiple civilians nearby."

The suit touched down in the school parking lot with a metallic thud. The drone detached, and the autopilot guided the final landing with surgical precision. Jordan flexed his fingers. The suit moved with him, perfectly in sync. He wasn't just a man anymore—he was the weapon.

"All right," he said, cutting through the tense silence. "I'm going in. Taser active to start."

The Gunman suit strode toward the school entrance. Its heavy footfalls echoed down the hallway. As Jordan approached the doors, he found them barricaded. In Omaha, he'd punched through air. In Boise, the suit forced its way through with a brutal slam, sending debris flying.

Inside, a school safety officer lay sprawled on the ground. His weapon was gone. One hand clutched a cell phone. The 911 dialer was still open.

"Jesus..." Jordan muttered. "This is for real... shit." His eyes scanned the screen. "The 911 dialer's still up."

"Peck, watch the language," came a voice in his helmet. "We're live. We can bleep it, but don't make the kids think their hero swears."

He crouched beside the officer and gently pried the phone from stiff fingers. A gold wedding ring gleamed on the lifeless hand. Jordan stared at it, something twisting deep in his chest. A weight settled on him. The reality, the cost.

Then the voice came, sharp and unfiltered.

"Peck, you idiot. It's McMann. Now listen, son—we've got this shit live-streaming to the fans. Kids think you're some fucking hero. So, here's the deal: Don't do anything stupid. And for the love of God, don't kill anyone unless it looks *cool* on TV. Got it?"

Jordan snapped out of it. "Yes, sir. Understood."

McMann's voice crackled again. "Good. We've got a delay on the feed, but a few seconds won't mean shit if you screw this up. Keep it smooth. Like my hand on a stripper's ass. Don't fuck up."

The suit surged forward. Jordan's heart thundered. His limbs moved with mechanical precision, but his thoughts were spinning. The psychological training kept him sharp—aware, but not afraid.

He thought of Emily. He didn't know where she was teaching. It could be this school.

But it wasn't. He remembered—this was a high school. She wouldn't be here.

He locked back onto the mission. This was it: the first real-world deployment of the Gunman program.

"Suspect's armed with a semi-automatic rifle, high-cap mags," a voice crackled in his earpiece. "No word on casualties yet. We're hearing gunfire and 911 calls. Local police arriving in sixty seconds."

"Confirmed," Jordan said, his tone cold and flat. "Tell them to stand down. I've got this. One casualty—*that's* all there's gonna be."

The suit moved with lethal speed, VR sensors feeding him real-time updates as he tore through the corridors. Classroom doors were locked. For a moment, Jordan felt a grim sense of satisfaction. This school had prepared well.

He rounded a corner—and saw him.

A young man, barely more than a kid, stood with an AR-15. He was advancing on a group of terrified students huddled at the end of the hall. The rifle rose.

Jordan's heart pounded. His mind cleared. There was only the mission now.

"Freeze! Drop your weapon!"

Jordan's amplified voice boomed through the Gunman suit's external speakers, its mechanical resonance echoing down the hallway.

The shooter spun around, eyes wide with fear and disbelief. For a split second, he froze—taking in the towering, metallic figure just thirty feet away. The rifle trembled in his hands. His breath came fast and ragged, his mind scrambling for a plan.

Then panic took over.

His grip tightened on the AR-15, and he raised it, the barrel gleaming under the harsh fluorescent lights. A violent burst of gunfire rang out, the sharp cracks reverberating through the corridor. The sound was deafening, drowning out everything else.

The Gunman suit absorbed the shots, bullets pinging harmlessly off its bulletproof armor—the impact sounding like raindrops on a steel roof. The sharp whir of internal mechanisms was the only response, the machine advancing, unfazed by the assault.

Inside, Jordan felt nothing but a deep, cold calm. The chaos outside faded, leaving only the mission.

Back in the control system, Jordan's instinct was to duck. His training kicked in—his muscles moved before his mind could catch up. But then clarity struck: he was invulnerable. Even to semi-automatic fire. For a fleeting moment, he let himself feel it—a rush of satisfaction, a flash of power, knowing the bullets would never reach him.

But it didn't last.

His mind snapped back.

A bullet could ricochet. Could hit a student. A teacher.

The exhilaration vanished, replaced by focus.

With one smooth motion, Jordan raised his right arm and selected the taser function. His HUD lit up green, locking onto the shooter's chest. The suit's AI had already calculated the perfect angle for a full-voltage strike.

He activated it without hesitation.

The sharp crack of electricity filled the hallway.

The taser launched, striking the upper chest just above the heart.

The shooter's body went rigid, the rifle falling from his hands as he collapsed to the floor. The entire confrontation had lasted less than three minutes—

No time for hesitation.

No room for error.

Jordan moved quickly. The suit's systems disarmed the shooter, restraining his wrists and ankles in one fluid sequence.

As the tension lifted, Jordan stood over the subdued assailant, breath steady, heart still pounding.
He'd done it.

It worked.

"Suspect neutralized," Jordan reported, voice tight with adrenaline.

"No additional casualties that I can see. The officer at the door —we need the coroner."

Local police began streaming into the building as Jordan stood guard over the fallen shooter. From the shadows of the hallway, he could hear sobs and quiet whimpers—students still huddled in fear, still processing what had happened.

Across the nation, millions were watching—on phones, tablets, TVs—subscribed to Gun-Watch.
Inside the control studio, the creative director erupted:

"Slow down the shot! Bring up the music—give me an inspirational crescendo! Now freeze it—graphic up!"

'Gunman has been successfully deployed to Lincoln High School in Boise, Idaho. One casualty: a school security officer. The suspect has been disarmed and secured. Local police will now transport the suspect to jail.'

"Alright, now play the song!" the director barked.

The screen remained frozen on the subdued shooter as local authorities took over. Beneath it, the aftermath unfolded—blurred motion, flashing lights, controlled chaos.

Then came the music.

Blaze Richboy's "Guardians of the Hall" thundered in, its triumphant beat punctuating every moment.

The shooter, still dazed from the electric shock, was hauled to his feet by officers. The cold clink of cuffs snapped around his wrists as they led him away. Students remained frozen, some trembling, others clutching the walls—caught between disbelief and delayed terror.

Inside the suit, Jordan softened the voice modulation—trading the intimidating mechanical growl for something more human, more comforting.

"It's okay now," he said gently.

The words echoed with sincerity, but they felt hollow against the weight of what had just happened.

No one moved. They couldn't.

Moments earlier, their lives had hung by a thread. Now all they could do was sit—stunned, silent, trying to make sense of it all... if that would ever be possible.

Back in Omaha, the command center erupted into raucous applause and cheers, the officers slapping each other on the back as if celebrating a victory. The first real deployment of the Gunman program had been a success. The mission was flawless. The suit had performed as expected—and it had looked damn good doing it.

CHAPTER 26: UNINTENDED ESCALATION

The door shut with a familiar, weighted thud. From inside, Mason Foster pressed the lock button, and the electronic beep that followed confirmed the seal. These days, with reporters circling like vultures and lunatics emboldened by headlines, the Secret Service had tightened their grip. One agent now sat inside the apartment. Another stood outside her door. A third was stationed in the lobby, and a fourth idled in an unmarked car out front.

Surveillance cameras tracked every angle—inside and out—but she knew their exact positions. None dared breach the boundary of her private quarters. Not yet.

It wasn't really her apartment, though—it was provided by the U.S. government. Carefully selected for both its location and defensive advantages, the apartment's orientation within the building and its distance from potential sniper vantage points had all been assessed. Her position didn't make her anywhere near the target the President was, but as America spiraled into chaos and proxy civil war, there was no limit to the crazy—or to what people might do.

Secretly, Lauren was pleased about the insistence that an agent remain inside the apartment, despite her outward objections. She liked having Mason there. He was a source of comfort, and she felt better when he was around.

She stood in the entryway, the routine well established by now. Mason moved past her, checking every room and alcove within the apartment before returning and reporting, "All clear," both into his microphone and for her benefit.

Lauren retreated to her bedroom for a moment, kicking off her heels into the wardrobe and peeling off the restrictive blazer and tight pants she'd worn all day. She folded them neatly and placed them into a laundry bag. As she did, she became aware of being watched. Turning, she found Mason leaning in the doorway, silently watching her undress. She smiled faintly, sighing.

"You know the Supreme Court upheld the executive orders again?" she asked.

"I heard, yeah. Reign really is a magician in the courts, isn't he? I mean, he's spent almost as much time in courtrooms as he has on the golf course, so he knows how it works."

"Between sexual harassment and breach-of-contract suits? Yeah, you could say that."
She suddenly remembered something an aide had mentioned earlier—something she had passed on to the President.

"Did you know the police captain Reign's been attacking in the media... committed suicide?"

"No, I didn't. That's terrible. I guess he couldn't live with it on his conscience. I mean, it's a lot for a man to deal with."

"It was already enough to bear without the pile-on. What about the bullying, Mason? Reign called him out of the blue and abused him—for no reason. Just before one of those social media posts. He abused the guy, then posted about him. His fans swarmed him with death threats, slandered him... it was awful. And Reign didn't even blink when he found out."

"We don't have much hope when the president's bullying people until they end themselves. Not much hope for our kids, is there?" Mason said.

"That's just an example of conspicuous manipulation. There was a reporter poking around early in the constitutional war—she was right onto it. They had her added to the DHS watchlist. She can't go through a security checkpoint without a strip search anymore. Reign said it was bound to happen if you're going to be hanging around a mosque."

Lauren glanced at her reflection in the full-length mirror inside the wardrobe. She'd once been slender, but now she just looked thin—her eyes bleary and sunken. She felt frail.

"I look terrible, Mason." She thought about Alicia Turner's words—that she'd never get a man looking the way she did. Petty, but effective in wounding her.

Mason looked at her with intensity, his gaze unwavering. "I think you look amazing. Maybe a little tired—but babysitting Reign and running the entire government? That's gotta wear you out."
"So... you think I look bad, then?" she probed.

"I think you're fuckin' gorgeous," he said, without hesitation, his eyes locked onto hers.
Her eyelids fluttered closed for a moment, green irises disappearing. When she reopened them, he was still staring. The light caught a small scar near his temple—a reminder that the gentleness he showed her was not extended to his enemies. She held his gaze, both of them frozen for a moment, until she broke first, smiling—genuinely happy, if only briefly.

"You want me to order some food for you, Lauren?"

He was always thinking about food. Talking about restaurants he saw on social media, or telling stories about some incredible burger he'd eaten. Sometimes—though she wasn't sure if he noticed, and far be it from her to tell him—he would unconsciously lick his lips when hors d'oeuvres trays passed at official events or when courses were brought out at state dinners.

"Sure. You have any recommendations for pizza? Maybe we could get a couple for the other agents working tonight."

"Oh, babe, let me tell you about this new place I went to a couple weeks ago—Capitol Crust. Get this: they've got a pizza called the 'Philly-Buster,' spelled P-H-I-L-L-Y. Get it? Like filibuster? Anyway, it's got this rich garlic butter sauce they spread all over, including the crust, and the sliced ribeye just melts on your tongue."

She watched him—a grown man in his forties, dressed in Secret Service attire, his service pistol flashing as he waved his arms describing a pizza. His suit jacket shifted with each gesture. She smiled until he stopped talking.

"What?" he asked, a slight smile playing on his lips, equal parts bemusement and confusion.
"Absolutely nothing. That sounds great. Can you get a pepperoni too? And whatever the other agents would like?" She held out her credit card in agreement.

He nodded. "Yes, ma'am." Walking into another part of the apartment, he activated his microphone and spoke into his wrist. "Boys, we're doing pizza."

Lauren stepped into the bathroom and into the shower. The hot water enveloped her, providing a cocoon against the stress of the day—the stress of every day. Each one seemed to intensify just a little more. She wondered how much longer she could survive in this job.

Sometimes, she forgot the predicament of her entrapment.

On one hand, there was the professional prison: she'd worked her entire life to get into a position like this, only to find the reality was nothing like she'd imagined. Maybe it would've been different under another president. Maybe her role could've been more traditional. But this hybrid chief-of-staff-slash-personal-assistant-slash-enforcer job? It was brutal. She wasn't out breaking kneecaps, of course—not literally. No, her work wasn't as classy as that. It was more like going to Darius Greene and setting him up to be destroyed by Reign and McMann.

Her conscience was already heavy. Her hands were already bloodied.

She supposed she could quit. But someone else would replace her by the end of the day. There was always a revolving door in Reign's administration—and what if the next person was even less concerned with checks and balances?

But there was another, bigger problem.

Her brother, Ethan.

He wouldn't last in prison. Physically, he was like her—tall and slim—but where she carried her height with elegance and femininity, he was lanky, nerdy, and had the intimidation level of a pencil.

It had all started at the beginning of Reign's first campaign —before he'd even solidified himself as a serious candidate. Back when his political ambitions seemed like an amusing side project.

Ethan had just made junior partner at a prominent New York real estate development firm. It was his big break. But things fell apart. Financial problems mounted. He altered contracts and invoices, inflating costs to secure more investor money. Blatant fraud—meant to be temporary. A bridge until the project turned around.

Maybe he would've gotten away with it—if an investor hadn't pulled out. That's when it all came crashing down. Reign never told her directly that he'd intervened. But Ethan had.

She remembered the night Ethan had shown up on her

doorstep, disheveled and broken. Reign had pumped funds into the project and made the legal mess disappear. Ethan was ruined, terminated, and blacklisted from the industry.

But he wasn't in jail.

And that was something.

Suddenly, the shower didn't feel like a cocoon. It felt like a cell.

She turned the water off.

Lauren had changed now. She had wiped the makeup off her face, her wet hair dangling just above her shoulders, curling slightly as it dried. She pulled on an oversized Georgetown sweatshirt—her go-to sleepwear since college—paired with well-worn pajama pants.

She wandered into the dining area and found Mason sitting in a chair facing the direction of her bedroom. He had been gazing intently toward the unopened pizza boxes on the dining table, but his eyes lifted to her as she walked into the room. He looked at her contentedly.

"Stop it. I'm wearing a sweatshirt, and I'm not wearing makeup," she reprimanded him.

"You stop it, woman. Imagine looking that good and not knowing it. You're the reason so many people tune in to watch Reign's rubbish press conferences."

She huffed, expelling air through her nose as her lips turned upward into a reluctant smile. Mason jumped to attention, pulled out a chair for her, and motioned for her to sit. He returned to his seat, rubbing his hands together in anticipation before tearing open the pizza boxes as if it were Christmas morning.

"So," he began, "can you get me one of those Gunman figurines for my birthday? You know, the one that says all the recorded phrases and comes with a drone it flies around on?"

"I suppose so. Do you want one of the smaller ones too, the kind you can clip onto your school bag? What about the lunchbox?"

"There's a hell of a lot of merchandise available, isn't there, Lauren?"

"We've put $8 billion into this program, you know. Merchandise returns alone—well, I only read the summary, but I think it was around $91 million. So we've got a way to go. Of course, the entire defense budget was over $900 billion, so the program is significant but still inconsequential when it comes to overall spending on keeping America safe."

"The problem is," he said, pausing for another bite of pizza, "this batshit-crazy program has actually stopped school shootings."

She nodded slowly, absorbing his words, her mind turning as she quietly chewed her own slice.
"There's something not right, Mason," she said suddenly.

"Of course it's all wrong. Everything is wrong. Everything's more wrong than right. But even by Reign's standards of... well, I don't know what his standards are. What I mean is—I don't understand why we have this program."

"Well, school shootings were a stain on our nation, Lauren. Something had to be done. Reign is... Reign. I don't understand his motivations sometimes, but maybe he's done something good this time?"

"That's my point, Mason. Reign doesn't do things for the greater good. He does things because someone slighted him, or someone posts something on social media and he happens to see it. He doesn't care about kids getting shot in public schools in the Midwest or down in Texas."

Mason's posture was relaxed, but his eyes were sharp—analytical. "Nobody wants their kids going to school and not coming home, Lauren. The program, with all its inherent failures, is saving lives. I think maybe you're being too hard on yourself. You're shouldering the responsibility of a nation. You're like Atlas holding up the world."

"You know, Mason, in Greek mythology Atlas holds up the sky, not the world. It's a common misunderstanding. And it was punishment for his role in the war between the Titans and the Olympians," Lauren corrected. "So, in actuality, I *am* just like Atlas—holding up the sky for my sins."

Lauren exhaled sharply. "I've been in rooms where the decisions we make sound good on paper, but when you think about them long enough, you realize they come with a cost. And no one ever tells you who's going to pay it."

She set her slice of pizza down on the table, her gaze drifting across the room, fixated on the wall—hypnotized by its mundanity, lost in thought. The apartment, with its modern trappings and sterile colors, felt at once constricting and imprisoning. She pushed back her chair and hurried across the dining room, her hand gripping the edge of the counter as she reached for a glass. She needed water. Now. The weight in her chest pressed against her throat.

Mason was instantly behind her. He gently took the glass from her hand and set it down on the kitchen counter. Then he turned her around and pulled her into his chest.

She sobbed quietly, tears running down her face.

"It's going to be okay, Lauren. I'm here for you," he comforted her, and she clung to him.

"It's not, though, Mason," she whispered. "It's not, is it?"

CHAPTER 27: THE BIG 'T'

The glow of monitors and the gentle hum of white noise wrapped around John McMann like a warm hug, filling his soul with joy. The way other people might feel their soul reset when stepping onto a sandy beach, crystal-blue waters beckoning them to frolic—that was precisely how McMann felt at this moment, bathed in the trill of computer processors and the flood of technical information displayed around him.

Standing beside McMann was a grunt named Derek Thorne. Thorne by name and a thorn in the side of anyone he determined to be an adversary. He stood at ease, arms clasped behind his back, the fingers of each opposite hand touching his elbows. He was one of McMann's "special guys," a select group of disciplined, handpicked men who solved problems where others feared to tread.

McMann surveyed the room with weathered eyes. No technicians were on-site tonight—only security. Security agents that McMann owned. Tonight's roster consisted of specially selected guards, men who loved America.

"What's the story here tonight, son?" McMann barked at Thorne.

Thorne wasn't a man who wasted time on anything other than facts. He spoke with the absolute bare minimum of words needed. His joys in life were limited to two things: killing people and the equipment that facilitated said killing. McMann loved him like a son—more than his actual son, who was a fuckup working on the East Coast as a therapist, dilly-dallying around with other failures and their feelings all day long.

"System is in full incognito mode and ready, sir. All systems online. Target confirmed."

McMann nodded, a glimmer of satisfaction in his eyes. Incognito mode was a special little Easter egg one of his top computer geeks had built into the system—unbeknownst to the other geeks. Some kind of computer joke, he had said. Effectively, it made any actions invisible to recording and documentation. Handy for the kind of work McMann needed to do.

For three months now, he had been making America safe. Three months of kicking ass. He had won. The program worked. Everyone was wrong. Some were even more wrong than others. He made a mental note to call that bitch Garrison at the UFAA.

He turned to Thorne. "Stand by me, my apprentice, as we make America even fucking better."
The younger man met his gaze evenly. "I'm ready, sir."

"Fuck, my dick is hard right now, son. Metaphorically speaking, that is," McMann informed him, clasping his hands behind his back, his biceps straining against the fabric of his suit. "The Gunman program really is making American schools safe. By default, son, if we make America safer, it stands to reason the schools within will also be safer."

As he spoke, McMann's mind drifted to the battles he had fought to make this program a reality—the politicians, the protesters, the handwringers who couldn't stomach what needed to be done.
But the public was coming around. How could they not? There hadn't been a single fatality on school grounds since the program launched—other than a security officer here and there and, of course, the shooters themselves. A couple of them had caught a bullet in the head.

Besides, America had already paid for the Gunman program. Paid in fear. Ever since 1927, when that Andrew Kehoe motherfucker let off all those bombs, killing 38 kids. If McMann had been around then, 1927 would have been the last mass shooting in an American school.

Columbine. Now, that was another good one. Those two little fuckers had set the precedent for a new era in killing children.

These days, you had to hit double digits to even make the national news for a school shooting.
Tonight wasn't about school safety though. This is the big league: National Security. The big 'T'; terrorism. The best defense against terrorism is offense. That's the name of the game tonight. He fixed Thorne with a penetrating stare.

"Are you ready, son? You ready to clean up America?" The younger man nodded crisply. "Yes, sir." It was a rhetorical question. Thorne was not the kind of man that wouldn't seize the opportunity presented to him here tonight. He loved America. Maybe not as much as McMann, but good enough.

As the gentle white noise bustle of the control room continued around them, John McMann allowed himself a fleeting smile. The Gunman program was his legacy, his mark on history. It was a beautiful machine of order, efficiency, and power. If the Gunman system was a woman, he would make love to it, twice. The first time would be with great intensity, rock hard with unrelenting fervor; she would be helpless against his powerful thrusts until ecstasy violently took hold of them both. In the morning, he would again make love. This time, lovingly, with tenderness and care. He would even see to it that breakfast would be provided.

The control room hummed with tense energy as McMann and Thorne took their positions; John standing at the ancillary systems and Derek taking his place within the control capsule. McMann's fingers punched into the keyboard, his eyes scanning the GPS coordinates of a location outside of Washington D.C. in the suburbs. "There," he jabbed a finger at a particular location on a zoomed-in map. "Tariq Al-Zahir. That dirty little fucker and his gay beard are going to be in there."

Thorne leaned in, intensely focused on the location. McMann pulled up a digital image of the target and Thorne studied the man's face one last time. He had already studied the subject in detail. This was just a matter of procedure. It was as much a psych-up exercise as an ID process. It wasn't that killing the wrong man would be anything to worry his conscience; he just wasn't going to give him a chance to escape if they hit the wrong target. He would be on alert then, making it harder, even with the greatest domestic weapon system the world had ever seen.

"There's that little fucker, formerly known as being alive." McMann's voice carried more than a touch of exuberance and excitement. He keyed in a series of commands, his gaze never leaving the screen. "He's at the location as intel provided, house just outside D.C." Al-Zahir hiding out in Silver Spring, Maryland, only a few miles away from the president in the nation's capital—that made John McMann very angry. Little rat bastard.

Al-Zahir wasn't actually hiding, he was just on an unofficial watch list because he was planning a major terrorist act on American soil. It's just those losers at the CIA couldn't prove it; he was a sneaky little snake, this Tariq. McMann had proven it, to himself and to President Reign, so technically, he was guilty. And besides, there was enough division in America at the moment, dissonance spurred by the loud vocal criticism of the government wasn't going to make this country better or safer. America had granted him citizenship years ago and now that little towel head Ali Baba motherfucker was funding extremist organizations back in the Middle East he was desperate to escape from. Fucking typical of these kinds of people. Run away from their homelands, not brave enough to fight and what's the first thing they focus on? Making America just as shitty as their empires of sand. Al-Zahir, pharisaic little bastard with his charity providing aid to his sycophantic AK47-loving refugee buddies. Yeah, not on McMann's America's Neighborhood Watch.

McMann continued punching into the keyboard, he was in full manual mode now; he manually entered the coordinates and selected suit number 116 from the hundreds for this mission. "Suit number 116, he's going to get a medal after tonight for his services to America. We're ready, son, launch in tandem – 3, 2, 1." Thorne didn't hesitate. He instantly punched the launch button in sync with his handler, and the suit launched from one of the launch sites on the outskirts of the city, covering the Washington D.C. area.

They didn't need rocket propulsion on this one, just the nice quiet motors of the drone to deliver the suit to its destination. The drone silently glided through the sky, arriving at its destination in just ten minutes. Thorne maneuvered it to the rooftop of a sizable three-story family home located opposite the house where Al-Zahir was staying; a smaller, single-story building, and the elevated position provided the Gunman suit with an excellent vantage point to aim down into the house. The suit detached from the drone as it dropped with a slight thud onto the rooftop, Thorne selecting a point in the roof where the trusses underneath would provide the most strength for the weight of the suit, the drone landing gently and powering down until needed again.

Through the video link, McMann watched as the suit provided him with a full 4K resolution view of the situation. He stared at the screen, focused. The house was basic, small—somewhat out of place between the larger, older-style multi-story homes.

"Sir, what do you think?" Thorne gruffly questioned.

"Turn on those famous scanners, son."

Thorne toggled on the plethora of scanners built into the suit. The screen flashed for a split second before displaying an outline of the building, revealing the silhouettes of three men sitting at a table in what appeared to be a small dining room off the kitchen. The curtains were pulled back behind the window to the room, but this was no obstacle for the suit's scanning tech.

"Which one is the target, sir?"

McMann continued watching the screen, focused. He didn't know.

"All three of these motherfuckers now, since they want to party with this asshole."

"Yes, sir. Sir, what weapon would you like me to use?"

"Give me a minute, son, I'm thinking here."

It was a difficult shot. Three occupants, an interior room of the house. No clear identification on which one of these sandbox boys was the actual target. They could go in closer—into the house—but that would require killing all three to avoid leaving witnesses. That was an option, but it would draw more attention. Quite the predicament.

"Son, does it appear to you that these gentlemen are engaging in the most heinous of crimes—smoking inside?"

"Sir, yes, their movements do look like that is the case. Do you want me to take a shot?"

"On what, son? All three at once inside the house? They'll disperse, and we'll lose our opportunity to do America a solid. No, son, what we're going to do here is have a barbecue.

Everyone enjoys a barbecue."

The suit, after reattaching to the drone, made a silent descent into the large suburban backyard of Tariq Al-Zahir's home. Once again, it detached, and the drone settled into standby mode, awaiting its next deployment.

At the command center in Omaha, McMann stood with his arms tightly folded. This was risky. A suit appearing in a Washington backyard at 2 a.m. would be hard to explain. If there were any witnesses, he might have to clean up—permanently.

Thorne guided the suit toward a rear basement door. He prepared to force entry, twisting the lock until it snapped.

"Turn your scanners on again," McMann ordered. "Make sure no one's been alerted to your presence."

Thorne complied. The display showed three men still seated at the table.

"Hell are these assholes doing, sitting at a table at two in the morning?" McMann muttered.
The suit twisted the lock off with a quiet click. Thorne pushed the door open and entered the basement.

"There!" McMann pointed instinctively at the screen, forgetting Thorne couldn't see him. "Son, you see the gas line running under the floor there?"

"Yes, sir."

"Good. Follow that line to the connection—should lead to either a stove or a hot water system. Then you're going to do some unlicensed gas work. You tracking me, soldier?"

"Yes, sir."

Thorne followed the line from where it entered through the

exterior wall to a junction beneath the floor. In a corner of the basement, he found the connection to the water heater. With the suit's powerful grip, he twisted the pipe a full 180 degrees, mangling it until gas hissed from multiple ruptures, torn from its seat.

"Gas line is punctured, sir."

"Alright. Look up at the door into the house. Open or closed?"

"Closed, sir," Thorne replied.

"Perfect. Now get yourself out of there, go find some marshmallows, and relocate to the rooftop across the street."

Under Thorne's direction, the Gunman suit exited the basement and reattached to the drone. It returned to its original landing spot atop a three-story home across the road. Another soft thud. The drone powered down to conserve battery.

"Now we wait," McMann said.

They waited. Twenty minutes passed. The men still sat at the table, smoking. No movement.

"The suspense is killing me!" McMann blurted out, a little too excited for someone orchestrating an extrajudicial killing.

But it wasn't entirely unsanctioned. President Reign thought it was a "tremendously great idea" to fix Al-Zahir's attitude. And nothing fixed an attitude like death.

Ten more minutes. McMann grew uneasy. Every second the suit remained exposed risked the program's discovery. They'd already taken too many chances to get this guy.

Another minute ticked by. McMann shifted from one foot to the other. Thorne knew better than to speak.

McMann walked to the closed control room door and peered

into the hallway. A security officer patrolled the corridor.

"Son, I need you to grab my briefcase from the vehicle. Time's tight—move it." Moments later, the guard returned with the briefcase. McMann opened it on a desk, revealing a collection of basic burner phones.

"Alright, Gunny. Let's speed things up. Looks like you're a better gas plumber than we thought. Now we're gonna ID our friend. I'm going to give him a call. You watch for who picks up. When we've got a positive ID, you'll use the rifle and take the shot."

He paused, smirking. "Sure, we could've done this from the jump, but hey—no harm done. Nobody's dead... yet."

"Yes, sir. Sniper rifle is equipped. Ready to take the shot."

McMann pulled up Al-Zahir's file—courtesy of the CIA, off the books, of course. He found the number, activated a burner, enabled a VPN with a German host, opened WhatsApp, and dialed.
"Get ready, son."

In the suit, Thorne was steady. The rifle's sight aimed at the center of the group, ready to shift in an instant.

The phone rang once. Twice. Nothing. McMann cursed under his breath—bad intel?

Third ring. One of the men reached into his pocket and pulled out a phone.

Inside that quiet suburban home in Washington, D.C., the last words Tariq Al-Zahir would ever hear came with a terrifying calm.

"Take the shot, son."

The crack of a suppressed rifle echoed through the control room speakers. One figure dropped.

A split second later, the screen flared—gas ignited in a sudden explosion. Fire engulfed the room, consuming the remaining two men as they ran around frantically, flapping their arms about before falling to the ground and rolling around helplessly. Flames began to spread through the house.

"Holy shit, son! Looks like your home improvement project worked! That's what I call irony."
McMann laughed, slapping his thigh. He was genuinely delighted. He loved his work. And as they said—if you love what you do, you never work a day in your life.

"Alright, son. Wrap it up. Time to disappear."

The Gunman suit lifted off into the night as flames consumed the home. McMann snapped the burner phone in half and slid it back into his briefcase.

CHAPTER 28: BULLETS FOR BEAUTIFUL BABIES

It was one of Reign's favored techniques for handling the media: using Marine One as a dramatic backdrop while he strode across the lawn. Lauren figured the spectacle served a dual purpose—foremost, it was theatrical and authoritative, but it also gave him a convenient excuse to walk away if a question rubbed him the wrong way. He could always claim he had urgent presidential business awaiting him. Unbeknownst to the reporters stranded outside, that "urgent business" was usually a Big Mac or two inside the chopper.

She was in her office, the small TV recessed into the bookcase overlooking the long conference table, broadcasting the president's address to the media outside. Mason was standing just outside the doorway in the hall, but she motioned for him to come in and watch beside her. They didn't speak, but Lauren found herself looking into his gray eyes for a moment longer than she should have, considering how many staff and aides might walk in or pass by at any time.

There had been another deployment of Gunman yesterday. The frequency with which he was being deployed—and how normalized it had become—made it far less of a novelty than in the beginning. Reign, of course, was very pleased with himself, failing to restrain his ego in the slightest.

"Folks, another school shooting tragedy was stopped yesterday. I mean, if you want to say this is one of the greatest political accomplishments in the history of the nation? I think that would be accurate. We don't have school shootings in this country anymore—we have *attempted* shootings. I suppose you could say this is what winning looks like?

"I mean, here we have leadership that said: hey, we don't think a mentally unwell person should be able to go into a school and start shooting at children. If it were the previous president? Well, he'd say, 'Oh, you know, these deranged people are confused because they aren't sure about their gender. Sure, you killed some people—but you're the good guy. Here's some money for your gender reassignment surgery.'"

Reign took on a sarcastically mocking tone, impersonating a child. In her office, Lauren stared hopelessly at the screen. He pushed forward, waxing lyrical.

"You know, in other countries, they used to *laugh* at us for failing to contain school violence. It's true. When the other guy was in charge, world leaders would call me and say, 'Hey Reign, how come your president can't handle a little school shooter?'

"Folks, let me tell you—no one is laughing at America now. Look at the past administrations: total disasters. Tragedy after tragedy."

He paused for dramatic effect, staring straight ahead.

"Under my leadership, we brought real solutions. We said no more bullets for beautiful babies. No more violence. We implemented the Gunman Protocol, and people said it wouldn't work—but guess what? It did work. It's the greatest security program the world has ever seen. School shootings? Over. Done."

He paused again, and the group of selected reporters knew it was their moment to ask questions.

"Mr. President, do you consider it a success that the program has only *stopped* attempted shootings rather than *preventing* them altogether? Critics argue this isn't a solution—just a more militarized response."

"Of course it's a success. I mean, let's use common sense. When someone commits a crime, the police stop them—they go to jail. That's law and order. What do you want? *Minority Report*? You want us to predict crime, locking people up *before* they do something? We don't do that in America. If we did, maybe the last president would've been in jail *before* he had a chance to wreck the country, tank the economy, and turn our great cities into crime-infested wastelands.

"Look at New York. Look at Chicago. San Francisco. They let criminals run wild. They let Mexico send us the worst of the worst—murderers, rapists—and now we have to clean up the mess. The real question is, why did we even need this program in the first place? Weak leadership. But now? We win."

Reign pointed at a different reporter.

"Does the government profit from the commercialization of the program—such as streaming revenue from *Guardians of the Hall* or licensing the technology to private contractors?"
"What kind of question is that? Do you even understand how business works? Because it doesn't sound like it. I think that's why you're a reporter—not a job creator.

"Look, smart leaders find ways to offset costs. You want security? You want safety? Well, guess what—patriotism and capitalism go hand in hand. We're creating jobs, we're advancing American technology, and we're making sure this program pays for itself. That's what winning looks like."

He scanned the crowd again.

"Is there anyone here that isn't from a *Fraudcast Media* outlet?"

He tried again with another reporter.

"Mr. President, several civil rights groups have raised concerns about excessive force and racial bias in the Gunman Protocol's implementation. How do you respond?"

"Well, I'd say that if you're concerned about excessive force being used against you, you should probably *not* attempt a mass shooting on an educational campus in the United States. It's very simple, really. I think even a reporter from Fictional News Network could understand that.

"And I don't think *you* understand racial bias. If you are white and you have a gun in a school, you will be captured—dead or alive—by the Gunman. If you are Black, or Mexican, or any other color, you could be purple for all it matters—if you aim a gun at someone in a school, you will be dealt with."

"Mr. President, some critics argue that the decrease in school shootings isn't due to the Gunman program itself, but rather the increased focus on safety measures—better locks, more drills, and staff training. Would you acknowledge that those factors play a role?"

Reign rolled his eyes.

"Oh, here we go. Here we go. Another genius who thinks they know more than the experts—more than the people *actually* doing the job. Let me tell you something—those things? They help. Sure, they help.

"But you know *why* they're happening? Because of me. Because of this program. Because when I said we were putting Gunman in schools, suddenly everybody started taking security seriously. Before that? Nothing. Nothing but excuses. Weak leadership. Total disaster. Now they're locking doors—imagine that! Locking doors! What a concept. I mean, they should have been doing that already, right? Unbelievable."

He paused again, certain he had said something profound.

"But let's be very clear—without Gunman, without our very tough, very strong response, none of this happens. You think some new locks and a couple of drills stop a shooter? Please.

Give me a break.

"What stops a shooter is the fact that the second they step foot on campus, there's a highly trained, highly advanced, very lethal response waiting for them. That's what stops them. And by the way—people *love* it. The students, the teachers—they feel safe. Safer than ever. They tell me all the time. Parents? They're thrilled. And the bad guys? They're *terrified*. So you can try to spin it, but the reality is simple: this works. It's working better than anyone imagined. And it's only getting better... Next question."

"Mr. President, Tariq Al-Zahir, a prominent activist and frequent critic of your administration, was recently killed under suspicious circumstances. Do you have any comment on his death?"

Reign scoffed and shook his head.

"Well, you know, I can't say I was a fan. A lot of people weren't. Let's be honest—this was a guy who, frankly, said some very nasty things about me, about this administration. Very unfair things. And that's fine—we believe in free speech. I'm a big believer in free speech. The biggest.

"But sometimes, you look at these guys—very negative, very nasty—and you wonder: what's *really* going on there? You know what I mean?"

He paused, shrugged with the petulance of a small child, then continued.

"Now, obviously, it's tragic. Very tragic. No one wants to see that. But look—bad things happen, okay? People have enemies. *He* had enemies, believe me. Some very bad people didn't like him. I hear that.

"You're talking about a guy involved in a lot of things—big business, international stuff. A lot of people weren't happy with him. And now, you want to pin it on me? Give me a break.

Total nonsense."

He waved his hand dismissively, as if swatting a bug.

"We're looking into it. We'll see what happens. But let's not pretend this was some angel, okay? He played the game—and sometimes, the game plays back."

As he spoke, President Reign raised a finger and circled it in the air, cueing the roar of Marine One's rotors. The wind whipped violently around the press pool. Reporters shouted questions as the helicopter's thunder intensified. Reign ignored them, flashing a thumbs-up and his signature goofy, closed-mouth grin before boarding.

In Lauren's office, she stood in stunned silence, her mouth slightly ajar as Marine One lifted into the air.

"He was really mean and nasty to the president."

"I'm sorry?" Lauren turned to Mason.

"He was really mean and nasty to the president," he repeated.

"Mason..." She began gently. "I can't have this conversation with you. Not here."

He nodded solemnly. His comment had been noted, but no further exploration would follow.

"Of course, Miss Chalmers. My apologies if my actions have made you uncomfortable."

His gray eyes lingered on hers a moment longer than needed. His tone and sudden formality hurt. It was intentional—a sharp reminder of the game they were playing. She looked him over, chastising herself for the risks she'd taken. It weighed on him, too. Otherwise, he wouldn't have reminded her with his tone.

Her eyes scanned his face—its features held in tension,

exasperation burning in his eyes. A plain, squarish face lacking the angles to be considered handsome. A blockish body without the taper between shoulders and waist. Her gaze caught the glint of light on the ring on his left hand, and a deep ache formed in her stomach. She looked back into his eyes, hopelessly filled with fondness.

Then he softened. The apprehension left his face.

He turned slightly, revealing the holstered firearm on his hip. Lauren's focus shifted—it was a reminder of why this man was in her life: he would kill anyone who tried to harm her.

He spoke with gentleness. "I'm sorry, Lauren."

Instantly, she repented the feelings that had risen moments ago.

"It's fine, Mason. We're okay."

She repented, then pivoted—melancholy settling in, resentment curling at the edges, and yet, beneath it all, a quiet, irrepressible thrill.

He was right, of course. He didn't need to say it outright—Tariq Al-Zahir's death in a gas explosion was a hell of a coincidence. In a world where flying robots patrolled schoolyards, it was almost laughable to think that a man loathed by the president just happened to die in a freak accident.

Almost.

"You know, Mason," she said, "I read an opinion piece the other day. It said that now that we have the Gunman program, political satire is dead."

Mason smiled, the tension in his posture finally releasing. Clearly, he was relieved to move past the awkwardness.

"Well... do you think it is?"

She exhaled, shaking her head. "No. I think we still have a few more punchlines in us yet".

CHAPTER 29: WE'RE THE GOOD GUYS WITH GUNS (ON DEFENSE)

Richard Garrison was feeling pretty damn good about himself. His phone buzzed relentlessly, notifications popping up faster than he could check them. His inbox? Overflowing with emails from fellow patriots rallying to action. He loved America—and he loved freedom even more. And if Reign's attack meant surrendering that freedom, he'd die first. Civil war? Fine by him. It'd been too long, anyway.

Alicia Turner knocked briefly, then stepped inside, standing close beside him, her presence almost magnetic.

"Look at this, Alicia," Richard said, tapping his screen. "Patriots mobilizing across the nation. Some states are more favorable than others, but we've got real representation today."

"It's great news, Richard," she agreed, her fingers brushing his shoulder as she leaned over to take a closer look. The touch lingered a second longer than it needed to. She didn't pull away, and neither did he.

"People are listening. The message is spreading. Reign's done for—like a roast at Thanksgiving."
They shared a brief, knowing look before turning their attention back to the digital firestorm they were fueling. Each retweet, each share, was a victory—each notification a spark in the growing wildfire of nationalism.

He stood, the Colt Python .357 Magnum thumping softly

against the desk. Its size was impractical for an office, but practicality had no place in a world this fragile. In times like these, making a statement mattered more than anything—and he wasn't about to settle for some sissy gun while the nation teetered on the edge. Besides, it was just a companion to his AR-10, should the situation call for it. He made sure it was always within arm's reach—whether in the car, at home, or in the office.

"Good Guys with Guns on Defense" Richard declared. "It just rolls off the tongue, doesn't it, Alicia?"

"Absolutely," Alicia affirmed. "Fantastic concept and marketing. The uptake has been outstanding."

Richard was proud of his work. It would be his legacy—and it was important for a man like him to have a legacy. Flesh and bones could only stand for so long. But history? History stood forever. It was fundamental, really. Even the most dangerously naïve, freedom-hating, radical, weak-kneed liberals could understand: a bad guy with a gun needed to be put down by a good guy with a gun.

Guns, to his mind, were the fixed equation. There was no other math to be considered. It was all well and good for the zealots to propose removing rights—to attack the Constitution in order to appease the bleeding-heart snowflakes—but the truth was simple: the bad guys would always have guns. So it was of the utmost importance the good guys had a bigger weapon.

That's why he created the GGGOD movement. His AR-10 was a serious weapon, but nobody ever lost a gunfight with Jesus on their side.

His idea was simple, straightforward, and powerful—like a Glock 19. The patriots would assemble, peacefully, with their legally acquired firearms, to stand guard at schools across the nation. Nobody was going to get hurt with their members on watch. No gutless, spineless, cowardly vermin would attack a school today. Punk little kids with big guns? No match for big men with bigger guns.

Garrison instructed Alicia to broadcast their final war cry before deployment across all channels—a last barrage across social media, mass email, and SMS messaging:

Patriots, today we stand united against tyranny and the greatest threat to our freedom ever known. The enemies of liberty seek to strip away our rights, but we will not falter. Man the guns, protect the innocent, and defend what is rightfully ours. Stay strong, stay vigilant, and show them that we will never back down. The fight for freedom is here, and we are ready. #GGGOD #UFAA #REIGNHIMIN

Liberty Oaks High School, Jacksonville Florida.

The sun scorches the pavement outside Liberty Oaks High School as Chet Daniels observes the swelling ranks of GGGOD members. A burly, proud Floridian man in his late thirties who wears an obligatory trucker's hat and sunglasses at all times that hides the lines etched into his forehead making it difficult to assess his exact age but does nicely compliment his well-trimmed goatee. He has a strong affliction for things that end with 'in. Huntin, campin, fishin and especially; shootin.

He's not a man who has a strong understanding of constitutional law, but he knows that Richard Garrison, a great American patriot says that the goddamned Gunman robot is going to be the end of freedom, guns and what about the children? Standing beside Chet is Brandi Daniels. She's a petite little blonde thing with perky fake breasts and tiny little shorts displaying her impressively toned legs for a woman who has popped out a squad of little Daniels.

Chet and Brandi's faces are etched with the weight of determination and duty. There is a tension within the crowd, humming with the responsibility of patriotism and duty. This is a peaceful protest, but as Chet always says, "It's better to be a peaceful warrior than a dead victim". The tactical gear and vest slipped over the AC/DC shirt, double denim jacket and jeans matched with a utility belt with extra mags adds grit to his ensemble; finished with combat boots he's dressed to impress. A perfect outfit for a day out protesting the rape of freedom and attack on the constitution.

On his person is a selection of personal protection equipment, his favorite AR-15, the .45 and a backup subcompact pistol hidden away, just in case. There's extra magazines of course, and a complimentary array of accessories; pepper spray and a large hunting knife.

"Steady Jolene," Chet half drawls to himself, as he scans the perimeter for threats against the high school. As an important member of the UFFA, Richard Garrison sent him a personalized letter, selecting him as squadron leader of the Jacksonville platoon. Brandi had that letter framed professionally, and it has pride of place in the den back at their trailer. She had to move some deer antlers, but it works and goddammit, is she proud of her husband. He stands as a beacon of strength within the sea of tactical gear. There were so many beautiful firearms in attendance today. During the morning, there is a constant rotation of other members exchanging words and handshakes with Chet, all unanimously committed to their cause.

A local news reporter moves through the crowd, her camera man following in close proximity, their relationship based upon trust, the man with the camera displaying a genuine care for his reporter as though she were his charge; realistically powerless among a sea of heavily armed men if it went wrong. She sticks her microphone in the face of any GGGOD member who appears approachable enough to do so. Some stare straight ahead; others make somewhat reserved statements that they are worried about the attack on the constitution.

Eventually the reporter reaches Chet.

The camera isn't recording yet. Lowering the microphone as if it were a weapon, the young woman speaks to Chet. She wants to win his favor, not ambush him.

"Mr. Daniels? Excuse, are you Chet Daniels?" Chet stares back at her for a moment. "Yep".

"Mr. Daniels, I've Savannah Reed, First Coast News, would you be willing to be interviewed for my report? Get your story across to our viewers?" She pressed him, despite his initial abruptness.

Chet looks at Brandi, she nods firmly, her lips tightened somewhere between tension and anger.
"Yeah, OK I'll be on the news." He reluctantly agrees. "Real news though, no fakery or bullshittin, alright?"

"Absolutely Mr. Daniels. I'll show the viewers exactly what you say, no editing, you have my word". Savannah reached her hand out to shake, but Chet notices the rage of jealously radiating from Jolene's glare; he doesn't raise his hand. Savannah turns to her camera man and nods "you ready?"

"Sir, you've come out today to support the UFFA and their stance on gun rights; what do you say to those who believe that these protests and calls for more guns only escalate violence and make our communities less safe?"

"Chet spits at the ground, narrowly avoiding the fancy pointed shoes the reporter's wearing. "Ain't nobody gettin' hurt here today, is there, miss? Guns ain't killin' kids, idiots with guns are killin' idiots. Why ain't we makin' bein' an idiot against the law, huh?"

"But don't you think that more guns in the hands of everyday people could lead to more accidents or even more escalation in tense situations? Isn't there a risk of making things worse, not better?"

"Nah ma'am, I do not think that. You explain to me how more folks having a firearm is more dangerous? It ain't. It means we are more equipped if the need arise that we can de-escalate any situation by using our own guns to protect them, like the kids and shit"

"Nah, ma'am, I do not think that. You explain to me how more folks having a firearm is more dangerous? It ain't. It means we're more equipped, if the need arises, to de-escalate any situation and protect folks, like the kids and all that."

Savannah pushes again, her tone flirting with hostility.

"So, just to be clear; you truly believe that the solution to gun violence is introducing even more guns into the equation? That arming more people will make us safer?"

It was at this point that Brandi moved across the pavement and between Chet and the reporter. She was not what you would call 'an educated woman' "She knew when someone was trying to make a fool out of her man, and she wasn't having it. Not for one minute.

"Listen here, princess, you done had your fun. Now take that little notepad and scoot."

"Thank you, Mr. Daniels, for your time. And thank you, ma'am." Savannah offered the exit with a polite nod, already stepping back. These people were heavily armed, and the heat wasn't doing them any favors.

"You havin' yourself a real good time there, Chet? Starin' at your little news lady like she's somethin' special?"

"Nah, baby, I was just tryin' to get our message out. I'm here as a patriot, you know, protectin' our freedoms."

Jolene stepped in close, tilting her chin up at him, her finger just shy of his nose.

"Yeah, well, you just make sure that's the only thing you're gettin' out, or God help you, Chet Daniels..."

"Yes, ma'am." Chet swallowed hard and nodded. He might've been in charge of this chapter of GGGOD, but he damn sure wasn't in charge at home.

The day dragged on, Florida's heat and humidity clinging to the militia like a second skin. Outside the school, they stood their ground, sweat beading on brows, rifles slung at the ready. Every so often, a patrol car crawled past, officers inside watching the assembly with quiet hope that things would stay peaceful.

The school bell rang, its shrill pitch cutting through the thick air, stretching out longer than it should. Someone muttered, "Just a few more hours."

Brandi snapped, "Hold your positions. Wars ain't won by losin' battles."

She yanked Chet down by the collar, close enough to feel her breath, but not for anything tender.
"You better keep these men in line and quit their hollerin'. What kind of regiment you runnin' here, man?"

Chet was beginning to wonder about that himself. Funny, he didn't recall the history books mentioning how damn thirsty the Confederacy must've been in the hot sun.

Gunman Control Center: Omaha Nebraska.

In the Gunman Control Center, Omaha there was a restless urgency with no particular use of the pent-up energy and frustration. Jordan was all out of routine; there had been numerous deployments of The Gunman, but they were far from a regular occurrence. He mostly kept to his routine of hanging about and going to the bathroom as often as possible.

There were more staff on deck today, and ancillary staff in the outer offers adjacent to the command room. They were needed to monitor the huge number of protests taking part across the country. Jordan held a tightness in his stomach, but that was nothing out of the ordinary for a man of his experience. Tensions were high across the nation, people used phrases like 'civil war, uprising and attack on America'.

He generally wasn't allowed access to social media, but he heard whispers. The country was divisive, torn between the mild concern for the inconvenience of school massacres, the fact that they had for the most part been stopped and the price they had for doing so. There was no tangible effect on the average person, yet the perception of the erosion of liberties and freedoms was enough to ruffle the most sensible citizen. Personally, Jordan didn't know, he ached for peace both within the nation and his mind. There would be no peace today though, frantic communications flowed through the command center, false reports and alarms. People were on high alert. The GGGOD protests, as had been explain to him by McMann—onsite today, which was unusual, but justified due to the tension, involved "stupid fuckers who think they're smarter than the US government despite the overwhelming evidence that our program is the greatest improvement to safety in the history of the world".

California and New York had their share of demonstrations, but the numbers paled in comparison to the fervor seen in Texas and Florida. The loudest crowds gathered in Arizona, Wyoming, and Kentucky, where opposition to federal overreach ran deep. Even in battleground states like Pennsylvania and Ohio, protests flared up, with rural areas clashing against urban skepticism.

It was only noon, and the stress and restlessness was wearing down the staff of the center. It was going to be a long day. It was going to be a long war.

Liberty Oaks High School

Detective Marcus Hensley pulled up and parked his nondescript, unmarked Chevrolet Impala a little way up the street from the entrance to Liberty Oaks High School. He was working alone today, in plain clothes as usual—his badge tucked beneath his T-shirt on a chain, easily accessible when needed, but discreet enough not to draw attention when it wasn't. His service weapon, on the other hand, was harder to conceal.

He'd been called out to the school to investigate yet another incident—one of these asshole kids using AI to generate pornographic images with the faces of their female classmates. The victim in this case was a Black student, so the captain had assigned him. It would've been better to have a Black female officer handle it, but there weren't any currently in the Special Victims Unit.

The captain had been blunt in his directive:

"Hensley, you've got a young, non-threatening pretty face—you're interviewing the fake porn victim."

He understood the sentiment. The captain genuinely cared about victims, even if her delivery sometimes lacked finesse.

The school was required to report it immediately, of course. But Hensley knew all too well how difficult it was to actually track down the culprit. These little motherfuckers doing this to young girls—it was an ongoing problem, growing more frequent and more complex by the month. Child exploitation, harassment, cybercrime, defamation. It was a legal minefield.

Why couldn't people just not be assholes? he wondered as he stepped out of the car.

Speaking of assholes—the picket line of protesters from the UFAA stretched along the perimeter of the school grounds.

What were these idiots calling themselves again? GOD or something? There'd been a briefing about them during shift change that morning. A heads-up to tread carefully. Tensions were running high.

Hensley didn't really have a strong opinion on the Gunman program, other than being amazed at the financial resources it was soaking up—especially when most police departments were chronically underfunded. It was just the new reality. We've got robots doing police work now.

Detective Hensley surveyed the group of GOD members. That many white dudes with guns in one place made him nervous.

Chet Daniels shifted his weight, fatigue beginning to wear him down. The tactical gear pressed heavily against his pudgy frame, sweat beading on his brow. Being a patriot and a soldier was hard work. He glanced at Brandi, who suddenly froze—her entire body stiffening like a coiled spring.

"Gun! Chet!" she barked, pointing down the street. "That man coming this way—he's got a concealed gun! That Black man, he's got a gun!"

"Gun!" The alarm spread through the crowd, echoed by a jittery GGGOD member—a young, wide-eyed kid with a mullet and a rifle far too big for his skinny frame.

Chet hesitated only a split second, deciding which of his many firearms to use. The AR-15. Most suitable for a threat like this.

The protesters erupted in chaos. He yanked the strap over his head, raised the rifle to his shoulder, clicked off the safety, and took aim. People screamed, some reaching for their own weapons, as the red dot sight locked onto the center mass of the approaching man.

Then came the cracks.

BANG. BANG. BANG. BANG.

Sharp and loud. The air hissed with the speed of the rounds. They tore into the young Black man's chest. One ricocheted off something metallic. Three hits to the torso and heart. He collapsed. Blood bloomed through his shirt and spread across the concrete. Chet's rifle still smoked, spent casings clinking to the pavement. The red dot remained, steady on the body now lying still.

A stunned silence fell over the crowd.

Inside the school entrance, a security officer fumbled for his phone and hit the Gunman panic alarm.

The skinny kid, now full of bravado, stepped forward and rolled the man onto his back. He lifted the shirt to reveal a holstered Glock.

"This is weird," he muttered. "Why would he show up with just a handgun?" He tugged on a chain around the man's neck, pulling it free from under the shirt. A badge.

"Y'all, that's a damn cop right there!" he screamed. Panic twisted his face as he shoved past people and ran. "Nah, bro, I ain't part of this!"

Brandi's voice cracked like a whip. "Chet, goddamn it—you shot a cop!"

Chet stood frozen, his rifle still in his hands. "I didn't know. Them kind of folks—them colored boys, they look like grown men when they still young. I just thought he was lookin' for trouble. He found it, didn't he? Should've had his badge out if he's gonna walk up on us like that."

In Omaha, a voice rang out.

"Jacksonville, Florida! Liberty Oaks High! Panic alarm triggered. ID belongs to a school S.O."

"Get me intel!" the commanding officer barked, snapping the room into action.

"Shots fired—no further details," another officer confirmed.

The commanding officer didn't hesitate. "Deploy Gunman."

Jordan moved on instinct. He dove into the control capsule and synced with the suit. A fist slammed the launch button. Another technician hit the dual-confirmation switch. The drone launched from Mayport Naval Station. Propulsion systems roared to life, AI calculating the fastest trajectory. It screamed across the sky—fifteen miles in under sixty seconds.

McMann was in the room now. Jordan couldn't see him through the VR headset, but the voice was unmistakable—and so was the phrasing:

"Go get those Walmart Warrior sons of bitches. Fuckin' Y'all-Qaeda—they're worse than the real terrorists."

Beneath the chaos, Detective Hensley stood still. He knew this was it. The mob's rifles danced above him, polished barrels glinting in the sun. He exhaled, heavy and final. Eyes closed.

A streak of white split the sky—smooth, merciless, machine-perfect. The drone arrived. And there, on the pavement, Detective Hensley died.

Killed by the Good Guys with Guns.

The mob spotted the drone as it slowed and descended. Jordan readied the suit for deployment.
On the ground, Chet Daniels trembled. His hands were stained with a cop's blood. His rifle still smoked. The crowd murmured, some crying.

Brandi screeched, "It's the goddamn Gunman—shoot that sonofabitch down!"

Her bloodlust hadn't been satisfied.

The mob raised their rifles skyward.

"**FIRE AT WILL!**" Brandi screamed.

They obeyed. Twenty rifles opened fire.

Chet stood frozen, staring at Hensley's body. "Goddammit, Chet—MOVE!" his wife shouted.

He raised his rifle haphazardly. Bullets ripped through the drone's rotors, sparks flying. The drone—a marvel of tech —could withstand moderate gunfire. But not this. The suit wasn't hit, but the drone was done. It spiraled down. Crashing onto a passing car that had stopped a hundred feet up the road. Steel and circuitry crushed the vehicle's cabin.

The Good Guys with Guns advanced on the wreck.

Brandi raised a hand. "Hold your fire—civvies in play!"

In the control room, Jordan shouted, "I'm down! I've been shot down—the suit's dead, nonresponsive!"

McMann scanned the monitors. "The suit's destroyed. Shit— we're down."

Jordan thrashed inside the control pod. Hopeless. He had seen the officer on the ground. Now, there was no way to save him— if he was even alive.

The commanding officer was stunned. This wasn't in the playbook. Shot down by amateurs?

He turned to McMann. "Deploy another suit? We can get one there in ten minutes."

McMann was quiet. Too quiet. His usual swagger gone. His voice cut cold and flat:

"No. Let local law enforcement handle it. But send a team to retrieve our hardware."

He turned and walked out.

Jordan watched him go, confused. This wasn't like McMann. The usual cold calculation had vanished. In its place, a heavy silence. Defeat hung in the air like smoke.

Jordan slumped. It settled in his gut. A slow, deep ache of failure.

The commanding officer stepped forward, his tone softened as much as it could be for a man of his background.

"You did everything you could. That was an unprecedented situation, sir." Jordan nodded. Humility washing over him.

The commander added, "We've still got a few hours left of the school day. I'll have someone bring you a cup of coffee."

Jordan blinked. The kindness caught him off guard. "Thank you," he said quietly.

He wasn't used to people being nice to him.

Reign was furious, of course. Rage surged through his lethargic body, channeled through his eyes—wide with maddened intensity. Lauren watched him make call after call, frantic and relentless, slamming the phone down after each one. Formalities were long forgotten. What spilled down the line was pure, unbridled venom—acidic and demeaning, directed at anyone who dared pick up.

This was going to end badly. There was no doubt in Lauren's mind.

He had already demanded a press conference. The halls of the White House were in disarray, a chaotic mess of fluster and noise. Everyone knew what was coming—Reign would explode, and the only way to survive was to facilitate whatever he needed, however outrageous the request.

By 7 p.m., all arrangements were finally in place. Nearly seven hours had passed since the events at Liberty Oaks High School, and every second had been spent scrambling. Lauren coordinated people and logistics with obsessive focus, losing herself in the tasks, using the chaos as a temporary reprieve from questioning her own role in it all.

Reign had insisted on optics. He wanted someone from the Black community to stand in for the slain detective and another figure to represent the victims of the drone-crushed car. The latter was easy—a distant relative lured in with the promise of a free trip to D.C., a few nights in a high-end hotel, and, just for good measure, a $5,000 cash bonus. Overkill, it seemed.

The Black community was a harder sell. No one was volunteering—until luck delivered a pastor who had known the detective. He was hesitant at first, but the offer of a national platform to speak for Black lives eventually won him over.

But once inside the White House, he quickly discovered the true cost of political theater.

Lauren felt bile rise in her throat. She knew the nausea would pass with a couple of Xanax later. The pastor was proud—controlled in speech, commanding in tone. But when Lauren calmly explained the consequences of deviation, the illusion shattered.

If he tried to turn the press conference into a political statement, the FBI would be more than happy to "discover" a string of backdated dating profiles, exposing his supposed fetish for subservience and domination by big, Black, beautiful women. What would his wife think?

His expression changed immediately—eyes wide in horror. He protested, vehemently, but the realization set in fast: he wasn't ready to play politics at this level. When he asked how Lauren could live with herself, she brushed the question off. But his words echoed in her mind, as she knew they would later, whispering in the dark just before she numbed herself to sleep —bitterly, and with two Xanax.

Meanwhile, the final details were falling into place. Only a handful of pre-approved reporters would be allowed in. Security was tight. Every protocol enforced to the highest standard before access to the Rose Garden was granted.

There was a time when Lauren had felt exhilarated by the fast pace of White House life. Now, standing in the shadows as camera flashes lit up the garden, she watched Reign striding across the lawn, maintaining the illusion of a man in control. He smiled and waved despite the fury simmering beneath the surface. He joined the pastor and the "relative" onstage.

Lauren felt the familiar ache in her soul—like a slow-growing cancer, poisoning her from the inside out. She stood opposite the press pit, beside the carefully tended roses, their sweet scent floating in the air, sickening in its contrast to the ugliness about to unfold.

Reign took the podium, framed by the elegance of the Oval Office windows and manicured hedges.
"Today," he began, his voice strained as he tried to contain his fury, "we are mourning lives lost to a tragic, senseless act. A detective—a hero—and two innocent Americans, taken from us by the very technology meant to protect them!"

He gripped the podium, jaw clenched, regaining his composure.

"You know, I said a few months ago, I said, 'Hey, we're not going to offer thoughts and prayers anymore. We're going to solve the problem.' But here we are—offering thoughts and prayers."

His anger began to crystallize into something more focused. This was his element. The stage. The spotlight. It was a drug to him.

Reign believed in Reign—and everything that entailed.

He motioned to the pastor standing solemnly at his side—a man now overflowing with the kind of patriotic cooperation one might expect from someone whose wife was about to receive anonymous emails advertising illicit services. Fabricated or not, doubt is a seed. It lies in the dirt until, one day, it blooms into something hideous.

"Pastor, folks—here we have a man from the Black community. A pastor from Florida. A man of God who knew the detective murdered today by the UFAA and their radicals. Pastor Omari Bennett, what do you have to say about the murder of this member of your community?"

Reign added, with a flourish, "And folks—he was a brave police officer. As you all know, I'm a big supporter of the police. This officer was attending a routine call, investigating some very nasty stuff. Criminals created some disgusting images of a girl—a beautiful young woman. This man was murdered by fanatics. Pastor Bennett, what would you like to say to America tonight?"

Pastor Bennett cleared his throat, stepping toward the microphone. He was stiff, uncertain, and paused awkwardly before beginning.

"This is a tragedy. A man who served and protected his community is gone—taken by violence. We should all mourn him, no matter our differences. I pray for his family, and I pray for healing in this nation, because right now... we are lost. Justice must be served, but we must also seek understanding. Hatred won't bring this officer back."

He paused again, the memorized lines falling flat now.

"May God be with Detective Marcus Hensley's family. And may He be with us all."

Reign nodded as Bennett stepped back, clapping him on the shoulder like a pet that had performed its trick. "That's right, Pastor. Very nice. Very thoughtful."

Then his tone hardened. "But folks, let's be clear. A police officer—a good man—was murdered. And who do we have to thank for that? The UFAA and their radical supporters. You know who else they killed today? An elderly couple. Just driving near the school. Shot down by the Gunman drone suit after it was brought out of the sky. That's an act of terror—on American soil."

He shook his head, letting the words linger.

"I'm going to introduce you to a relative of the victims. Folks, these were hard-working Americans. Retired to Florida. Imagine that—spending your whole life working, only to be murdered by people who call themselves the 'Good Guys on Defense.' Who are they defending? It's not brave to kill retirees."

A woman stepped forward, eyes blinking in the lights. Her hands were clenched, her voice shaky and rehearsed.

"My name is Diane Walker, and I'm here tonight because my aunt and uncle, Harold and Linda Mayfield, were taken from us in a senseless act of violence. They were good, honest, hardworking Americans. They didn't deserve to die."

She glanced at Reign.

"They were just going to the store. Like we all do. And then— boom. The Gunman drone crashes down. They didn't stand a chance. And now my family's left to pick up the pieces, while the people responsible try act like their fighting in the Civil war."

She looked down, then back at the crowd.

"We need justice. We need answers. And we need strong leadership of President Reign that won't let this happen again. Thank you, and God bless America."

Reign beamed, barely concealing his glee. Lauren braced herself. She could feel it coming—the moment. The explosion. She didn't know what kind of bomb it would be, but it was about to go off.
He returned to the podium.

"Fellow Americans, today we witnessed a terrorist attack—on American soil. Carried out by the United Firearm Advocates Association. Let me tell you something, folks—the only thing they advocate for is violence against this country."

He leaned in, almost spitting the words.

"The United Firearm Advocates Association. Today, they mobilized their guerrilla armies in an attack on our safety. So tonight, I am signing an executive order classifying the UFAA as a terrorist organization."

The press pool erupted. Flashes burst like lightning. Reporters shouted over one another.
Lauren's heart pounded. Her thoughts spiraled.

Oh God, no. Why?

The noise, the lights—it all blurred. Her mind fragmented, overwhelmed. She grasped for clarity and couldn't find it.

Breathe. Steady.

This would never work. The executive order was theater. A threat with no substance.

She forced herself to act. Reaching into her handbag, she pulled out her phone and blocked Alicia Turner's number with practiced precision.

No tremble. No shake. Not yet.

Too many cameras.

Too many eyes.

CHAPTER 30: MASON INVESTIGATES

It was just before 11 p.m. when Lauren readied herself for bed. Or, at least, she was getting into bed. The weight of the day sat heavily on her chest, but the racing thoughts in her mind were far too much for her to quiet. She had swallowed a Xanax and an OxyContin pill earlier, hoping it would dull the chaos in her brain. As the drugs began to take effect, her reality softened, and she started to float in and out of her own head.

But then, the ringtone shattered her fugue— a jarring, high-pitched tone that felt wrong, foreign. It wasn't her cell phone. It was the burner phone, hidden deep in the bottom of her bedside drawer under a sleep mask and a trashy romance novel she'd never finished.

Her fingers fumbled as she dug through the drawer, clumsy from the sedatives, struggling to unlock the device and answer the call. The low hum of the ringing seemed to fill her ears until she finally managed to press 'accept.'

"Lauren?" The voice on the other end was unmistakable. It was him. Of course, it was. Nobody else had this number. It had been carefully arranged. Safer to talk through burners than risk being overheard. Only her apartment, and even then, only when she made sure everything else was secure, was safe enough for conversations like this.

"Mason, I'm here..." she answered, her voice feeling distant even to herself.

"Alright, Lauren, listen carefully. I need you to pay close

attention. After I tell you this, you'll confirm you understand, then hang up. Understood?" His voice was authoritative, clipped. There was a cold certainty in the way he spoke, a flush of excitement deep inside her. His voice had power over her, even now. She tried to focus through the fog in her mind, pushing past the haze to stay alert.

"Yes," she said, the word slipping from her lips like a confession. Obedient. Yielding.

"Okay," Mason continued, a pause in his words as though making sure she was listening. "First, we need to be damn careful. Don't trust anyone right now. The FBI? It's all a fucking joke. You think they're the good guys? More like glorified bureaucrats. Trust no one—especially in the Bureau. There are moles, traitors, and a whole bunch of dirty, compromised shitheads. The real work's not written up and documented in an official report, you know?"

"Yes, Mason, I know that," she said, her voice shaking slightly, despite her attempts to steady herself.

Mason's voice softened but grew darker. "Now here's the shit that matters. The kid who did the shooting at Hope Valley? You know what they didn't release? The toxicology report was buried. The kid had high levels of Scopolamine and Phencyclidine in his system. Scopolamine's also known as Devil's Breath. That shit's no joke. And Phencyclidine—PCP. Together? It's a fucking cocktail for chaos."

Lauren felt her pulse spike. Her mind struggled to catch up, the words swimming through her head like they didn't belong in the same sentence. "Wait, Mason. What are you talking about? These drugs? What?"

"Devil's Breath and PCP. Combined? It makes a normal person violent, paranoid, out of control—confused as hell. But when you have someone with mental health issues already, it's like handing a loaded gun to a guy locked in a fucking prison. You understand?" His voice was sharp, each word cutting through the fog in her head.

She swallowed, trying to process it. "That... would make him a good person to agitate and send into a school if that was your intention," she whispered, more to herself than to Mason.

"Exactly," Mason said with grim satisfaction. "And there's more. There were other bullet casings at that school. They don't match any of the firearms the kid used, or Peck's gun or Rodriguez's gun. So unless the kid had another gun that he hid somewhere in that school, and nobody has been able to find it after extensive fucking searches..."

She felt it. The awful feeling of betrayal, heartbreak, and absolute fear. "Mason... do you understand what you're suggesting here?"

"Lauren," he sighed heavily. "You know I think the world of you. You're one of the smartest people I've ever met; you're fucking gorgeous, and I'm always thinking about those legs that go all the way up and never end, but you're a kid from a privileged world and upbringing. There are evils in this world that you're not ready to understand. This shit gets people killed. And you—" He paused for a moment, his voice low. "You've asked me to pull back the curtain. But you're not ready for what's behind it. You wanted to know? Are you sure you want to know this shit, Lauren, or do you want to go on in denial?"

His words stung a little, but he wasn't wrong. Still, she felt the weight of them. Too much. It was too much to absorb all at once. She was numb, but the undercurrent of fear ran deep, somewhere in her chest, where her heart was trying to fight against her rising panic and that damn feeling again—her stomach falling and falling.

"How do you know all of this?" she asked, her voice hoarse now.

"I broke into Reign's office," Mason admitted, the words heavy and reckless. "Went through his shit. He's a slob. Files everywhere. Couldn't give a shit about national security. Fucking moron."

Her pulse quickened, her head spinning, fighting against the fogginess from her bedtime cocktail. "OK, OK, so you think someone else was involved in Hope Valley... is there anything else?"

He hesitated before answering, and when he did, it was with the weight of someone revealing too much. "Tariq Al-Zahir —the gas explosion? That's what you know. What you don't know is that there was a sniper round in his head. The report's in his office, Lauren. Right there. Evidence. I have no idea why they shot him and blew him up at the same time."

Lauren's mind raced, struggling to connect all the dots. Her breath caught in her throat. Her hand shook as she clutched the phone tighter. What was she supposed to do with all this? Mason's words hung in the air, suffocating her. She wanted to shut it all out, block it from her mind. But now that she knew, there was no going back.

"Lauren, I've got to get off this line, and so do you. Do not do anything with this information at this stage. Do you understand?"

"Yes, I understand." Sudden silence on the line. Lauren was unsure if he had ended the call.

"I love you," she whispered into the dead air. But there was no response. No reassurance. Just a cold click. The line went dead.

In downtown Washington, Mason gripped the wheel of his personal vehicle tightly, alert and focused on his surroundings. His eyes constantly scanned the movement of vehicles around him, checking the rearview mirror to ensure the headlights behind him held no pattern or rhythm.

He kept moving when he made the call to Lauren. It was dark, and he didn't want his senses dulled while talking and monitoring his physical surroundings. There were only so many things a man could focus on at once.

He'd been too harsh on her—angry, confused, and a little resentful. She had asked him to look, and now he couldn't un-look. He'd apologize to her in person. He hadn't meant it. She was right to ask him; this was some high-level shit. It didn't get much higher than this. He wondered what life would look like as a whistleblower if he took it to the media. Maybe Lauren would do it; she'd weather it out better than he would. He'd never work again. She could use it, weaponize her position. He'd lose everything.

The red light ahead forced him to stop. On the pavement to the left, a war veteran sat on the cold, heartless street with a sign identifying his service, asking for money for food.

"Thank you for your service," Mason muttered to himself, thinking of Peck and the Gunman program. He wondered what would become of him if he ever made it out of the situation he found himself in. That guy was a ticking bomb —his flinching stability barely concealed beneath the façade of his marketed image. That thousand-yard stare betrayed the inevitable detonation.

It was just after 11 PM now. The traffic lights felt out of sequence, taking too long to change. Paranoia, maybe. But that didn't mean they weren't after him.

It was only another ten miles to his home, to his wife and two young daughters. At this time of night, the drive would take about 20 minutes. No one would be reckless enough to hit a Secret Service agent at home, not with his family there.

Behind him, a vehicle pulled up slowly, determined, coming way too close to the rear of his car at this late hour. Mason paid full attention to the glare of light in the rearview mirror and the pending green signal. The very last thing he noticed was a flash of movement to his right.

Death for Mason was neither painful nor conscious. He existed in one moment, and then, the next, he did not. The bullet from the assailant easily penetrated the passenger-side window at close range, passing through his skull and out into the street, executing an awful finality to it all. The homeless veteran scrambled in fear at the sound of gunfire.

CHAPTER 31: DEATH BECOME US

It had been almost a week since he was murdered. Nearly a week and fifteen minutes since they last spoke. The words from that final conversation kept rattling around in her head like a roller coaster that never stopped at the platform. She was sick of riding it—moments of exhilaration in the split seconds she momentarily forgot he was dead, followed by a rapid plunge into the depths of grief and despair.

She knew her mind couldn't take much more of this existence. The pressure was building inside her head; her thoughts offered no solace, no injunction for rest. She needed rest—desperately—but there was no escaping herself.

Staff and aides had stopped by her office to offer condolences for the loss of her primary protective agent, unaware of the depth of that loss. She felt like a fraud, hiding beneath the superficial expressions of sorrow for what they assumed was a professional relationship.

The FBI had taken point on the investigation. He'd been off duty at the time, and there was no apparent link to his work. A carjacking gone wrong—that was the prevailing theory. Not much more to it. He was shot in his car, from the passenger side, while stopped at a light downtown. No threats had been made against Lauren, her office, or the president. If the FBI said it was a carjacking, then that was it. That was a much cleaner, neater conclusion than a complex conspiracy implicating people who could not afford to be implicated.

The president had called her in to speak about it. Completely devoid of human emotion, he promised to get "the very best investigators at the FBI" on the case. "They had some very good agents there, the best." He wasn't about to let them assign "some DEI hires to fumble the investigation." Then, as if that covered everything, he added that he would get her another suitably qualified Secret Service bodyguard.

The funeral was scheduled for the middle of the following week. A couple of days after the murder, Lauren made the obligatory call to his wife. Her heart pounded with terror. Words fumbled—stuck somewhere between her mind and tongue—lacking eloquence or structure. Guilt purged her thoughts. What if she knew? Knew everything? Lauren could wear her professional title as proudly as she wanted, but beneath the façade, she was a liar, a manipulator, a woman without morals. Dissolute and debauched, she had used her body and mind to ensnare this man—squandering his life for her own needs.

She didn't want to call. Not at all. She fumbled around with the handset in her office, the phone number jotted down beside her. It took several attempts to dial correctly—the tone would cut out before she finished. When she finally entered the numbers fast enough, the ringing thundered in her ears so loudly it startled her, and she inhaled sharply, her body flinching. The conversation was terse and contrived, flowing as naturally as water uphill. His wife was as courteous as could be expected, but abrupt. She didn't want Lauren's thoughts and prayers any more than the parents of school shooting victims wanted them. She just wanted her husband—the father of her child—back.

It was by mere chance that she came across Jordan Peck in the White House corridors that morning. An unscheduled photo op with the president—another media stunt. Propaganda, she supposed, if she was being honest. Or maybe it wasn't unscheduled. She couldn't keep pace anymore. The cracks were beginning to show in what had once been her perfectly managed professional life.

Her personal life had always been barren: no real relationships, a disorganized apartment, a near-empty fridge, no interests outside of work—but dammit, she had been good at her job. Not anymore. It didn't matter. She was adapting to a new routine: pretending she was in control, functioning like an addict, dulled by exhaustion and a carefully calibrated mix of prescription medication to numb the pain.

She should get out—out of this job, out of Washington. But she couldn't. She was trapped. If she ran, they'd know she knew the things she pretended not to. It had to be McMann. Maybe he didn't need to kill her—she was already pinned in place. She couldn't walk down a hallway without a dozen people wanting a piece of her.

She was surprised to see Jordan exiting the president's office. Something was off. He was massive, powerful, but diminished somehow—like a loyal dog that had just been beaten by its owner. A far cry from the action figures and official photos that framed him as the embodiment of American justice and ingenuity. Now, he was alone, lumbering down the hallway with a clunky, unnatural gait.

Lauren didn't know what compelled her. Despair, anger at her own imprisonment in the political machine, Mason's death... or maybe it was just poor judgment dulled by medication. Whatever the reason, she acted without thinking—timing it perfectly as the hallway emptied like the parting of the Red Sea.

She grabbed the fabric of his jacket and pulled him into her office, slamming the door shut. He didn't resist, allowing her to guide him—her willowy frame like a tugboat hauling a freighter. She pushed him gently against the closed door, his mass more than enough to deter anyone from interrupting.

She stepped closer, the way she'd seen the president do countless times, weaponizing proximity. But her reasonable height was dwarfed by him—even in heels, she couldn't meet his eyes. This approach felt wrong. She stepped back, recalibrated, and then unloaded everything. Her delivery was precise and passionate—an execution of facts as clean as it was damning.

She told him what she knew: that Mason had been killed because he asked the wrong questions, that the Gunman Protocol was being used for clandestine ops. He showed no reaction. No response. No emotion. Just... stillness. His eyes didn't look at her. They looked through her.

But then she said it—the words that ignited something behind those empty eyes.

"There's some suggestion—evidence—that the Hope Valley Massacre was assisted by some kind of outside force..."

"What the fuck do you mean?" he asked. His voice was calm—but it was the calm at the eye of a hurricane.

"There were other bullet casings in that school that didn't belong to Lamar Williams. Or your partner. Or your weapon."

And then... he was gone again. The flicker of life vanished. His face emptied. His eyes—God, those eyes—so vacant and yet somehow filled with everything at once. Lauren was terrified. She had made a terrible mistake. A catastrophic miscalculation.

Oh God... was it treason?

It was treason. She was going to disappear. Military prison. An "accident" like Mason. No—wait—it wasn't treason. Unless Reign spun it that way. Was it aiding the UFAA? She couldn't think.

Dammit, Lauren, think. She wasn't giving aid to enemies or levying war against the U.S. No, it was just espionage. Disclosure of classified information. Fuck—it was conspiracy.

She collapsed to the floor, nauseous and shaking, curling into the fetal position. Peck just stared, unmoved. She lay there for what felt like forever, hyperventilating, lost. She was alone. She had no one. Nothing. She was dead already. Pulling herself up, tears streaked down her face.

"Please... help me."

He just stared. That vacant, inhuman stare. She wanted to hit him. Mason was gone, and she was left with this hollow shell.

Eventually, he spoke.

"Lauren... give me a way to contact you. Off the record."

She hesitated. The burner phone. Bottom drawer. Hidden under the paperback novel and her personal items. That was the only way. But giving it to him meant giving the government everything they needed to prove collusion. Espionage. Treason.

She walked to her desk, scribbled the number onto a scrap of paper, attempting to disguise her handwriting. It wouldn't matter. The FBI, the CIA, the Secret Service—they could prove whatever case they needed. Her prosecution would benefit Reign. He could show no one was above the law—if it suited him. Draining the swamp. She had nothing left to lose.

Peck took the paper, folded it, tucked it into his pocket, and left.

Almost immediately, a female aide appeared at the door, knocking once before stepping inside. She announced a revision to the president's briefing schedule and emphasized the need for Lauren's approval on a minor wording change in his upcoming remarks.

She glanced at Lauren—disheveled, pale, eyes red, clothes wrinkled—and tilted her head with a smug little smile.

"You're a lucky girl. Wouldn't mind a few minutes with him myself," she said with a smirk.
Lauren didn't acknowledge it.

She had fucked him all right.

Just like Mason.

CHAPTER 32: GOOD INTENTIONS

Vic Rodriguez unzipped his black duffel bag with a quick, smooth motion. The sound of the zipper reminded him of a dozen other times in his life—packing most of his worldly possessions into a bag and heading out, never really sure if he'd come home again. Not that it really mattered. He didn't have a home anyway.

All he had ever had was the army—and now, his diminished role as a police officer. His career had become a fragment of the semi-tolerable existence he once knew before Hope Valley. Working a desk, writing reports, filing paperwork? That wasn't him. He was handy with tech in the field—give him a battlefield tactical assault computer and some geospatial software any day. Data entry at the precinct? Hell no.

His country—well, the one he resided in now, anyway—had given him the opportunity to be taken whole, shattered into pieces, and reassembled with precision into someone trained to kill with efficiency and vengeance. Jordy was the same, except he'd fared much better after Hope Valley. At least career-wise. There wasn't much else for a man like Vic to do around here.
Honestly, he didn't really care if he lived or died. He missed the action. But he was terrified of it, too.

Still, Jordy was, in a way, a brother to him. And when a brother calls on you? That's an honor you answer—especially when it's someone who's had your back for years on the streets of Philly. They'd saved each other more times than they could count.

Besides, a man who's seen the horrors of war, the destitution of urban policing, and the soul-wrenching aftermath of a school massacre—each one worse than the last in a trilogy of boundless terror—doesn't usually live long. Men like that either die young on their own terms, or they fade into old age, withering, atrophying, pissing themselves in a bed somewhere while their minds replay dementia-riddled flashbacks of a pile of children's bodies stacked in the corner of a classroom.

Yeah, there weren't many options left for men like Vic and Jordy.

It was time to leave the apartment. He glanced around as if it might be the last time he'd ever see the place. He didn't care. It was nondescript, functional. He didn't bother with many possessions—just essential furniture and a PlayStation for first-person shooters that helped release something buried deep inside him, something he didn't fully understand. He considered grabbing one of the novels on a shelf, then changed his mind. Reading bored him. Still, it might serve a purpose —like shielding him from someone's gaze or suspicions. He grabbed a book anyway.

He was ready. He checked his reflection in the mirror. It was fine—discreet. Nothing to draw attention. Nothing memorable. Bland. Boring. He was an average-looking man. No one would remember him. Of course, if this went wrong, **everyone** would remember him—for a very long time. He had an exit plan. But if it failed? He could live with dying.

He had planned the journey meticulously—approximately twenty-six hours of travel. He'd nap during one leg of the trip. That was no big deal. He could sleep standing up if he had to. The first step was the subway to the Greyhound terminal on Filbert Street. He arrived just before 7 p.m., blending effortlessly with the evening commuters, using cash to buy a ticket before boarding the bus to Harrisburg. Everyone was distracted—on their phones, a few reading.

Bigger issues loomed—rumors of civil war, states openly discussing secession. It was the closest the country had come to the edge in a long time. War felt imminent. Tension gripped every corner of America. Anger, hostility, restlessness, and paranoia—thick in the air for anyone old enough to understand.

The bus pulled away, and the familiar world faded. Outside the window, the landscape rolled by—at once familiar and foreign. The same chain stores and brands, just in different buildings. The low hum of the engine and occasional rattle of the frame offered him a strange comfort.

The next leg was Amtrak to Pittsburgh. He arrived just after 9 p.m., using a burner phone to call a taxi. That was crucial —if the phone were ever traced, it would only tie him to Harrisburg, a place he'd never actually visited before.

The cab ride lasted ten minutes, paid for in cash, of course. The air inside was stale, matching the silent, strained atmosphere. Vic didn't enjoy being unfriendly, but he couldn't risk leaving a lasting impression.

The station was quieter now, its lights dimmed for the night. The ride to Pittsburgh wasn't bad—mostly empty. No one wanted to talk, not at that hour. Everyone else looked just as tired and indifferent. He took a window seat, his duffel bag secured between his legs. The train's gentle rhythm lulled him into a nap.

The journey took five hours. When he stepped off the train, it was past 3 a.m. Pittsburgh was quiet, but not enough to make him careless. He moved with purpose, no hesitation in his step. From there, he caught a Megabus to Chicago.

Cops were dumb—he knew plenty of them. The FBI? Probably not as dumb, but still. He was betting they wouldn't connect the dots. Not for a while, anyway—and even then, it'd take some luck. There would be traces, sure. There always were. But it would require an extraordinary turn of events to uncover the full truth.

Nine hours later, walking a short distance from the Chicago station, the city's bustle offered him invisibility. He didn't expose enough of his features to be identified by cameras. And besides, who was checking bus stations in Chicago? If they were, well—then hats off to them.

He could still abandon the mission. The point of no return hadn't been reached. So far, he'd committed no crime. Just a long, odd road trip across the states. No one would ever know. And that was the problem—**no one** would know. He didn't have anyone. His movements, though calculated and discreet, were invisible to the world. He could simply vanish. Aside from a few dumbass cops he worked with, no one would even notice.

But if he followed through, he could leave an indelible mark on history. He could have just as easily died in a foreign land and been buried with a military funeral—forgotten after a few years by the handful of people who once called him a friend.

Maybe he should've left a note back at the apartment.

This was the final leg now—a FlixBus. Perfect for a budget-conscious traveler like himself. They still took cash. Unfortunately, he wouldn't be writing a glowing review. But he would have, if things were different. He decided to take another nap. The novelty of cross-country travel had long worn off.

Nearly nine hours later, he arrived.

He used a payphone inside the bus station to call a cab, directing it to a location a couple of miles from the real destination—just outside the main part of town. He walked the last stretch. He had time to kill. He grabbed a large coffee from a gas station and found a dark, empty park. A bench beneath tall trees gave him the cover he needed.

He'd already scoped it out on a map, but it was even better in person. Shadowed. Isolated. As risky as it was to stay still in public, there was no other option. Otherwise, he'd create a witness—and killing a random cab driver wasn't something that would help him sleep any better.

And besides, timing mattered. This needed to go down in the early morning hours.

It was a little after 9 p.m. now.

Just a few more hours hiding in the dark.

CHAPTER 33: OF NO GOOD, COMES AFTER 2AM

Her eyelids grew heavy, tugging downward and cocooning her inside her mind—a place she didn't want to be. Intermittently, she closed her eyes and checked the time on her phone, consciousness slipping in and out. Each time, the clock had leapt forward. Each leap more agitating than the last. She just wanted to sleep through the night. Bedtime had passed over three hours ago, and her nightcap of prescription meds— combined in ways God never intended—was failing her.

So, too, had her personal collection of toys in the bottom drawer of her bedside table. The same drawer where she kept her burner phone, as though she were some kind of secret agent.

Realistically, she was neither—just a grown woman with no real friends, shadowed all day by people assigned to protect her. That might've been worse than the unknown people who wanted her dead. It seemed like everyone these days wanted to kill her. She was a nice person. She didn't deserve that.

She played with the idea of giving one of the toys another go, a distraction from the fear and panic inside her. Her chest was heavy, her heart fluttering so violently she was sure she was shaving years off her life. No. She wasn't interested in vibrating herself again. She needed solutions.

She should've taken a private-sector job out of college and married someone with a nice house in the suburbs. Someone like Mason.

That was it.

She tossed angrily, flipping over to bury her face in the pillows. She tried not to think of him, but now it was guaranteed—she wouldn't be sleeping for a couple more hours. Just in time to get up again.

God, she couldn't keep doing this—one of the most visible positions in the country. She couldn't keep up. Details were slipping. The President had noticed. His grace wouldn't last much longer. She'd be fired, dragged through the media, ridiculed. That would be bad enough—except that she'd probably be executed the same way Mason had been. Not right away. They'd wait until she was forgotten, replaced. But not long enough for the story to fade from the headlines.

She could already hear the commentary: a 38-year-old unmarried professional woman unraveling under pressure. Sleep deprivation had only accelerated the decline. Her face felt unfamiliar in the mirror—faint ghosts of old age in the lines, the sagging around her mouth and eyes. She didn't want to grow old and die alone.

She forced the thought of Mason away, but in the void came the intrusion of other sins.
Darius Greene.

His kindness. The way she'd helped steal his work. He had been restrained, intelligent enough to avoid attacking the administration—or her—directly. But she knew. He said it between the lines.
"I'm deeply disappointed by the direction this has taken," Darius had said. "But I remain committed to ethical innovation and trust that history will judge these actions accordingly."

Some men let hatred spill in ugly, acrimonious tones. Others held their tongues—letting silence do the heavy lifting of bitter disappointment. Lauren had memorized his words.

She'd scanned every media report after it came out. Reign, of course, spun Darius's minor assistance, only for Wolfe to be credited with the original idea that saved the day.

At least she could argue her actions helped end school violence. There hadn't been another massacre.

But the pastor she helped blackmail in Florida—that was a different story.

She wasn't sure about religion. She participated when it wormed its way into congressional proceedings, but as for what happened when you died? No clue. It seemed strange to think Mason might be up in heaven enjoying himself while his mistress and family lived in misery. The point was, blackmailing an honest man probably wouldn't go over well with God. She wondered if she could repent—if religion could still offer comfort.

McMann. She hated him. The way he spoke to her—condescending, belittling. The power he held over her. The fact that he would order her death, and the President wouldn't do a damn thing to stop it. Probably release a statement: she'd been involved in some *very bad stuff*. The worst kind of stuff.
Letting McMann get close to the President had been the greatest mistake of her career. They had created a monster by combining forces—and now it was unstoppable.

The fucking UFAA. Richardson. His guard dog, Turner. The pettiness didn't escape her, but the way Alicia had attacked her that day—*that* day Mason made that joke about her—was unforgettable. That was the day she first really noticed him.

And Alicia? She should've had her back. They were both in the same position, opposite sides of the same room. Why was it always other women who tried the hardest to pull you down? There was always another intern or aide, younger and perkier, ready to do whatever it took to get a leg up.

They all wanted her job.

Fine. Take it—if you think $200K a year is worth it. They were staring down the barrel of a civil war, and that still wasn't enough to make people come to their senses.

The phone rang.

She was lost in the recesses of her mind, confused and barely cogent. The burner phone. Its ringtone shrill and empty, the speaker tinny and cheap. She scrambled for it, ransacking the drawer until she found it.

No number.

She answered.

"Hello..." Just one word, two syllables—and all her fear came rushing in. Her voice was barely audible, the pitch shifting halfway through.

"I want you to be very clear with me. When you spoke with me in your office, you suggested the Hope Valley massacre was staged. Are you absolutely certain that's the truth?"

It was Peck. It had to be. She didn't know his voice well—he rarely spoke—but it had to be him.
"Yes... I'm as sure as I can be. We looked into it—"

"No. *Looking into it* isn't going to cut it. Do you know?"

All the clutter in her mind was gone now. The sharp tone of his voice had swept it away. The anger was palpable, bleeding through the speaker.

"Mason broke into Reign's office. I found an FBI report —confidential, restricted from release. There was another shooter. And the kid was drugged—to make him paranoid. Aggressive."

Silence.

She could hear him breathing heavily on the other end.

Then finally—

"Okay, Lauren. You think Reign was involved?"

"I don't know if he was directly involved... or just aware. I think McMann is running it all. I don't know how, or the ways he's controlling things—but Reign definitely knows. That's all I can tell you for certain."

She was unraveling, spewing information, rattled and irrational. She tried to rein it in.
"Jordan... Our nation is on the brink—of war, or collapse. The UFAA, the media—it's all heading toward a point of no return. Garrison's just the spokesperson. Turner—she's the brains. She controls him. She controls the UFAA.

You know what kind of men let women like that control them, Jordan? Weak men. Cowards. Men who watch while the brave fight their battles. Men who stand by while their brothers are slaughtered. While their country is ripped to pieces. But you're not like them, are you? You never have been."

Silence again. The emptiness of sound filled her ears.

"Jordan?"

Finally, he responded.

"All right. I want you to destroy the phone you're talking on as soon as we hang up. Then go back to bed. Try to sleep... And Miss Chalmers... I want you to promise you'll do something for me."

She shuddered. Terrified of whatever the next burden would be.

"That depends, Jordan... on what you're asking me."

CHAPTER 34: THE LIST

John McMann - 293
Derek Thorne - 043
Xavier Wolfe - 198
Alicia Turner - 354
Richard Garrison - 354
Douglas Reign - 449

Jordan had scribbled the names and numbers vertically on a small scrap of paper. He wasn't a man who spent much time with a pen in hand or danced effortlessly across a keyboard, the written word manifesting neatly on a screen. His handwriting was childlike and unsure, letters jumbled in his attempt to spell them correctly. A moot point—misspelled or not—the outcome wouldn't change. The pen might be mightier than the sword, but men like these didn't listen to peaceful, well-constructed arguments.

Besides, he had a pretty big sword. 448 swords, in fact.

There was always room for error in a plan like this. He and Vic had investigated hundreds of crimes—some simple, some complex. No matter how diligent the planning, no matter how thorough or brilliant, there was always a thread exposed. A single flaw could unravel everything, shining a light into the darkness.

Right now, that liability was Vic, waiting in a public park a couple of miles away, needing to make his way to the control center. All it would take was some beat cop responding to a call about a suspicious Mexican sitting alone in the park or drifting through the industrial zones surrounding the base. He'd likely be arrested. Maybe even shot. He was a suspicious-looking little fucker in the dark.

Jordan had made a promise to himself—he would get him out alive. Vic seemed nonchalant about the whole thing, but it mattered to Jordan that his friend made it. What happened after was out of his control, but Vic was a capable soldier, fluent in Spanish, of course. Plenty of countries he could disappear into. Or maybe he'd just stick to the plan—make it back to his apartment and play dumb. He was good at playing dumb. Maybe he just didn't care anymore, and Jordan could respect that.

The world had never felt right for them, no matter where they went or what they did.
In the end, it worked.

At a quarter to two in the morning, Jordan slipped out of his quarters in the command center—the might of the U.S. government, the pinnacle of security—grossly inept. Otherwise, he wouldn't have been able to escape through a service chute, make his way to the exterior fence, and slip past it undetected.

A few hundred yards down the road, he spotted Vic—hooded, wearing dark sunglasses in the middle of the night. As if he didn't look suspicious enough.

They embraced, Jordan's larger frame enveloping the smaller man. They didn't speak. There wasn't much to say. Jordan was sorry—for everything he could be, and even for the things he couldn't. Brothers sometimes fought. But they were still brothers.

"Let's move," Jordan said.

The two men hugged the shadows, using vehicles and buildings to obscure their movement. This was the point of no return. Five minutes ago, the worst outcome was Vic getting picked up by a local cop with no good reason to be where he was. That would have led straight back to Jordan, but there had still been plausible deniability.

Now? Now there was none.

The plan had consumed Jordan's thoughts ever since that woman at the White House pulled him into her office—a bigger mess than he was—babbling and collapsing onto the floor. She was right, and he knew it. She might not realize it, but what was about to go down? That was on her. If you're going to report a crime to the relevant authority, you'd better be ready for that authority to *do* something about it.

McMann was a crafty son of a bitch, his physicality exceeded only by his intelligence. Gruff, crass, designed to be underestimated—just like Jordan. For all the offensive nonsense McMann spewed, his words were carefully measured. He didn't make mistakes.
Except once.

Early in the training program, McMann had mentioned The Gunman had a built-in safeguard—a security measure to prevent a rogue operator. He caught himself immediately, but Jordan had already clocked it. It wasn't a dead man's switch —it was the opposite. Activation required a second person, positioned on the other side of the room. No lone wolf. No unsanctioned operations. A fail-safe against the very kind of betrayal McMann expected from everyone.

At the time, it had seemed irrelevant. Jordan was part of the protocol—why would he ever be alone in the command module? But now, it meant something. If Lauren was right, if The Gunman had been used for black ops hits, someone would have had to be in that room with Thorne. It had to be McMann. Or someone Thorne trusted enough to keep that kind of secret.

It could have been one of the inner-circle mercs at Warlord Peacecorp. There was no shortage of shitty human beings in that place.

McMann had hated Jordan at first, and Jordan never quite understood why. Maybe McMann had wanted one of his own men in the role. But somewhere along the way, that hatred had softened. The insults lessened; the occasional grunt of approval slipped through. It was the kind of relationship a soldier had with his drill sergeant—cruel to be kind. Almost a shame, given their bond, that Jordan was going to have to kill him.

But there were no friends in war.

And if McMann was involved in Hope Valley, that was a debt he would have to pay.

McMann. Thorne. Wolfe. Turner. Garrison. Reign.

That was the list.

And that was the order.

McMann first—he was the most dangerous. He could assemble an army faster than any government or police force. Thorne was his attack dog. Under normal circumstances, that would have bought him a stay of execution. But those shells at the school... someone had been there. There would be no due process, no judge or jury—just Jordan and a multi-billion-dollar network of machines capable of killing whoever the hell he decided.

Thorne was an evil little shit. A mercenary running black ops for the highest bidder. He was the one operating The Gunman for the President's side jobs. And now? He was next.

Garrison might be excessive; Jordan didn't hate guns per se—only that they'd never really solved anything for him. Every bullet seemed to make things worse. Killing Garrison would send a message to America: violence begets violence. Live by the gun, die by the gun.

Wolfe? He needed a hard reset. The *country* needed a hard reset. His control was too great—his ownership of social media, his influence over the President. A false god among evil men. His death would be the kind of catalyst the country needed to finally take a hard look at itself.

Turner was the newest addition. Jordan didn't feel great about the idea of killing a woman, but Lauren had been insistent. *She's the real brains behind Garrison,* she pleaded. *The June to his Johnny Cash. The Yoko Ono to his Lennon.* Neutralizing Garrison alone wasn't enough; without eliminating Turner too, that pot would just keep boiling.

President Douglas Reign.

Jordan wasn't the kind of man who grew up wanting to assassinate the president. He was a soldier. A cop. He felt angry and frustrated that it had fallen on him. That now, this was the only way to save America. Reign had to be the last and biggest target. Once he was dead, it would all be over—maybe within seconds, at best, several minutes. He *had* to be last.

At 1:00 a.m., Jordan commenced the mission. His dormitory within the complex allowed for movement at all hours— nothing suspicious. The two guards on the security desk weren't surprised to see him. He'd made a habit of waking up at odd hours, wandering the halls, chatting with the boys on the desk. "Can't sleep," he'd say.

They liked him. He liked them. That's why they were going to live—though they'd be in a lot of trouble tomorrow.

One of them was a former grunt. He knew what it meant. Habits had formed. Jordan would offer to make hot drinks for the three of them—cocoa for himself, coffee for the guards.

Tonight, he slipped 200 milligrams of diphenhydramine into each cup. Stockpiled Benadryl from the supplement program. It was almost unbelievable that McMann had actually provided an illegal supplement stack just to make him look like a superhero.

But Jordan was a soldier, and all soldiers knew:

The road to hell is paved with good intentions.

It was possible the antihistamine wouldn't knock them out completely, but they weren't going to be paying much attention when there was some movement at the maintenance and delivery entrance in an hour.

At 1:50 a.m., Vic arrived. Any remnants of doubt melted away, as if they had never existed. The truth was, Jordan didn't *know*. He only had Vic's word since their reconciliation a few weeks earlier, during a rare window of sanctioned leave. He'd been shadowed by security the whole time, but as they sat across the room, oblivious to his whispered conversation, he knew one thing:

They were still oblivious.

Because he was still alive.

The personnel door beside the large roller gate was unlocked. The guards didn't notice. They weren't quite asleep, but they were incapacitated. No trouble.

At 2:00 a.m., Jordan Peck and Victor Rodriguez stood side by side in the Gunman command center in Omaha. Vic's appearance was fully concealed, hands gloved in thick latex with extra padding around the fingertips. There wasn't much more to say. Jordan began instructing him on the system. Vic understood now. It was a two-man job.

He looked like a man carrying the weight of the world.

"Vic? What we're about to do—there's no turning back. This is going to be one of those days. Like 9/11. Like the Kennedy assassination. History will split around it. And there's only a small chance you survive this."

"I know, Jordy... Let's fly this plane, buddy."

"Alright, but listen. The only shot you've got at making it out alive is the next thirty minutes. The second we go after Reign, you run. Run like you've lost your papers and the whole damn Border Patrol is chasing you. Got that?"

"I've got this, Jordy. Thanks for everything, man."

CHAPTER 35: THE GUNMAN

John McMann usually slept deeply. Tonight, though, something gnawed at him—deep, uncomfortable, unfamiliar. As a man who'd always prided himself on his unshakable confidence, he found this feeling disorienting. He lay in a bedroom that wasn't shared with his wife, once again relegated to the spare room. There was no shortage of women in his life, but the sterile, transactional nature of paid encounters had long since lost its appeal. The fervor of those girls had waned as his looks had aged, and he couldn't ignore the sinking truth: their enthusiasm was fading, just like him.

Lately, the thought of reconciling with his wife had consumed him—a disease as relentless as the cancer that ravaged her body. Their marriage, now a tired formality, existed only in name. He realized, too late, that he loved her and owed her the man he could have been. Loyalty was rare in his world, but she had been fiercely loyal to him, despite their estranged relationship. In that moment, he knew it was all a little too late. Anger simmered at the thought of her standing by his graveside, indifferent, quietly relieved that he was gone. Tears shed only for the pain of a life that could have been better lived. No peace for her to find as she fought another unwinnable battle—his considerable resources worthless in her protection.

McMann knew he was dead before Peck did, like a coward, thousands of miles away when Peck came for him. Neither of these men were fools, but McMann was less of a fool than Peck. He knew the Gunman suit had launched—suit number 293, to be precise. There was nothing he could do to ensure his survival. He knew Peck wouldn't harm his wife or anything else in the house. He had only a moment to spare, and only one priority: kill Peck. He could have scrambled any number of responses to incapacitate him, but there was only one man he trusted to kill him in revenge for his own death. He made the call.

After retrieving an HK MR762A1—he kept one in every bedroom for emergencies—he stood in the middle of the room, fully exposed to the exterior window. He began firing into the darkness, desperately trying to hit the Gunman suit. Seconds later, the sniper round from the suit punched through his skull, and he collapsed to the floor, the rifle slipping from his grasp.

Within the Gunman control room, Vic confirmed the kill. The brief moment of vindication was soured by the sudden realization that Derek Thorne was on the move. The software tracking system pinpointed his location a few miles away.

"Mission parameter change, Vic. We're going after Wolfe instead. Looks like Thorne is coming to us, and we'll go more hands-on."

Xavier Wolfe wasn't a man who slept much—only a few hours a night. Fueled by relentless ambition, he was dogmatic and hubristic in whatever he set his sights on. Tonight, it was his latest, and in his mind, most groundbreaking project: a new AI-driven social media platform. He was going to call it XOX. It was revolutionary—a curated feed designed to cater to every need, want, and whim. A constant source of affirmation, no arguments, no disagreements, just unyielding support for the user. The best part? The reciprocation of sexual attention. No matter how unattractive or socially awkward you were, the opposite sex would always welcome you. Advertisers were going to love it.

Wolfe was no stranger to security threats. It came with the territory when you were an important, influential figure—

someone who, in his mind, was changing the world for the better. Sure, it was bound to upset a few nutjobs. His primary residence was designed with that in mind. Short of flying an attack helicopter up to the heights of his living area and opening fire, he was well-protected. An attack helicopter, or maybe a rapidly deployed high-speed drone, he thought —until a Gunman suit crashed through the large windows overlooking the ocean below.

He marveled at the ingenuity of the design in the few seconds he had left before the FN P90 submachine gun embedded in the suit discharged dozens of bullets into his body.
They left the suit standing in the middle of his mansion, its purpose fulfilled—now useless.

Alicia Turner and Richard Garrison were holed up in a hotel room in downtown Denver, preparing for the rally the following morning. They were going to protest outside Columbine—the birthplace of the nation's oppressive policies. Garrison was determined to reclaim the narrative. The gun-free zones hadn't worked back then, and they wouldn't work forever—not with the public's ever-shortening attention span and the looming threat of the goddamn Gunman. Columbine had marked the beginning of the assault on constitutional gun rights, and now, it would mark the beginning of the end for Reign, the Gunman program, and the attack on liberty itself.

Garrison stood in the corner of the room, pouring himself a strong drink, his gaze flickering toward Alicia, sprawled out on the bed. She was tired but satisfied after the big, gun-loving Texan had finished with her. Her husband—a weakling of a man—had never been a concern for Garrison. His own wife was smart enough to know her place didn't involve questioning him about his movements outside their marriage.

Inside the control room, technology of the sort that tin-foil-hat-wearing conspiracists could only dread in their worst nightmares hummed to life. Advanced AI systems capable of accessing financial records, facial recognition programs, and a plethora of other data streams. It took Vic only minutes to confirm Turner and Garrison's whereabouts—on the eighth floor of the hotel, in adjoining rooms.

Jordan wasn't surprised to find that their rooms weren't the only things adjoining. The heat signatures confirmed his suspicions as the suit touched down on the rooftop of another hotel across the parkway.

"Doesn't anyone have any moral integrity these days?" he muttered, the question more to the air than anyone in particular. He fired, and Richard Garrison dropped, a sniper round driving clean through his skull.

Alicia Turner's scream pierced the air as her brain struggled to catch up with the reality of what had just transpired. She shot out of the bed, arms flailing around, darting about in small, rapid movements as if she were a mouse with a cat on her tail. If she had been as skilled with weapons as she claimed, she might have survived by staying low, buying Jordan enough time to reposition the suit for a cleaner shot. But her frantic movement only made her an easier target. She'd been the target all along, though her death wasn't Jordan's immediate priority, despite Lauren Chalmers' advice. Still, better to be safe than sorry—her and Garrison's deaths would stifle the UFAA's momentum for a while. At least they wouldn't be leading any rallies outside Columbine tomorrow. Jordan couldn't help but think that if they had more guns, they might have stood a chance.

It was time for the big one—President Douglas Reign.

Vic's voice broke through the silence, his hesitation palpable. "Jordy, I don't understand which suit you want to launch. 449?"

It wasn't an error, of course. Officially, there were 448 suits scattered across mainland America, 448 launch sites, each with an armed suit ready for deployment. Suit number 449, however, was different. It was unarmed, stationed in the Entrance Hall of the White House—part art installation, part demonstration of power. Though it lacked any firearms, it was otherwise fully functional. The suit was capable of being piloted remotely, but that presented its own set of challenges.

This was the linchpin of Jordan's plan. If things went wrong, if the suit wasn't fully powered, if he couldn't remotely access it, or if the Secret Service overwhelmed it with enough firepower before he could get upstairs, everything could unravel.

"OK, Vic, here's the plan. We're activating suit number 449. The second we do, you're running like Speedy Gonzales, and you get the hell out of here. Stick to the plan, get back to your place, and don't look back."

Vic nodded solemnly. They'd already taken out some important people that morning, but assassinating the sitting president? That was a whole new level of escalation. There wasn't much left to say.

The door to the command room slammed open. Derek Thorne bypassed the security system with his top-level code, and as he stormed in, Jordan realized they had let their focus slip amidst the chaos. Thorne went straight for Vic, isolating the easier target first, leaving only Jordan to take out.
What Thorne didn't anticipate was how fast Jordan could move. His massive frame surged forward, overpowering Thorne in a heartbeat. Grabbing him by the throat, Jordan slammed him to the ground, then stomped on his wrist with brutal force. Thorne's firearm clattered to the floor, useless now.

The moment Thorne hit the ground, he knew it was over.

Jordan loomed over him, eyes wide with an untamed rage that made Thorne's blood run cold. He recognized that look—the look of a killer—and lying there, unarmed, was the worst possible place to be.

Jordan didn't speak, didn't ask any questions. He didn't need to. Thorne had been in Hope Valley that day. Jordan knew it, and Thorne knew it too.

With grim finality, Jordan's hands wrapped around his neck. Thorne fought weakly, but the power in Jordan's grip was unstoppable, fueled by blind hatred. A minute later, Thorne's body went limp.

Jordan spoke only once more. "Thank you for serving with me today, Vic. We're gonna activate suit 449, and then... you're gonna run."

It was almost ironic. Jordan had been mentally trained and conditioned to feel nothing about using deadly force, first as a soldier, then as a cop, and now as The Gunman. Standing in control of the decorative suit in the White House's entrance hall, he felt little. Calm. Focused. There was no fear—just an unwavering commitment to his cause.

He knew he was likely within the last few minutes of his life, but for the first time in a long while, he felt a strange peace.

He wasn't sure if the suit would respond to his commands, but he didn't need to worry. The U.S. government was remarkably good at missing the details. And now, here he was, controlling a robotic suit making its way up the grand staircase, heading straight for the President's bedroom.

The suit worked. Vic activated it without hesitation, pausing only to steal one last look at his friend before running out the door. He looked as if he'd aged ten years in the span of a single breath, his sudden rise from foot soldier to kingpin settling heavily on him—a moment that would never be forgotten.

It took the Secret Service only about 45 seconds to realize something was wrong. Initially, there was confusion. Was the suit there to protect or to attack? Their commands were meaningless to Jordan, thousands of miles away.

As the suit approached the bedroom door, the decision was made. The Secret Service opened fire. Their handguns were ineffective against the suit's armored exterior. Jordan turned his back on them, no agents directly in his path now. With a decisive move, the suit kicked the bedroom door down, the loud crash echoing through the White House.

For a fleeting moment, Jordan felt a pang of guilt. The destruction of property in an iconic American building was unavoidable, but it stung nonetheless.

President Douglas Reign sat up in bed, his movements slow and unsure. As quickly as his aging body would allow, he stood, his feet uncertain as they found the floor. Disoriented in the early hours of the morning, fear soon became his sharpest ally. He was awake now, acutely aware of the danger staring him down. There was no mistaking it. The realization hit him hard: death was imminent, and he was facing it in nothing but his presidential pajamas.

He was humbled, stripped of the power that had once shielded him. There were no words of privilege left to wield, no wealth to manipulate, no security in the fear he'd so often used as a tool. He was just a man now, standing before the very thing he had once denied—a fate he could not escape. As wrong as wrong could be.

Jordan wanted to linger in the moment, to make Reign face his inevitable demise, to let the fear shatter the arrogance and megalomania that had once defined him. This was a moment in history, a moment that would freeze in time. No need to prolong it further.

And so, with a single, brutal motion, Jordan punched Reign in the face with enough force to kill instantly. The blow sent the president's body swaying for only a moment before it collapsed, lifeless, to the floor. The once mighty figure, dead in his own bedroom, his life extinguished with terrifying ease. His wife lay in another room, oblivious, unaware that the most powerful man in the nation was now nothing more than a corpse on the floor.

The Secret Service swarmed in; their purpose rendered moot. Guns were drawn, but their training faltered in the face of shock and confusion. They were powerless, moving in hesitation as they aimed at the now-motionless suit.

Jordan stepped out of the command module; his work was done. The suit, now inactive, stood silent in the president's bedroom. The mission was complete.

Jordan hadn't expected to get this far in the mission, expecting to be executed in a hail of bullets when security flooded the command room, shooting him as he sat entrapped in the module. As it was, Derek Thorne had provided him with a far more fitting solution than the expected outcome. He knelt beside him, gripping his broken wrist, and took a moment to position his own hand over Thorne's, the dead man's index finger clumsily inside the trigger of his handgun. Jordan considered multiple angles before settling on one directly through his heart—a fitting conclusion, given the pain it had given him over the last part of his life. There was no pain when he pulled the trigger. The close range of the shot almost muffled against his mass.

He fell backward more suddenly than expected, the force of the bullet forcing his movement. His hands fell away from the handgun after some effort in using Thorne's trigger finger to discharge the shot. He didn't bother to move from the position; it was as good as could be given the circumstances, instead allowing the blackness to engulf him, falling and falling until there was nothing.

CHAPTER 36: THE ASHES OF ASSASSINATION

They were in the Situation Room again now. Lauren found it almost ironic—the full circle that had led to this day. This was the same room where President Reign, God rest his soul, had first posited the idea of using robots to protect schools against violence. The irony was not lost on her: in the pursuit of peace, great violence had been achieved. But then, that was always the price of war.

They were seated at the long desk, surrounded by an overload of information. All the usual clowns from the circus were there: the newly promoted Vice President, the National Security Advisor, Secretary of Defense, Chairman of the Joint Chiefs of Staff, FBI, CIA, Homeland Security, the Attorney General, and Lauren—White House Chief of Staff. And these assholes were going to listen to her.

She was functioning without any sleep at all. It hadn't taken long for the Secret Service to breach her apartment and remove her just after 3 a.m., muttering phrases with stern authority like, "Ma'am, we need to move you to a secure location," and "The United States is under attack." The confusion had been real. Clarity came many hours later, after a handful of important Americans had been assassinated—most notably, the President of the United States.

The Vice President, a grossly incompetent man, had been carefully selected to ensure he posed no threat to the President. Now, he was deeply out of his depth, struggling to navigate the crisis he found himself in. It was the biggest news story since

September 11, compounded by the fact that just yesterday, there had been a very real possibility they were on the brink of civil war. The United Firearms Advocates Association was pushing for the secession of several states from the Union. The Constitution was in tatters, and the country had never been more the Divided States of America since the last civil war.

By morning, the agencies that handled these crises had already taken control. The FBI led the charge, devoting full federal resources and manpower to the case. It hadn't taken long to identify the assassin.

It was The Gunman.

In the small hours of a Sunday night, The Gunman had deployed from multiple points across the nation, executing its targets with chilling precision: President Douglas Reign; John McMann, the CEO and appointed government head of the Gunman Program; Xavier Wolfe, a tech mogul and self-proclaimed genius; and Richard Garrison, the president of the UFAA.

The problem with it all was that The Gunman wasn't legally, technically, or ethically an actual person—and the FBI wasn't going to arrest him. The real issue lay in the discrepancy about who had been in the command module in Omaha, executing these people.

There were two dead men in that control room: Jordan Peck and Derek Thorne. While there were two very clear initial theories, proving either beyond a shadow of a doubt would be difficult, leaving the nation in uncertainty.

The Vice President, tense under pressure, his jaw locked and sweat visible through his shirt, struggled to hold on to any sliver of stoicism. The voices of the assembly roared around him, clearly overwhelming whatever small degree of competence he had. He looked over at her. Sitting there, she was in control. Nobody else in that room was. All of them were fazed by the very real possibility that The Gunman could have killed any number of them if it had chosen.

"Lauren, what in the hell are we going to do?"

They continued to talk, ignoring the question directed at her. He couldn't handle it; his stress level impeded his sense of ceremony.

"Everybody shut the hell up. I asked a question...I want an answer."

They fell silent. Reign had been dangerous, and this man was incompetent—but he was the President. Lauren felt strangely calm. Collected and sensible. She reverted back to her old self, if just for the moment.

"Sir, let's just lay out our options on the table here, okay? I think we consider it all and work out our approach from there."

He nodded, and she continued. All eyes in the room were on her.

"Right now, we have two competing theories about what happened in Omaha. The first: Peck went rogue, betrayed his nation, and assassinated half a dozen very important figures, including the President. The second: Derek Thorne, a mercenary who worked for McMann and, from what we're led to believe, undertook some very serious operations under his direction, went rogue for reasons we do not yet fully understand and executed the targets. In both cases, either Jordan Peck intervened to stop him and lost his life in the process, or it was the other way around."

"Okay, we know this, Lauren, but what the hell are we going to do?" he grumbled, gruff and sullen.

"Sir, President Reign believed in The Gunman. He believed it represented a symbol of hope for our nation—that it stood for something. That it made a difference. And right now, our country is on the verge of self-destruction. We're legitimately discussing the possibility of civil war and deploying our military against our own citizens. That situation needs to be de-escalated immediately. For all its flaws, the Gunman Program did reduce school shootings. And regardless of the political firestorm surrounding it—the constitutional debates, President Reign's failed attempt to classify a legal entity as a terrorist organization—The Gunman, as a symbol of hope, was the one redeeming feature of the predicament we're in."

"The problem is this: if Jordan Peck went rogue, that's going to be bad news. It's going to cause even further tension, and we're already at a boiling point. We need a symbol of hope right now."

"Front the press and tell them that Derek Thorne, a rogue mercenary who we believe engaged in acts of illegal warfare on American soil, betrayed his country for reasons we do not fully understand. That he launched an attack on the United States. That Jordan Peck discovered his plan, attempted to stop him, and lost his life in the process."

"And if we're wrong, Miss Chalmers? If Peck was the assassin?"

"You're the goddamn President of the United States, sir. Let me bring you up to speed fast. The truth is whatever you say the truth is. There are only two kinds of truth: the truth we need, and the truth we don't. So, the way I see it, you can go out there and lead us either into, or away from, war."

His eyes gave him away. It was dawning on him—he might be about to celebrate a traitor while condemning the man who tried to stop him. One way or another.

"Give us the room," the President stated. There was no movement. "Get out! All of you! Lauren, stay."

When the two of them were alone, he dropped all pretenses.

"You knew it all, didn't you?"

"I did, sir. The black ops, the involvement of McMann at Hope Valley. President Reign read me into everything. I aided as ordered."

Lauren felt rather pleased with herself. It was just like that time in the second grade, except it wasn't Mrs. Whitmore. It was the President of the United States of America. And she was Lauren Chalmers, Chief of Staff to the President.

And nobody fucks with her friends.

She waited a couple of weeks for it all to die down. After all, no matter the headline, nobody can hold their attention for long. There was always another disaster waiting in the wings, ready to take precedence. No matter how great the tragedy, it eventually becomes history against the present. Still, even by American standards, the violence and tension had been excessive—enough to create breathing room for calmer heads and a great de-escalation. There was no more talk of a pending civil war, just a consensus that they should all work toward a more peaceful nation.

The Gunman protocol had been deactivated for the time being. There was a strange sense of calm over the country, despite the perceived lack of protection. Maybe—just maybe—people were beginning to believe in each other, if only a little. That was until a few days ago, when a kid in Mississippi killed eight of his classmates, driven by a thirst for infamy and a burning desire to take lives. The Gunman suits had stood idly by. A new wave of anger swept the nation. They could have ended it— if not for the grave price of protection. There was talk now of reimagining the program: full government oversight this time, perhaps a specialized military division to operate the system.

The truth was, they had built a weapon of immense power. But who was virtuous enough to wield it without corruption?

The night after the press conference—where Derek Thorne had been given full credit for the assassination of the president, alongside some others the country wasn't particularly worse off for losing—she slept like a baby. It would take more than one good night's sleep to recover from the trauma of the past few months, but at least Mason's death had brought real change. The nation could begin to heal. So could she.

The president hadn't been thrilled to comply with her request for personal leave. But it wasn't really a request. It was an ultimatum: he could go without her temporarily—or permanently.

And so, she found herself honoring her promise to Jordan Peck, somewhere in the backwaters of Iowa, in a little town called Hickory Springs—and the cemetery of the same name.

It didn't take her long to find the grave. The Secret Service agent assigned to her while on leave waited in the car. This was private business, and he knew better than to involve himself. He was a smart man—and smarter still for not asking questions.

And suddenly, there it was in front of her, just as Jordan had said.

She stopped for a moment to pay her respects, marveling at the chain of events that had unfolded because of this woman. The headstone had a polished plaque and a high-definition photo etched into the surface. Lauren had done some quiet research when she could—away from the prying eyes of the White House. She was adorable. Her online presence revealed a sharp sense of humor and a vivid, vivacious spirit. Lauren could see why he loved her.

She laid the flowers down and took a breath.

The small cemetery was serene, shaded by towering American

elms. Their branches stretched overhead like the beams of a cathedral, forming a natural canopy. It was peaceful. She and Emily had much in common, despite their differences, and Lauren felt—deeply and empathetically—that she could finally rest in peace.

The photo on the headstone showed Emily smiling, surrounded by the elementary students she had given her life to protect that day at Hope Valley. A tear rolled down Lauren's cheek as she read the inscription one last time:

Emily Carson

October 12, 1991 – November 24, 2025
Died protecting the most innocent of all

ABOUT THE AUTHOR

Theo W. Pitchstead

Theo W. Pitchstead is a chef, father of three, and lifelong observer of the absurd. This is his debut novel. Written between kitchen shifts and school runs, Bullets for Beautiful Babies reflects his deep discomfort with violence, power, and the performative theatre of modern politics. He plays several instruments, cooks a mean brisket, and never thought he'd actually publish a book — but here we are.